The Absence of Olivia
© *Copyright Anie Michaels 2015*

Edited by Hot Tree Editing.
Cover design © Sprinkles On Top Studios

For Kamryn ~

My wish is for you to always be your own first choice.

Prologue

It had been forty-seven minutes since my best friend passed away.

Forty-seven minutes.

And I already had no idea how to live my life without her.

I was already lost.

I had no idea how to move forward, how to live, in a world she wasn't a part of anymore.

She was the biggest part of my world since I was fourteen years old. She was the first person I made eye contact with on my first day of eighth grade. My first day at a new school, just having moved to New Haven the week before. I sat down in the first empty desk I'd come to in my first period homeroom class, and she'd been sitting in the desk right next to mine. She turned to me, her long, blonde, sleek ponytail swinging to the side with her movement, and she smiled.

I couldn't help but smile back.

Then she spoke and, we didn't know it then, but we'd started a lifelong friendship that day.

Well, lifelong for her. Cut drastically short for me.

Olivia Marie Wright wasn't the most popular girl in school, mostly because the most popular girls in school got that way by kissing boys at the bottom of the hill by the soccer field. She wasn't the smartest girl in school, and she wasn't the prettiest girl in school. But she was all three – popular, smart, and pretty. And she was the *best* girl in school. Hardly a person didn't like Olivia and those who didn't like her, only disliked her out of jealousy or spite, and Olivia was always the nicest to those people.

She sang in the choir, was in the school plays, participated in student government, and was even on the drill team. There wasn't a single thing she wasn't good at. And I was happy to know the one thing she particularly excelled at was being someone's friend.

That very first day she had turned her head to me, smiled, and said, "Hi, I'm Olivia. Are you new?"

I smiled back, albeit, a shy smile, and said, "Yeah, I moved here last week."

"Well, I'll ask Mr. Marshall if I can show you to all your classes. Usually, they let someone show new students around, and I'd love to help."

Thus, a fourteen-year friendship was born. And today, it died, along with Olivia.

Just yesterday, I sat in her hospital room, holding her frail, cold hand as she looked at me with eyes missing so much light and tried to say her goodbye. She was weak, the cancer taking everything from her right up until the very last moment, so her words were thin and soft; but she'd said them, so I'd listened.

"Evie," she whispered, her eyes trying to remain open, but closing every few seconds, just to flutter open again.

"I'm here, Livy," I said, scooting forward on the chair, rubbing her hand with a little more force, but still gently. "I'm here," I repeated, not certain what else to say to her, not even sure I had words to say to my best friend slipping away right before my eyes.

"Evie, you're my best friend," she breathed, "so I need you to promise me something."

"Anything," I whispered back.

Her eyes found mine again, and the dullness of them wasn't lost on me, the absence of everything bright that had once been in her eyes was nearly as devastating as the condition of her body. There was nothing left of any part of her.

"I need you to take care of Devon, Ruby, and little Jax for me," she said, her eyes rolling back in her head as her voice tapered off. Then they fluttered open again, finding me, searching mine. "Promise me."

This wasn't the first time she'd asked me to take care of her family after she was gone. However, every other time we'd talked about it, she'd been well enough that it had been something far away, or just some smoky idea that would disappear when you really tried to grab hold of it. When she'd been diagnosed with breast cancer two years prior, she'd almost jokingly, with a smile, asked me to take care of her family if anything should happen to her. Of course, I agreed. Of course. Then, again, when her health turned poor and there was that moment when everyone realized that, eventually, she wouldn't make it, she'd asked again. And I'd agreed, of course.

But she'd never asked me before while she'd been lying at death's door and the request had never seemed so final. To agree to this would mean I agreed to her dying; it would be to accept that the end was really here, and Olivia was really leaving. To agree to take care of her family would be agreeing to give her up, and I wasn't sure I could do that.

But I looked at my best friend on possibly the very last day of her life and realized that anything I could do to ease her mind or make her last day easier, I would do, of course. So I nodded, tears streaming down my face, and agreed to care for her family.

"Of course, Livy. I'll always take care of them," I muttered through tears. She smiled, and she looked like she was drifting away from me, which I'd come to expect since the pain medication they had her on was strong. However, a few minutes later, when she opened her eyes again, she looked at me and said the very last words I'd ever hear from her.

"You're my very best friend, Evie. Promise me you'll be happy."

I nodded, not able to say anything in response, because I knew there would be no happiness in the absence of Olivia.

Chapter One

Spring of Freshman Year of College

Nothing in the world felt worse than ice-cold soda running down the front of your body. Forget that it was hot outside. Like, blisteringly hot. Forget that there had been many times that week I'd thought about dumping a bucket of freezing cold water over my head. Having diet coke fill your bra cups, ice cubes included, was not how I wanted to cool off. Not only was the sensation alarming, you know, ice cubes in my bra and all, but I was humiliated. My white linen sleeveless shirt was now sticking to the same bra filled with soda and giving everyone in the campus café a sneak peek at my goods. Everyone, except of course, for the guy who'd run into me, spilling my soda down the front of my chest, and then continuing on his way without so much as a "sorry," or even a "get out of my way."

"Oh, my gosh," I whispered to myself, leaning forward slightly and pulling the drenched fabric of my shirt away from my body, trying desperately to hide what I'm sure everyone had already seen. My purse strap slid off my shoulder, and before I could catch it, my entire purse fell to the ground, all its contents splaying across the floor in a brilliant display of girl-shit pyrotechnics. Not only had everyone seen my bra through my soaked shirt, but also now, everyone could clearly see I was on my period and had to use moisturizer for people with oily skin. I tried to keep in both a groan of embarrassment and the tears that were currently pooling in my eyes.

"Here, take my shirt."

I heard him before I saw his face, and even in my state of absolute embarrassment, I noticed his voice. Heard its deep timbre and felt the way my body leaned toward it before my head tipped up and my eyes found his. I saw his face first. I saw the way his jawbone was prominent, as were his cheekbones. I saw the blue of his eyes and the way his blond eyebrows only made them look bluer. I saw his lips that were a shade of pink that, alone, would seem feminine, but coupled with all the maleness of the rest of his face, seemed to fit him perfectly.

Then my eyes wandered and I realized his chest was bare. His chest was bare because he was offering me his shirt.

"Here," he said gently, motioning for me to take it from him.

I finally regained the use of my arms, and opened up the plaid cotton shirt he offered and pushed my arms through the sleeves. I did so while keeping my head low, but not low enough that I couldn't see his absolutely and ridiculously muscled chest. He had more abs than I'd ever seen up close and in person. More breadth to his shoulders than should have been physically possible. He was wide in a way I couldn't have ever imagined. But he was also lean. There was no fat on him. He was tight and long and huge.

"Thanks," I mumbled as I tried to give him a small smile. I probably looked like I had tasted something bad. Instead of buttoning up the shirt, I just wrapped it around me, and stood there in front of him, huddled like a loser, feeling the soda squish from my shirt and drip down my legs.

Suddenly, his face was gone from my sight and I realized he'd bent down to pick up my belongings. My tampons.

"Well that guy was a big asshole," he said, grabbing my purse and opening it up, reaching for all my girl things laying on the floor. I dropped to my knees as quickly as I could and reached for the first tampon I could see, trying desperately to get to them before he did. Luckily, it looked as though he was aiming to collect everything *except* tampons, so I shoved them in my purse and tried to pretend like I wore hot strangers' shirts every day while flinging feminine hygiene products on the floor.

When everything had been collected, we stood up, both still holding on to my purse, him shirtless, me trying not to stare. He finally let go and I watched as he raised a hand to his too-long hair and ran his fingers through it.

"He should have at least apologized," he said finally.

"Who?" I asked, confused.

"The guy who totally ran you down and then took off."

"Oh, right. Him. He was probably in a hurry."

"That's no excuse for being a douchebag."

"You know what? I agree. That was kind of a douche move." I laughed and then laughed a little more when I saw him smile. "Um, thanks, again, for the shirt."

"No problem. You were a little, uh, on display."

"Oh, you noticed?" I asked him this question in a totally innocent way, hoping that perhaps, even though I felt like everyone's eyes had been on me, no one really saw much. But when I saw his face turn red, the blush creeping down his neck, I knew he'd seen more than enough.

"Hard not to," he said, blushing even deeper, but this time the corner of his mouth tipped up in a lopsided grin I liked way too much.

"What dorm are you in? So I can return your shirt after I wash it?"

"It's no problem; you keep the shirt," he said easily.

"Oh," I said, a little dejected, thinking he didn't want to tell me which dorm he lived in because he didn't have any interest in seeing me again. I wasn't a bad looking girl. I liked the way I looked and tried hard to look my best each day. I was satisfied with my body, only really longing to be a little taller. But I had great hair and knew my boobs and butt were assets the opposite sex found attractive. I didn't flaunt them, but they weren't a hardship to have. I had an hourglass figure and was proud of it. So when he'd basically seen my chest through my see-through shirt and didn't want to see me again, I was a little confused and more than a little hurt.

A woman wearing the instantly recognizable uniform for the campus café showed up with a mop and bucket. Obviously there to clean up the mess my soda had made, she shoved in between us with a huff and a few choice words about spoiled college kids. I stepped around her and gave him another smile.

"Well, thank you...oh, I didn't catch your name."

"I'm Devon," he said, reaching his hand out.

I kept one arm wrapped around my middle, making sure his shirt stayed in place, and shook his hand. "My name's Evelyn, but people call me Evie."

"Nice to meet you," he said, still shaking my hand, looking right into my eyes. He held on to my hand a little bit longer, all the while my stomach was doing a tumbling roll. When he dropped my hand, his smile grew larger and he put his hands in his pockets. That action must have reminded him he was shirtless because he suddenly became acutely aware of his naked chest and seemed uncomfortable. "Well, I better get back to my room and find a new shirt."

"Are you sure you don't want this one back? I promise I'll wash it."

He smiled again and I found myself smiling right back.

"Really, it's okay. You keep it. Maybe I'll see you around sometime." He gave me a small wave and then turned around, walking out through the doors that led to the courtyard at the apex of all the dorm buildings. I watched him until he disappeared around a corner, then sighed, and started toward my own dorm.

My shoes squelched and squished the entire way, and with every step on every stair all the way up to the third floor I left footprints that I knew later would be sticky. *Just another job for housekeeping, I suppose.* I made it to my door and found it unlocked, which made me happy because it meant Liv would be home and I could share my embarrassment. I opened the door and with only two steps into my room, I was put in a situation even more mortifying.

There, on Liv's bed, was another topless man, only I was pretty sure he was pants-less too as he was thrusting vigorously *into* my best friend. It took approximately three thrusts for him to notice me.

"Holy shit," he said, startled, and then fell off the bed, pulling the blanket with him, leaving Liv naked and spread eagle, but thankfully, facing away from me.

"What the hell, Brandon?" Liv shrieked.

"It's the middle of the day, Liv. And the door is unlocked." I tried to sound surprised or shocked, but it was difficult, seeing as how this wasn't shocking or surprising coming from Liv.

She turned her head sharply to see me, my hands on my hips, obviously irritated.

"Oh, hey, Evie. You've met Brandon, right?" she asked, as if nothing in the world was the matter. As if she were standing on the street, totally clothed, not mid-coitus. He was quickly finding his clothes and putting them on even quicker. "I think I introduced you at the Beta house last weekend."

"Well, now that he's wearing clothes, you're right, he does look familiar," I said, not trying one bit to hide my sarcasm.

He threw the blanket over Liv to cover her, and then slipped his shoes on his feet. "I'm gonna go. This is really awkward." He leaned down and kissed Liv quickly on the lips, then walked right past me and didn't even say goodbye.

"Liv," I sighed, putting my purse down on my desk and sitting on the edge of my bed, facing her. "What are you doing? You don't even know that guy."

She shrugged. "I have my lit class with him. I've sat next to him every day for two months. Plus, he's a Beta. I've seen him at all the parties and last weekend we hung out quite a bit."

I tilted my head to the side and raised my eyebrows. "Oh, well then, obviously, sex is the next step."

She shrugged again and then stood up and walked to her closet. "You don't have to be in love with everyone you have sex with, Evie."

This is where I was realizing, recently, that Liv and I differed on our opinions about sex. I wasn't a virgin, hadn't been for over a year, so it wasn't that I thought everyone should save themselves for marriage, but I couldn't imagine having sex with a guy I wasn't in a committed, loving relationship with. Liv was more of the free love variety of girl, and usually, that was fine. Until I saw some random dude's sex face.

"Your antiquated views of a healthy sexual relationship are setting the women's movement back at least thirty years," she said from behind the door of her closet.

"Antiquated? My views aren't antiquated. They're emotionally safe and your sexual relationships aren't even *relationships*. They're like, encounters, at best."

I saw her head lean just around the door, her captivating and gorgeous smile beaming. "Conquests," she said excitedly, her eyebrows moving up and down suggestively. I couldn't help but laugh. Liv had been my best friend since we were fourteen and she had always been boy crazy. Living on our own during our first year of college, she seemed to take the bull by the horns and took her liberated stance on sex very seriously. In fact, she'd slept with more guys during our first term of college than I had hoped to sleep with in my entire life. The thing was, you couldn't hate her for it. Sometimes, I was even envious. She had this confidence about her. She knew guys wanted her and that gave her some sort of power over them. And to be fair, it wasn't as if she slept with just anyone. She was picky and usually chose guys who were respectful and nice. And some of them, I'm sure, would have loved to date her – like, for real – but she was never interested, always claiming she was too young to be tied down.

She also had rules. Rules she was perfectly up front and open about with her partners. 1) No cheating, as in no sleeping with a guy who was in a relationship. She didn't invite, participate in, or tolerate "girl drama." 2) No communication drama; she didn't expect them to call her, and she didn't plan to call them. If they called, they called, but no expectations. 3) Safe sex – always. This was one of the rules she had that I fully supported. 4) The minute it wasn't fun anymore, it was over. 5) No one stayed the night, not at our dorm or wherever he lived. And I swear, the minute the guys got even remotely territorial, she bailed.

Even I could recognize she had a view of sexual relationships beyond her years. I thought maybe she'd watched too many episodes of Sex and the City while we were in high school.

I let out a sigh because I knew there was nothing I could say to make her change her ways, and if she did, she wouldn't be the Liv I loved. I walked to my closet, which was just across from hers, and started peeling off my sticky-wet clothes.

"What in the world happened to you?" Liv asked, noticing my predicament.

"Some jerk ran into me at the café and my soda spilled all down my front." I took off the borrowed shirt to show her the damage, tossing the handsome stranger's plaid button up into my laundry basket.

"Oh," Liv said, staring at my shirt. "I love that bra."

I laughed, because, of course she did. "Yeah, well, so did everyone else who saw it through my drenched shirt." I pulled the linen tank over my head, not enjoying the feeling of the wet fabric peeling away from my skin at all. "Luckily, some nice guy literally gave me the shirt off his back."

"How gentlemanly of him. At least he didn't just stare at your boobs," she said as she pulled on some shorts.

"Well," I said, taking off the rest of my clothes and wrapping a towel around my body. "I think he got an eyeful before he offered his shirt. But he *was* a gentleman. He let me keep the shirt." I grabbed my shower caddy and turned to her just as she pulled her top over her head. "I'm gonna grab a shower. Are we still doing dinner tonight?"

"Sure thing. I'll meet you here right after my last class."

"Okay. Try not to be in the middle of a sex act next time I come home."

"How about I just lock the door?"

"I'll settle for that," I said with a laugh, then paused before heading to the shower. "See you later. Are you headed to your lit class?"

She smiled wickedly. "Yeah. And it should be a lot more exciting now that Brandon's, um, unsatisfied." She continued to smile as she adjusted her hair in the mirror. Hair that looked like sex hair but also fantastic. I rolled my eyes and left the room, shaking my head all the way to the shower.

It had been three weeks since the soda incident and I would have been lying to myself if I didn't admit to looking at every guy I passed on campus for the first two weeks trying to find Devon. I wasn't sure what I would have said to him had I seen him on the sidewalk or as I walked to class, or in line at the bookstore, or even back at the café where we had met. And I couldn't help that my eyes roamed to every face, searched the back of every guy I saw for those wide shoulders and too-long blondish hair.

So, I struggled with both surprise and relief when I finally laid my eyes on him, as he approached me, Liv's arm threaded through the crook of his elbow.

"Evie," she said, her words slurred, most likely from the copious amounts of vodka she'd consumed. "This is Devon." She motioned toward him then swung her arm toward me. "Devon, this is my best friend and roommate, Evie."

I should have said hello, should have reached out to shake his hand, but all I could manage to do was stare at her hand on his forearm.

"Oh yeah, hey, Evie. Nice to see you again." His deep voice accosted me just like it had three weeks before.

"You know Evie?" Liv asked with a little too much drunken enthusiasm.

"We met a few weeks ago when some douchebag spilled her soda."

My eyes managed to tear themselves away from where her hand rested on his arm, which was causing me to feel things I wasn't used to, only to see Devon's eyes dart back to my breasts, obviously remembering what I looked like in a wet white shirt.

"You're the guy who gave her his shirt?" she squealed. If the music hadn't been so loud, it surely would have been deafening. "She sleeps in that shirt sometimes," Liv offered, much to my complete embarrassment.

"Liv!" I shouted, mortified. I immediately heated, starting in my cheeks. I knew I was blushing furiously. My eyes darted up to Devon, but I couldn't look at him. I did sleep in his shirt, it was true. It was also mortifying.

"You sleep in my shirt?" His voice, even over the music, sounded soft and sort of gentle. It wasn't critical, or even playful. He wasn't making fun of me. So I answered him honestly.

I shrugged. "It's pretty big, so it works as a nightie."

Before he could respond, I steeled as Liv curled up around his large, muscled arm. "Devon was just going to take me to the dance floor." Her eyes were dreamy, probably a mixture of lust and drunkenness.

"Well, have fun dancing. I'm probably going to head home soon."

"M'kay," she slurred. "Remember your rape whistle."

I laughed because that was a typical, snarky Liv remark, but Devon's brow furrowed.

"You're not going to walk home alone, are you?" He sounded concerned.

"Well, yeah, actually. I am. Don't worry though, Liv and I took a self-defense class fall term. No one's gonna get the drop on me. Plus, I have pepper spray."

"Let me see your phone," he demanded, but in a weirdly nice way.

"What?"

"Let me see your phone." He held his hand out and looked at me expectantly. I sighed but complied, digging around in my purse and finally handing him my cell phone once I'd located it. He immediately started thumbing it. "Text me when you get back to your room safely." He held my phone back out to me.

"Are you serious?" He couldn't be serious. He just stared at me, his hand out in front of him, my phone resting in his palm. I could have sworn he didn't even blink. "I don't need another father. I have one already. And he lets me stay out past dark and everything."

"Devon, I wanna dance," Liv whined, still clinging to his muscular and attractive arm, batting her eyelashes at him.

"Just text me, Evelyn. I'd say text Liv, but she's too drunk to remember where she put her purse." He shook my phone at me again. I reached out and took it, but huffed out a breath so he knew it was under protest. "You'll text? I just want to know you're safe."

Some part of me that had been angry just moments before melted a little at his concern and I relented. "I'll text."

I walked home that night in the dark and alone, but I was smiling the whole way because I knew he was waiting for my text. Devon was huge, but he was sweet, and for some reason that combination of traits made him undeniably attractive. He'd give you the shirt off his back and make sure you got home all right. But I got the feeling he could also protect someone if they needed it. Not only could he, but he would without hesitation.

Something about him called to me. Opened me. Woke me up.

And even though my stomach was still doing the flippity thing as I sent him my text to tell him I'd made it home safely, I knew it was something I couldn't hold on to or hope for – that I would be the person he'd be opening up for or waking up for – because he was with Liv at that exact moment. And even if I thought I could compete with Liv, I wouldn't want to.

Chapter Two

Present Day

"Ruby. Jax. It's time to wake up, guys," I said gently as I flipped on the light switch, just like I had done every school day for the last three months. And like most days, neither one of the kids budged. They slept like rocks and woke up slower than molasses. I walked to the foot of Ruby's bed and sat down slowly, trying not to jar her.

"Ruby, sweetie, time to get ready for school." I reached out and rubbed my hand gently down her back, feeling her finally wake up a little underneath my touch. "Come on, Rubster. Time to wake up." I watched as she stretched, her head of brown, curly hair emerging from under the covers, little hands reaching out as if to hold on to sleep a little bit longer.

"Aunt Evie?" she asked, her voice heavy with sleep.

"Yes, baby?"

"How many days until summer break?"

I laughed. Ruby loved school, but she loved sleep more. "Quite a few, honey. You've got two months left." A loud groan came from under her blanket. Then I heard her brother grumble too, although, he was less resistant to waking up.

"Jaxy, you awake?"

"Yeah," came his little voice from the other side of the room. When Liv and Devon had first gotten married, they purchased a smaller, two-bedroom house. That had worked fine for them for a while. A couple years later, however, when Jaxy was born, they started to feel just a little cramped. When they finally moved into a bigger house, Ruby had cried and cried when they told her she was going to get her own room. She was devastated she wouldn't be sharing a room with her baby brother any longer. So, just like any parent trying to deal with a four-year-old's tantrum, they gave her what she wanted. Ruby and Jax had shared a room since his birth and Liv and Devon figured eventually one or both of them would want their own space. When that time came, there was a spare bedroom waiting for one of them.

"Okay, kiddos, let's get up and get going."

This was our routine. Every school day, I came over to get the kids ready in the morning. Devon was here, but he had to leave for work before the school bus came. Before, Liv would have been here doing this – being a mom – but I stepped in after the funeral as a way to help. Liv had been a stay-at-home mom and loved every minute of it. So, in her absence, Jax had recently adjusted to going to preschool. Another heartbreaking change to his regular routine. But he was a trooper. Both of them were.

"You guys get dressed and meet me downstairs for breakfast."

I had just finished packing Ruby's lunch when I heard the unmistakable sounds of Devon coming down the stairs. Longer strides, heavier footfalls. It was only moments before I saw his frame fill the doorway from the living room to the kitchen.

"Good morning, Evie," he said when he saw me. That morning, not unusually, there was a smile on his face. It wasn't the best smile I'd ever seen him wear, but he was slowly improving.

"Morning," I responded, smiling back at him. He turned sideways to squeeze between the kitchen counter and me, and I had the same thought I'd had for ten years whenever he was close. I remembered him as he was the first time I met him, shirtless and huge. I hadn't known it at the time, but he was a player for the college football team, which explained his size.

After college, however, when his job became more of the suit and tie variety, his bulk went away. He was still tall, and still very much an overwhelming presence, but he wasn't nearly as *huge* as he used to be. What I'd seen from summers at the lake house, Devon was still built and still had every muscle imaginable, they were just less enormous now.

"You'll be here when Ruby gets off the bus this afternoon, right?" he asked as he grabbed a mug out of the cupboard.

"Oh." I paused and turned to him. "Remember last week when I told you I couldn't be here this afternoon? I have a meeting with a client. Remember?"

"Shit," he whispered, closing his eyes. I hated this. I hated this part. The part where I could see the ache in him, could see how much he missed his wife. I knew that was what was going through his head. He would first berate himself for not being able to remember our conversation, and then he would think about how none of this would be a problem if Liv were still alive. I hated that even though I did everything I could for him, for his kids, I was never enough.

"I can cancel," I said quickly, trying to smooth over the situation, to fix it before it caused him any more pain. "Or reschedule. It's really not a big deal." I waved my hand, as if I could magically erase the agony that came with losing his wife and all the pain in the aftermath. If I could have waved it away, I would have. Devon had suffered a lot in the last three months and sometimes, I was at a loss as to how to help him. But I could cancel my meeting.

"Evie," he said, his voice so low and so sad. "You can't keep doing this."

"Doing what?"

"Giving things up for us. Rearranging your life for us. It's not fair to you." His back was to me and I was facing away from him, but the tension in the room was zipping between us like lightening.

"It's really not a big deal," I said as I turned my attention back to the lunches I was preparing. Just like every other time since I'd met him, his rejection hurt me in a way I didn't like to acknowledge. I knew Devon cared about me, knew from the moment we met I was important to him, but I felt differently for him and I always had.

"Are you sure?" he asked, even though his tone made it clear he wasn't.

"What other choice do we have?" My work was very much fluid and I was my own boss. I had no one to answer to besides my clients. Devon worked for a corporate conglomerate and the chances of him coming home early were slim. He'd taken a lot of time off when Liv had been sick, and then again when she had died, and even though his job was understanding to a point, he'd used up all the time allotted to him for the death of his wife and had none to spare. There was a long pause, and the silence was filled with so much angst and emotion. Perhaps, and most likely, I was the only one feeling everything between us. After all, that was usually the way it worked. I watched from afar with a veil over my real emotions, only letting the outside see what I wanted to show, while on the inside I was waging a war I never wanted to fight. What other option did we have? I'd had a thousand options. But I gave them all up when I decided to bury my emotions.

"All right," he finally sighed. "But this is the last time, Evelyn."

Something dangerous rolled through my body when he used my full name. Just another feeling to bury.

I turned my head just enough to meet his eyes over my shoulder. I smiled at him. He didn't return it, just stared at me over his cup of coffee. Before either of us looked away, two small children came bounding into the kitchen, running directly to their father.

"Dad, Jax didn't change his underwear," Ruby tattled as she wrapped her arms around her father's middle. I smiled at the image and then turned again to the lunches.

"Jax, did you put on clean underwear?" Devon's fatherly tone indicated he already knew the answer to his question.

"I looked in my drawer and there was none."

"Shit," Devon murmured. "I forgot to do the laundry again."

"Jaxy, I think I put a load in the dryer yesterday afternoon. Why don't you go check?" I held my breath, knowing Devon would view this as me doing too much. I couldn't help it. He needed my help. I listened as Ruby told her father about the tigers she was learning about in school, and as she jabbered, he inserted the appropriate responses.

I turned to watch Jax run through the kitchen on his way back upstairs as he yelled, "Found some!" and waved his clean underwear over his head.

Breakfast was served, lunches were packed, and as Ruby, Jax, and I sat at the table laughing at something Jax had said, Devon walked through the kitchen, stopping to kiss both of his children on the head as he passed.

"Ruby, be good for Aunt Evie this afternoon, and Jax, I'll pick you up from preschool on my way home."

"Bye, Daddy," Ruby said with a smile.

"Can we have pizza for dinner, Daddy?" Jax asked.

With a laugh, Devon responded. "Yeah, buddy. We can have pizza. Love you both."

"Love you too. Bye, Dad," Jax said, mouth full of pancake.

"Thanks again, Evie. I'll see you this evening." His voice was back to being friendly, but his words were still a little cold. That made me feel guilty. I was trying to help him, but he wasn't comfortable taking it from me.

"Have a good day." My voice was quiet and I didn't bother looking at him. I knew what I'd see – a man who missed his wife.

Chapter Three

Last Day of Freshman Year

"I don't think I've ever seen so much alcohol in one place." My eyes swept over the counter in the kitchen of the Beta house, which had been transformed into a temporary bar. At least fifty bottles of liquor were all lined up, and a few of the freshman Betas were manning them.

"Betas take end of the school year extremely seriously," Liv said, her voice already a little deep, her words slurred, the alcohol having its desired effect.

"Ladies, welcome to our little get together." My head turned toward the voice, and I smiled when I saw Elliot walking toward us. Since Liv and Devon had started seeing each other, we'd spent a lot of time at his house and I'd gotten to know quite a few of the brothers. I knew I was only accepted because I came with Liv, and without her, I would have been painfully out of place. However, a few of the guys genuinely seemed to like me, Elliot being one of them.

"Hey," I said, my smile brightening at his familiar face. "How'd finals go?"

"Well," he laughed, "I probably could have done better. My statistics class kicked my ass."

"But everything else went well?"

"I think so."

"Elliot, what exactly are you going to do with a sociology degree?" Liv's words were a little sharp, but he didn't seem to pick up on her tone.

He shrugged. "I'm not sure yet. I've still got another year to figure it out." He gave her a wink with his answer, which made me smile, but didn't amuse her.

"See, that's why I like Devon. He already has a plan. Business major then on to his master's in business. His track is all laid out for him. None of this uncertainty you seem to thrive on."

It had become obvious to me as I watched Liv fall for Devon, that his ambition and direction in life was something she latched on to, something she admired. His strong current down the river of his life pulled her right along with him. They balanced each other out in that way. She had been a free bird. She did what she wanted, when she wanted – not to mention *whom* she wanted. Now, she was his free bird and she followed him around. As long as she was with him, she felt like she had direction.

"I'll figure it out eventually," Elliot said, not unkindly. In fact, he'd never taken an annoyed or angry tone with Liv. Not even when she'd been completely out of line. That was one thing I really liked about him. "How about you, Evie?" His eyes found mine, his smile still friendly. "How did your finals go?"

I opened my mouth to answer, but Liv's voice rang out before I had a chance.

"Evie's finals were a piece of cake because she was taking mostly art courses where all the answers are subjective. How do you feel about this painting? What did this sculpture make you feel?" Her voice was exaggerated and haughty, making a show out of impersonating my professors. She wasn't far from the mark, I had found my finals kind of easy, but they were intro classes and hadn't been too difficult to begin with.

I laughed but then answered when she was finished.

"I think I did all right."

"Well then, let's get you a congratulatory drink." He held his hand out to me and offered me his ridiculously cute smile and I found myself putting my hand in his before I gave it a second thought. He immediately palmed my hand and then twined our fingers together as he pulled me through the crowd gathered in front of the bar. As we got closer to the liquor, the crowd grew thicker, and I pulled myself closer to him, my front pressed up against his arm. It felt nice to have my body pressed up against a man.

He made it right up to the counter and I saw his brothers nod at him in recognition. "Just get me a beer," he said, and then turned back to me. "What'll it be?" he asked, his lips moving closer to my ear. The movement of his breath on my skin sent prickles down my spine and I couldn't ignore how much I liked the feeling of them.

"Can I just have a vodka cranberry?"

"You can have anything you want." His eyes sparkled as he spoke, and I found myself smiling at him, feeling particularly punchy even without any alcohol in my system yet. He gave me a wink and then told the bartender my order. After a moment or two, and a much shorter wait than anyone else in the room had, we were handed our drinks. Elliot nodded toward the sliding doors, indicating he wanted to go outside, and I nodded in agreement. He then led me through the throngs of people, like fish swimming upstream, until we were finally outside.

I thought, since we weren't surrounded by people, he'd want to let go of my hand, but when I started to release his, he strengthened his grip and pulled me closer. It was impossible to hide the smile that stretched over my face. We walked to a bench overlooking their house's underwhelming yard – a large patch of grass with one sad, sagging volleyball net stretched across it, drooping in the middle. I sat first and then inwardly warmed when he sat down right next to me, even though it left plenty of empty bench on the other side of him.

"So," he said before sipping his beer. "You know all about my lack of ambition, tell me about your plans. You're a sophomore next year, right?"

I nodded. "Yeah, and I might be even more unmotivated than you."

"Well, now there's a challenge I will gladly accept. What makes you so unmotivated?"

"I don't know." I shrugged. "I guess I just don't really have the urge to find the career that will make me the most money."

"Ah, I see. You're not motivated by greed. Satan would be very disappointed in you."

"No," I laughed, "I suppose I'm not. And I make my lack of greed up to Satan by being really good at gluttony."

I watched as Elliot's eyes floated down over my body. He tried to hide it by bringing his red cup up to his lips and taking a drink, but there was no use, the heat his gaze caused followed the trail of his eyes. When they met back up with mine, and it was obvious he'd been caught ogling me, he simply smiled.

"Gluttony looks good on you." His comment floated in the air between us, both of us smiling like fools. "But seriously," he finally said, breaking the electric silence between us, "what is it you want to do after college?"

"Honestly?"

"Of course honestly. I never want you to lie to me."

I ignored the flip of my stomach at his use of the word never, as if we'd have an always. "I want to be a photographer."

"That's pretty ambitious," he said, his tone argumentative.

"You think so? I don't know. I think it sounds kind of lazy."

"I mean, I totally get why you feel that way, but when I think of people who do photography for a living, or art in general, I think of people relying on inspiration for their next paycheck. It's easy to show up for a desk job and get your monthly check, but a photographer's got to actually work for their money."

"I guess that's true," I replied, feeling a little better about the quiet dream I'd never really shared with anyone. "So, what are you really going to do with your sociology degree?"

"That's a good question. You'll be the first person I tell when I decide."

We sat on that bench for the majority of the evening, only leaving after we'd both downed multiple drinks and were feeling a little fuzzy. He asked me to dance and I had not one reason not to. Also, I was hoping I could feel my body pressed up against his again.

It was with my front pressed to his, my hands wrapped around his neck, his thigh between my knees, that I found a place in my mind where nothing else seemed to exist. I was just drunk enough to feel happy, slightly weightless, and loose, but not drunk enough to be stumbly or obnoxious. His hands were moving up and down my back, each downward swipe coming closer and closer to my backside. On each pass, I silently begged for him to graze his hands over my ass, to show me in some physical way he wanted me, wanted to do more than sit on a bench and drink with me.

"You're killing me here, Evie," he said in my ear, sending shivers throughout my body. He must have felt me tremble because his arms squeezed me gently. I took his admission as a clue that he needed me to move us forward, needed me to give him permission. I leaned away from him, feeling the scruff that had grown on his face throughout the day scrape against my cheek. My hands slid from the back of his neck to his shoulders, and I pulled him toward me, angling my face up to his.

The kiss, our first, was hesitant, soft, and mostly sweet. His lips brushed over mine, their lushness a surprise to me. They were plump and made it almost impossible not to kiss him a little harder, to use them to their capacity. We both inhaled, simultaneously pulling each other closer with the breath. His hand came up to grip the back of my neck and then his tongue was gently teasing. I opened, thankful he'd made the move and not waited for me, and I lost a little bit of myself in that kiss.

His tongue traced mine, and I let out a whimper. I couldn't find it in myself to be embarrassed by my sounds and, in fact, he seemed to like them. He responded with a low growl, which only made everything that was already burning up in my body liquefy. I forgot I was at a frat party, forgot I was on a dance floor surrounded by people, forgot about everything except Elliot and that kiss.

When he pulled away it was with a gasp, as if he'd forgotten to breathe while worshipping my lips, but then his mouth found my neck and slowly slid down, leaving a trail of wetness as his tongue darted out. I dropped my forehead to his shoulder, just trying to stay upright as his mouth assaulted me.

"I've wanted to kiss you for weeks, Evie."

Something about his words, the idea that he'd been thinking about me, wanting me, sent me over some proverbial line. Suddenly, I was desperate for his mouth. Hearing his need for me was more of an aphrodisiac than I'd ever experienced. My lips found his, and I kissed him with renewed vigor, my hands taking more liberties with his body, running down his chest, over his ribs, around his waist. He seemed to be enjoying the new enthusiasm with which I was kissing him, and before I was finished, he'd pulled away and grabbed my hand, leading me across the dance floor.

I followed him into the house and we made it to the staircase before he stopped and pushed me up against the wall, his hands spanning the sides of my hips, his tongue brushing up against mine again.

"I want to take you to my room," he rasped, his mouth against my neck again. I arched my back, pressing my breasts into his chest, aching for some sort of contact.

"Um, all right..." I responded.

"We don't have to have sex."

"Um, all right." He pulled away at my response.

"If you don't want to go upstairs, just tell me. Honestly, I just want to be alone with you, kiss you in an empty room, instead of being surrounded by a bunch of other people."

"Um, all right," I said, that time smiling. Luckily, he smiled in return. He grabbed my hand and led me further up the stairs to the second floor, then up to the third. We walked down a corridor of closed doors and I wondered how many of those doors had people behind them, and what state of undress they were in.

We stopped at a door and I watched as he pulled keys out of his pocket and unlocked it. He swung the door open and then motioned for me to enter first. I was pleasantly surprised that the room wasn't a disaster and it didn't smell. I'd been on the boy's floor of my dorm before and was appalled at how smelly boys could be when their mothers were no longer cleaning up after them. Elliot's room was neat, organized, and odor-free.

All thoughts of his room were pushed from my brain when his arms wrapped around me from behind and his luscious lips made contact with the skin just below my ear.

"I can't believe I've finally got you in my room," he said, his words breathed against my overheated skin. My hand gripped the overly long hair at the nape of his neck, my back arched pushing my backside right against the erection I felt there. "Every time I see you here, you're attached to Devon and Liv by the hip, and I always got the feeling I wasn't supposed to try to get with you."

All the heat disappeared at his words, and I was left cold. The sheen of sweat I'd built from the kissing was now a layer of cold wetness that blanketed me, causing me to shiver.

"What?" I asked, my hands paused in his hair, my back straightening, and hair on my arms prickling and standing up. He must have noticed the change in me, must have felt the shift in my arousal, and his hands stopped moving over me. "What do you mean?"

"Nothing, really. It just kind of always seemed like you were off limits."

I pulled away and turned to look at him, trying to find the real answer in his face. "Off limits? Why would I be off limits?"

"Evie, I'm not trying to upset you. It just always seemed like if I tried to talk to you or anything, Devon would have been upset about it."

"He's with Liv."

"I know. That's kind of why I always thought it was weird." His eyes never left mine, but they were filled with question and honesty. "Did you guys date before or something?"

I shook my head. "We've never dated. He's just my roommate's boyfriend." It was the truth, but for some reason, it felt like a lie.

"I don't want to step on anyone's toes, but I really like you, and I've wanted to kiss you ever since I first saw you." His hands came up to frame my face and my eyelids fluttered at his touch. "I don't like to share, Evie. So if you're with someone, let me know."

I shook my head slightly, my gaze darting back and forth between his lips and his big brown eyes. "I'm not with anyone. I want to be here with you."

"I'm going to kiss you now, but that's all tonight, okay? I just want to kiss you."

A big part of me was irritated that he was vowing only to kiss me, but a bigger part of me remembered his kisses and wanted them badly. "Okay."

He walked me backward slowly until my calves hit his mattress, and I landed on my butt with a bounce and a small laugh. He stood over me, his legs straddling my knees, which I was forcefully pressing together in an effort to relieve the pressure building between my legs. His hands came back to my face as he bent down and pressed his lips to mine.

He kissed me and I slowly fell backward on the bed, loving the delicious pressure of the mattress at my back and his body on my front. The noise from the party downstairs faded away and all I could hear were his breaths and low groans, which slipped out of him every once in a while. He kept to his word of just kissing, although his hands roamed over my clothed body.

He made me feel special. Wanted. Like he really had been wanting to kiss me forever and was so grateful finally to have me under him, to be able to kiss me however he wanted.

When a loud knock came at the door, he paused, almost as if he was waiting to see if the person knocking would go away. They didn't. The knocking came again along with a loud groan from Elliot.

"What do you want?" he yelled at the door.

"Elliot, is Evie in there with you?" Devon's voice sounded concerned from the other side of the door, and we both sat up, surprised to hear him.

"Shit," Elliot muttered as he stood and walked to the door. I sat up and watched him, using my fingers to straighten out my hair. When he opened the door, it was obvious he was irritated. I watched as he flung the door back and nearly barked, "What do you want?"

Devon looked surprised by Elliot's anger, but blinked it away, his eyes moving past Elliot to find me sitting on the bed. He looked me up and down, which embarrassed me as he was obviously looking for some evidence as to what we were doing on the bed. "I need Evie."

"For what?" Elliot growled before I could even respond.

"For Olivia."

Elliot scoffed, and then ran his hand over his chin. "Sure, man. Whatever."

Devon stared at Elliot for a few moments, neither one of them backing down. Finally, unable to stand the tension any longer, I stood and walked to the door.

"Where is she?"

"In the bathroom. She's drunk and wants to go home. Wouldn't let me take her myself."

I nodded, understanding. Sometimes, Liv wasn't a happy drunk. In fact, she was usually angry. And that anger was usually aimed at the male sex. "Give me a minute. I'll meet you down there."

Devon's eyes bounced between Elliot and me, looking uncomfortable with leaving me alone with him again. But after a few awkward moments, he walked away toward the stairs. I turned to Elliot, took his hand off the doorknob, and closed it slowly.

"It's not his fault," I said softly, hoping he'd calmed down a bit. "Olivia isn't a great person to be around when she's been drinking." I tentatively reached out my hand and wrapped it around his forearm, hoping he wouldn't pull away. I wanted to go back to five minutes ago when all I could feel were his hands on me and his mouth kissing me senseless. He let out a sigh at my touch, as though he was releasing some of the tension I could feel coiled in his muscled arms. When I slid my hand lower to his palm, he linked his fingers with mine and tugged me closer. It was my turn to sigh when he ran the back of his free hand over my cheek.

"You're oblivious and I can't tell if it's cute or irritating."

"I'm not oblivious," I whispered, even though I had no idea what he was referring to.

Elliot didn't respond, just ran his thumb over the line of my jaw, then up and over my bottom lip. He slowly leaned forward and kissed me without urgency or need. It was soft and warm. When he pulled away, I wasn't ready for his mouth to be gone, so I bit my lip to keep from frowning.

"When are you leaving to go home for the summer?" I was glad to hear all the anger had left his voice and he was back to the calm and gentle Elliot he'd been all night.

"Day after tomorrow."

"Can I take you to breakfast in the morning?"

I nodded.

"I'll pick you up at ten, okay?"

I nodded again. He leaned forward and pressed a kiss to my forehead.

"I'll see you then."

"Okay." He squeezed my hand just before he let it go, and then I opened the door and left to find my friend.

When I found Olivia, she was sitting on the floor of the communal bathroom down the hall from Devon's room. I cringed, thinking of how filthy the bathroom was and how her hands were lying flat on the nasty tiled floor. She was leaning up against the wall, head hanging low, her hair creating a veil over her face. One of her flip-flops had come off, and her purse was three feet away from her, splayed on the gross tiles.

"Okay, Livy, time to go." I knelt down and tried lifting her under her arms, not wanting to touch her hands. She didn't budge much, but she did grumble at me about wanting to go back to sleep. "Liv, seriously, get up off the floor. You're going to catch chlamydia down there." I tried to lift her again, but it was no use.

"Do you want some help?" Devon appeared in the doorway, arms crossed over his chest, watching me struggle.

"Would you mind?"

He didn't answer, but he walked to her, bent down, and with one arm around her back, the other behind her knees, he lifted her as if she weighed nothing. He moved to the door and I picked up her loose flip-flop and her purse, following behind.

"You can't carry her all the way home. Let's call a cab."

"Evie, it's not that far. I can make it." He punctuated his words by adjusting Liv in his arms, her body jumping but falling back closer to his. She was out. I'd never seen her that drunk before.

"How'd she get this drunk?" I asked as I followed him out of the house, the telltale sounds of the college party muting the farther we walked from the door.

"She just kept going back for more. I tried to get her to slow down, but when I realized she wasn't going to, I stopped drinking so at least one of us would be sober."

The thoughtfulness of his actions wasn't lost on me. Not all college boys would stay sober to make sure their sloppy-drunk date was safe. I imagined most boys would drink right along with her hoping it would lead to drunken sex. Liv looked anything but sexy right then.

"Liv has some issues. When she drinks, all the walls she usually puts up to protect herself fall down and she starts to feel things. Don't take it personally. It's not you she's angry with."

He was silent for a while and I just listened to the sound of our footsteps on the concrete.

"How high are her walls?" His voice was rough, a mixture of emotion and exhaustion.

"What do you mean?"

"Her walls. Are they so high that no one will ever be able to get over them? Or are they just, like, intimidatingly high?"

I thought about his question, picturing him on one side of a cartoonishly high wall, Liv on the other, back leaning up against it, hair fallen around her face, head bowed. "I don't think anyone's ever really tried to climb them."

"You're on the other side," he said in argument.

"I didn't climb it, though. I watched her build it and just happened to end up on the right side." It was true. I'd been a part of her life before she'd been damaged and, thankfully, she'd never pushed me away. He let out a loud sigh, either from frustration or from exertion. "No one's ever really stuck around long enough to try to break through, Devon. She's never let anyone get that close."

I saw determination in his eyes and again, couldn't tell if it was his will to carry her all the way to our dorm, or his need to get through to her. I figured it was probably a lot of both.

We were silent for the rest of the walk to our dorm, which was fine with me. I didn't want to talk about imaginary walls or how just having Liv in his arms, he was literally and figuratively closer to her than anyone else she'd been with in years. She looked good in his arms and he looked good holding her. I tried to ignore the small part of my gut that ached with that realization.

We made it silently up to our room and I watched as Devon laid Liv down with ease, gentleness, and care on her bed. He had beads of sweat on his brow and his biceps were flushed red under the sheen of the fluorescent lights. He pulled her covers up over her body and then pulled our tiny wastebasket to sit right on the floor next to her head. Thoughtful. I watched as his eyes roamed around our room and then he moved to her desk, grabbing the water bottle she usually took to the gym, and then disappeared into the hall. He returned just a minute later, the water bottle full from the drinking fountain. He placed it next to the wastebasket, and then turned to me.

"Do you have any pain killers?"

I opened my desk drawer and pulled out my generic bottle of Tylenol. I handed it to him and he placed it on the floor next to the water bottle.

"Make sure she takes the pills and drinks the water whenever she's conscious enough."

"Do you think she has alcohol poisoning?"

"No. She didn't drink enough for that. She's just passed out. Hopefully, if she gets sick, it'll make it in the garbage."

I scrunched up my nose, making a mental note about how I wasn't going to clean up her vomit.

"You're a good friend," Devon said, pulling my eyes from Liv back to him.

I shrugged. "I just carried her flip flop."

"No. You left the party, and Elliot, to help your friend." His voiced steeled a little at the mention of Elliot's name.

"She'd do the same for me," I said.

"I hope so, but I'm not entirely sure." A silence fell between us again and I wasn't sure what to say. I knew it was time for him to go, but I couldn't find the will to send him on his way. "Listen," he finally said as he pushed his hands into the pockets of his jeans. "Elliot's an okay guy. I don't have anything bad to say about him to try to steer you away, but something just doesn't feel right about it."

"We were just hanging out," I said quietly, suddenly feeling like I had to defend myself.

Devon held up his hand, palm out, to stop my words. His face was contorted as if he were in pain. "I don't want to know what you were doing with him."

"Okay," I whispered.

"Just..." he started to say, but his words tapered off. "Just promise me you'll be careful."

I nodded at his words and whispered again, "All right."

He nodded and then turned, walking to the door. Just before he walked out of it, he turned to me, gave me the saddest, weakest smile I'd ever seen, and then closed the door behind him as he left. I heard his heavy footsteps until he got to the stairs, and then I released the biggest breath I'd ever held. I grabbed my nightgown, locked the door, then proceeded to get ready for bed, trying desperately not to think about Devon, his face when he pictured me with another guy, and the way my entire body filled with butterflies at his reaction.

Chapter Four

Present Day

"Great. Perfect. Now, tilt your head just a little to the left. Right there."

My finger hit the shutter button furiously as I snapped the picture I'd been trying to create all morning. The light was battling me at first, then the wind, but finally, I was able to capture the perfect image. Or so I thought, anyway. My model, a woman I'd worked with more times than I could count, knew what I was looking for, and gave me gorgeous shot after gorgeous shot. My adrenaline was pumping, knowing I'd found my little pot of gold.

After a few minutes of my suggesting poses and Shelby, my model, doing beautiful work, we both paused as a cloud shrouded the sun. Usually, losing light in the middle of a good round would piss me off, but I knew I'd already gotten the shot I wanted, so I could do nothing but smile furiously.

"That was amazing, Shelby. Thank you. I think we got it." She smiled at me and came to look at my camera over my shoulder as I showed her the images I'd captured.

"You're brilliant," she said, her voice full of wonder, as she looked at the screen on the camera.

"Well, you're pretty damned amazing yourself." She laughed and we both got to work cleaning up our supplies. Shelby was a great model, but what made her even better was that she was a licensed cosmetologist, so I never had to hire a make-up artist. She was a twofer. I loved it, and sometimes even used her to do make-up when I wasn't photographing her. She'd been with me for a few years and we definitely didn't have a strictly professional relationship. As many women tended to do, when we worked together, we talked about our personal lives. I knew about her husband, and their troubles getting pregnant, and she knew all about the hardships I'd faced in the last few years.

"How's Devon doing?" she asked as she slipped a hooded sweatshirt over her head, covering up the sweeping lace dress she'd worn for the shoot.

I shrugged. "I guess he's doing fine. Although, we don't really talk about Liv often. I'm usually only there to get the kids ready for school and then in the evenings until he comes home."

"And the kids?"

"Better every day," I said with a small smile. "They miss her, obviously. Some days are harder than others, but the sadness is lessening, and they're having more good days than bad, I think. I hope."

"And how are you?" This question was asked with even more gentleness than the others, her voice soft and full of genuine concern.

I sighed, zipped up my camera bag, and then looked at her. "I'm all right, I think."

"That was the least convincing of all your answers," Shelby said, cocking her hip out to one side, resting her hand on it, waiting for me to elaborate.

"I don't know. I've been so focused on keeping her family together, I haven't really been able to mourn her." I shook my head at myself, feeling guilty for even uttering the words. "As soon as she passed, I immediately wanted to help her family, like she asked me to. But it almost feels like I'm stepping in for her while she's away on business or something. Especially, with Devon." I paused, trying to put my thoughts together. "Every day he expects me to be there and I am, and I don't mind. But he hasn't fully tried to live life without her, because I'm always there, pretending right along with him, that everything is fine. That this is all normal."

"Have you talked to him about it? Explained how you feel?"

My hands fell limp at my sides, tears threatening. "I couldn't say that to him. He just lost his wife. He doesn't need her emotional friend making things harder for him."

"You're not just her *emotional friend*," she said, using her fingers to make quotation marks in the air. "You were her best friend, Evelyn. You're those kids' honorary auntie. You're a part of their family."

Trying desperately not to let my voice crack, feeling the pinch of sobs in the back of my throat, I responded, "My link to that family died. I've got no claim on them anymore." From day to day, the worst part of losing Liv changed. At first, I was sad because I'd lost my best friend. Then I was sad because she was so young and the tragedy was too much to handle. Then I'd think about her children and how devastating it was that they'd lost the chance to be raised by their mother, the one person in the world who loved them the most. But today, the saddest part of losing my best friend was that, with losing her, I lost her family too; lost my link to them, my connection. My head dropped into my hands as I tried to fight off the cries wanting to rip free from me.

"Evelyn." Her voice was soft and full of worry. I didn't want her pity. I hadn't lost a mother or a wife. The sadness I felt was almost as bad as the guilt it caused. "It's okay for you to mourn her, to feel the loss. You lost her too." I felt her hand come to my shoulder and I tried not to shy away from it, knew she was just trying to comfort me.

"It's just hard," I said with finality, even though the hardness – the wake in my world caused by the disruption of her death –

was never final. It felt like it would last forever. I would be feeling her loss forever.

When the pinching in my throat had lessened and my breathing was under control again, I moved to continue packing up my gear. I kept my gaze from Shelby, but sensed she'd moved away to pack as well. Minutes later, after everything was picked up, I raised my head to see Shelby loading up her car. I walked hesitantly toward her, biting my lower lip, not wanting to have another breakdown in front of her.

"Hey," I said as I approached. She turned to me as she pulled the trunk of her car closed.

"Hey." She smiled and it was friendly. It shouldn't surprise me, we were friends, but it did.

"Thanks for listening and trying to help."

"Anytime."

"Okay. Well, I'll call you when I've got the proofs," I said, motioning to my camera.

"Sounds good, but Evelyn, you can call me anytime, for any reason."

"I'll remember that. And thank you." We both smiled at each other, and then I turned toward my car, glad the exchange was over and I'd made it out without shedding any more tears. Once I was seated behind the steering wheel, I reached into the center console to get my phone. I tried never to keep it on me during a shoot because it was distracting. I noticed I had a text from Devon.

I've been called into a last minute dinner meeting. Is there any way you can pick Jax up from school and stay with the kids until I get home? I'm really sorry, Evie.

I sighed. I hated this conflict; wanting to be supportive, to help him in any way I could, but knowing my help was enabling him, making it impossible for him to heal entirely.

Sure. I'll be there when Ruby gets off the bus then pick Jaxy up from school.

It wasn't even ten seconds before I got a reply.

You're the best.

I couldn't find a response to that, besides my mind yelling loudly that I wasn't the best. Not even close. The best for him and his children had died, leaving me to pick up the pieces.

Ruby had come home from school announcing she had a project due the next day, which she hadn't started. So, even if I had planned a quiet evening at Devon's house, I didn't get one. What I got was a rambunctious Jax and a bossy, temperamental Ruby, stressed out about how she was going to make a mummy for her report on ancient Egypt.

After we'd eaten a quick dinner of hot dogs and macaroni and cheese, I sent Jax to watch his favorite cartoon, while Ruby and I molded the shape of a small person out of newspaper.

"Auntie Evie, this isn't going to work." Ruby was turning into a tiny pessimist.

"Ruby, a positive attitude is much more attractive than being a whiner."

"I'm not whining."

"If I looked up the word whiner in the dictionary, it would have a picture of you right next to the definition."

Her mouth fell open in offense, which only caused me to laugh.

"Tell you what. I'll finish building the mummy and get the goop ready for the papier-mâché. Why don't you take your bath and get ready for bed? Once you're all pajama'd up, we'll finish this together."

"Promise you won't start gooping him up without me?"

"Promise."

"Okay." I watched her hop down from the dining room table and run through the living room, then listened to her footsteps go all the way up the stairs. I took just a moment to pop my head into the family room to check on Jax, only to find him passed out on the couch, sleeping the way only children and drunk adults could, oblivious to the world around him. I decided to leave him to sleep, planning to transfer him to his bed after our mummy adventure was over.

The shower ran and I finished building a small person made of crumpled up newspaper, then dug in the cupboards for the flour. I pulled out a large bowl and got to work mixing a little bit of water with the flour, trying to get the right consistency. I heard the front door open and close, figured Devon had come home, and kept working. I heard his footsteps come closer to the kitchen and just when I opened my mouth to utter a greeting, my heart stalled and my pulse paused.

I felt his hand before I saw it, starting at my hip, squeezing gently, and then sliding over my stomach. His front pressed into my back and his lips brushed gently over my temple. It was just one and a half seconds of my life, but it exploded in my mind, grew to infinite proportions and I knew whatever axis my world had been spinning on three seconds before, it was now careening in a new direction. My hands came to grip the counter in front of me, holding me up because my legs were useless.

"Devon," I whispered, clearly shocked. At my voice, I felt his entire body still; he went positively cold.

"Shit," he said, stepping away from me as if I'd just burst into flame. "Shit," he repeated.

I slowly turned, my face clearly showing my confusion. I could feel my eyebrows were very nearly into my hairline. I still wasn't breathing normally, still hadn't found the regular beat of my heart.

"I'm so sorry, Evie," he said, running a hand down his face. "I came home and saw you there, where Liv used to always be... and your blonde hair..."

He'd seen me and thought I was her. He'd forgotten his wife had died and he'd wrapped his arm around me like I was her. He held me for just a moment like he held the woman he loved. I was cracking on the outside. He could see it. He watched as I started to fall apart, but whatever he could see on the outside was only a small fraction of the destruction going on within me.

A part of me had wondered what his hands felt like. For years. Ever since the day we'd met. Now I knew. Now I knew they were incredible.

"I have to go," I said quickly, turning and reaching for my purse on the table. "It's two parts flour to three parts water."

"What?" he asked, confused.

"The papier-mâché for Ruby's mummy. Two parts flour to three parts water. Just dip the newspaper strips in the goop and cover the mummy. I have to go." I fled the kitchen like a murderer escaping from the scene of a crime. I absolutely could not think about anything besides Devon's hand covering my womb.

I'd made it half way down the front porch steps when I heard his voice call out my name.

"Evelyn, wait!"

My feet stopped moving like the traitors they were. I stopped, but I did not turn around, could not see his face as he processed that he'd touched the wrong woman. The heat coming from his body alerted me that he was just inches away, this time on purpose.

"Evie," he whispered. I waited a beat, giving him a second to get his thoughts together, but when no more words came from him, I spoke.

"It's okay," I said, my voice sounding so much stronger than I actually was. Inside I was crumbling.

"No, it's not. Please, don't leave like this."

"It's not a big deal."

"It *is* a big deal."

"It was a mistake. An accident." It was true, but it didn't make me feel any better.

"The first time I kiss you shouldn't be a mistake." His voice was so quiet, the whisper barely even audible, but I heard it and I tucked it deep inside of me, hoping it was buried deep enough that it would never surface again.

I made my feet press forward, made each foot step in front of the other until I made it to my car. Then I got in and I drove away.

It was hours before I made it home. I'd spent the late evening driving as far from my town as I could get, trying to escape the feeling of my spirit being crushed, but after driving for two hours, I realized the feeling wasn't attached to the town; it was attached to me. I turned around, stopped for gas, and pulled into my driveway around midnight.

When I finally made it to bed, I couldn't sleep. I lay there all night wondering what in the hell I was going to do, how I was going to proceed. I could pretend as if nothing had happened, but it had. I could pretend as though it meant nothing to me, but it meant everything. I could laugh about it, pretend like it was amusing, when actually it was devastating. The only thing clear after a night of tossing and turning was I would be doing a lot of pretending.

However, that wasn't something new for me.

Chapter Five

The Next Day - College

"Why are you moving so quickly?" Liv groaned from her bed, the first intelligible words I'd heard from her all morning. Up until then, all I'd heard were groans and possible swear words. In the middle of the night, I'd woken her up enough to give her the water and the pain pills, but she seemed to be coming around now.

"I'm meeting Elliot for breakfast in twenty minutes."

"What time is it?" She was speaking, but she wasn't moving.

"Nearly ten."

Another loud groan came from her bed.

"Just go back to sleep. I'll be back later." I sat down on my bed, pulling on my ankle boots.

"How'd I get back here anyway?"

"Devon carried you," I said, my snarky tone implying I didn't approve of the method, still remembering the way his biceps were twitching by the time we got to our dorm. The way his arms were wrapped around her.

"He *carried* me?"

"Yeah, you were passed out." I stood up and walked to the large mirror, which hung on the inside of my armoire. It wasn't full-length, but it did a good enough job. I turned from one side to another, trying to inspect my outfit from all possible angles. I was wearing a cotton skirt that flowed down to my knees with a tank top. I pulled on my worn-soft jean jacket, knowing it wouldn't be too warm outside yet. I flipped my blonde hair from the collar as I turned back to Liv. "Go back to sleep, Liv. You're still drunk."

"You're probably right," she said from under her covers.

"I'll be back eventually. Then we seriously need to pack if we're going to be ready to leave tomorrow morning." Her groan was all the response I needed. I grabbed my purse and headed down the stairs to wait for Elliot. I'd been sitting on the bench in front of my dorm for what seemed like forever, about ready to call it quits and go back upstairs, when a big red pickup truck parked in front of the lawn. I watched as the window rolled down, Elliot's face appearing from inside the cab, smile shining brightly.

I couldn't help the way my lips tipped up at his smile, and I didn't try to stop it. It felt natural. As I walked toward his truck, I saw him come around the bed, looking just as cute as I remembered him.

"Hey," he said easily as he opened the passenger door for me. I looked up hesitantly, and then looked down at my skirt.

"I didn't dress for mountain climbing." His truck was big.

"Just step on the rail there and you should be fine."

"Oh," I said, just noticing the little step seemingly made for situations just like the one I was in. "How convenient."

"If you're gonna drive a truck this big, gotta make it skirt friendly," he said with a wink. I couldn't help but roll my eyes, laughing all the while. He shut my door then climbed up into the driver's seat, started the truck, and pulled out onto the street.

"How's your roommate this morning?" he asked once we'd made it back onto the main road.

"She's as well as can be expected. Devon carried her the entire way home last night and she didn't wake up once."

"That's rough. Should we bring her back some greasy food?" He turned to look at me, waiting for my response, his expression soft and expectant. I felt the tiniest flutter of wings in my belly at his thoughtful gesture.

"I'm sure she'd be really grateful," I managed.

We made small talk about classes and finals until he pulled into the parking lot of what looked like it might have been an abandoned building.

"It doesn't look like much, but this place has the best food in town. No one talks about it though because we don't want the secret to get out." His words were tumbling out of his mouth, right past the beautiful smile he'd been wearing since he picked me up and my cheeks heated with a blush as I thought about how good looking he was. He wasn't rugged and he wasn't tall or dark, but he was the typical All American, Boy Next Door, cute. I watched as he walked around the front of the truck, opened my door, then gasped a little as his hands grasped my waist, gently lifting me from the truck and depositing me safely on the ground.

"Thank you," I managed to whisper.

"I'll help you out of my truck any day, Evelyn." I thought I'd reached the pinnacle of my blushing's capabilities, but when his hand reached down and wrapped around mine, my face heated even more. Something about the way he was upfront with his feelings for me was undeniably attractive. He was so easy with me, so open. It was just as refreshing as it was unusual. I was used to guys playing cool and not paying me too much attention, which was frustrating. Elliot seemed to be transparent, which I couldn't deny was attractive.

We entered the restaurant and I was pleasantly surprised to find the outside did not reflect the inside. The interior was straight-up country diner, with red checkered tablecloths and everything. Cute little salt and pepper shakers adorned each table, along with red and yellow squeezy bottles for ketchup and mustard. It was clean, adorable, and the waitress who approached us was all smiles.

"Elliot, didn't think you'd be around after classes let out." She was a round woman in her mid-forties, wearing a waitress uniform you'd imagine someone in a movie wearing: blue dress, white ruffled apron, and a pad of paper and pen sticking out of its pocket.

"Well, I promised Evelyn here a breakfast date before we both left town."

The waitress, whose nametag read Marianne, turned her attention to me and said, "Lucky girl," with what sounded like affection. She grabbed two menus and we followed her to a booth where Elliot and I sat across from each other. After we'd ordered our drinks and Marianne left us, I attempted to make small talk.

"So, why does the waitress know your name?"

He smiled and then responded. "The frat house can be a hard place to study. It gets loud and the guys aren't always willing to quiet down so I can cram for a test." He shrugged. "It's just part of frat life. Anyway, this place is open twenty-four hours and they're really cool about letting me study here, you know, as long as I order some food and stuff."

"So, you're here a lot."

"You could say that. Plus, you can't get biscuits and gravy like theirs anywhere else. In fact, I'm gonna miss this place over the summer." He smiled again, and then laughed softly. "I'm not sure who I'm kidding; I'll probably drive down once or twice just for the food."

"How far away do you live?" I asked, curious about him.

"I'm about two hours north of here, in Bakersfield. What about you? Where are you headed tomorrow?"

"Liv and I are from Portsmouth, about three hours east."

"Well, that's good news."

"What is?" I asked, confused.

"That you're not getting on a plane or going somewhere really far away." He reached into his pocket and pulled out his cell phone, typing furiously with this thumbs. Finally, he held his phone up, screen pointing at me, and I saw what looked to be a page from Google Maps. "See, look. If I take the bypass it's only a three hour and forty-five minute drive to your town."

My cheeks blushed at the thought of Elliot driving nearly four hours to see me. No one had ever made such an effort. "Don't you have some girl back home waiting for you?" I couldn't imagine someone as charming and courteous as Elliot without a band of girls vying for his attention. He gave a small cough at my question; apparently, I'd struck a nerve.

"No one's waiting for me, no. My high school girl friend will probably be home for summer, but we haven't been together in over two years. She's moved on, so have I. But, we have the same friends, so I'm sure I'll be seeing her."

"Elliot, I was kidding. You don't owe me any explanations."

At my words he reached across the table and took my hand in his, gently squeezing it. "I might not owe you an explanation, but I want to give it to you anyway." Then he shrugged and laced his fingers with mine. "Last night wasn't just some hook up. I've wanted to ask you out for weeks. I totally understand if you want to just say goodbye today, and maybe see each other in the fall, but I'm kind of hoping I can see you this summer."

I swallowed thickly, a little caught off guard by his declaration. "I'd like that."

A gorgeous smile spread slowly across his face, his brilliantly white teeth showing, eyes sparkling. "Great," he said confidently. I couldn't help but smile back at him, it was impossible to resist.

The rest of our breakfast date was effortless and comfortable. We ate, laughed, shared about our families, and talked about plans for the summer. He was genuinely interested in whatever it was I had to say. He listened with rapt attention, laughing when appropriate, smiling, and nodding. Listening. Aside from Liv, I'd never felt so comfortable talking to someone.

We sat at our table for hours, Marianne never making us feel like we had to leave, even though we took up a table for the entire lunch rush. Elliot never stopped touching me. When we ate, his foot pressed up against mine under the table. When we talked, his hand was holding mine, his thumb making soft circles on the inside of my wrist. His touch slowly built a fire inside of me, and by the time we decided to leave the diner, I could hardly wait to be alone with him in the privacy of the cab of his truck.

We took a to-go order for Liv, which I still thought was incredibly sweet of him, and he helped me into the passenger side of his truck. I placed Liv's food on the bench seat nearest my door, and scooted more toward the middle. I watched as Elliot opened his door, reaching in, grasping the steering wheel, the muscles in his forearm rippling. Then, suddenly, he was next to me. Strong biceps pressed into my shoulder. The hand that had just been gripping the wheel landed softly on my leg just above my knee.

My eyes darted to where his hand made contact, and then slowly made their way to meet his gaze.

"Thank you for breakfast," I said, as my sight wandered to his lips.

"It was more like brunch," he said, his lips lifting into another beautiful smile.

"Thank you for brunch," I acquiesced. He nodded slightly, and then I saw his free hand rise. He pushed some wayward hair behind my ear, and then his large hand slid around to the back of my neck, gripping me there softly, but with just enough force to take my breath away completely.

"I'm going to kiss you now." His voice was low, his smile had disappeared, and in its place was a serious expression, one of longing.

"Okay," was all I could manage before his impossibly soft lips touched mine.

I breathed in his kiss, taking everything from him in that moment. My hands pressed against his chest, slowly folding my fingers around the soft cotton of his shirt, pulling myself as close to him as I could. The night before, our kisses had been passionate and new, exciting and hurried. But in that moment, with hours of conversation and laughter between us, we were connecting on another level.

His hand slid slowly up from my knee, smoothing over the bare skin beneath my skirt, but only came to grip the fleshiest part of my thigh, inches below the elastic of my panties. I didn't want to go any further, sitting in a restaurant parking lot at a diner, but a large part of me wanted to know what it would feel like to have his hands all over me, his fingers inside of me. A flash of heat climbed through me at the thought of him being inside of me at all, and I pulled him closer.

When we finally pulled away from each other, we were both panting. He rested his forehead against mine and his hand came back up to frame my face.

"I foresee myself coming to visit you a lot this summer."

I smiled, and then pressed a small kiss against his lips. "I foresee myself enjoying that a lot."

"I hate to even tear myself away from you, but I think we should get going. Another kiss like that, and I'll lose my mind."

Laughing, I disentangled myself from him, sliding carefully toward the center of the bench, but before I got too far, his hand was back on my leg. This time, though, his fingers were higher up and just barely under the hem of my skirt. Just the sight sent shivers up my spine and goose bumps along my thigh. Whether or not he noticed, I'd never know, but his thumb grazed the sensitive skin all the way back to my dorm.

When he pulled up to my dorm, a wave of sadness washed over me. Why had he waited so long to make his move? Now it was summer and we were both headed in different directions. The excitement of new romance was being squashed by our separation.

"Elliot, why did you wait so long to ask me out? I mean," I said nervously, tucking my hair behind my ear. "I'm glad you did, but, now it'll be really hard to see each other. We could have been doing this for weeks by now."

He turned the ignition off and turned to face me on the bench seat. "Can I ask you a question before I answer you?"

I shrugged. "Sure."

"What's your history with Devon?"

His question caught me off guard and my head pulled back as my face contorted into a look of confusion. "What?"

"Don't get upset. It doesn't matter to me, I'm just curious."

"I don't have a history with Devon. He's my best friend's boyfriend."

His eyes were darting back and forth between mine as he was silent for a few moments. Then his thumb and forefinger came up to touch my chin, looking directly into my eyes, leaving me even more confused than before. When his hand fell away, his forefinger trailed down the front of my throat and my body immediately reacted, my breath shuddering. "Sometimes," he started to say, his voice low, and then it looked like he changed his mind about his words. "Before, when you'd come around with Liv, it was obvious Devon and Liv were together, or, that he was interested in her."

"Yeah?" I urged him to continue.

"But it also kind of seemed like you were into Devon."

"Oh," was my response. Without thinking about it, I pulled back, putting a little distance between us.

"If there's nothing there, I totally believe you. But, before last night, I was never sure and I didn't want to pursue you if it was going to be a waste of time."

My mind was racing, thoughts pinging back and forth inside my head, making me feel mentally dizzy. It never occurred to me that strangers would think that about me, that people who just observed me would think I was interested in Devon. When we'd first met, I'd been insanely attracted to him, hoped with almost embarrassingly frequency that we'd run into each other on campus and we'd laugh about our first meeting, then we'd fall in love and have a dream life together. The night I realized Liv was dating *the guy* who I'd met and been harboring a teenage crush on, for just a small moment, I was devastatingly jealous.

But to think other people could see the feelings I thought I was hiding so well..., well, that made me nervous. I was sure the silly feelings I thought I had for him had been buried a while ago. Once he and Liv were a real thing, I had tried to turn it all off. I tried to ignore the way my eyes always found his form at a crowded party, ignored the way his hand always pressed into the small of my back when I went through a door ahead of him, and the way my heart reacted to his hand there. I was suddenly extremely nervous that not only Devon had noticed my not-so-well-hidden feelings, but Liv might have as well.

"Elliot, listen, I'm sorry if I gave you the wrong impression. There's nothing going on between Devon and me. There never was."

He was quiet for a moment. "I'm glad for that, honestly, because I'd like to see what could develop between us. But, I just wanted to make sure you weren't hung up on someone else before I got invested."

I shook my head, even though there was a tiny voice inside my head questioning the very idea. Was I hung up on Devon? I didn't think so. Sure, he was cute and sweet. And he treated Liv so well. But it wasn't anything more than a stupid crush. That was it. Not serious enough to turn Elliot away. "I'm not hung up on Devon," I stated, with just the tiniest roll of my stomach that felt like betrayal.

"Good," he said as he smiled and leaned in toward me. "Because I'm pretty sure I'm gonna like getting hung up on you." Then his lips were on mine again, sweet and slow, making my heart rate accelerate and my fingers ache to run through his hair.

"I'd better go," I said on an exhale as I pulled away minutes later. I watched his tongue dart out and lick his lips, as if he were trying to taste every last drop of me, and my breath caught in my throat.

"Okay," he said, sounding like he regretted it. "But let me see your phone first." I smiled and handed him my cell, watching as he programmed his number in, and then called his own phone. "Expect to be hearing from me. Soon." He said it with a grin as he handed my phone back to me.

"Great."

"Yeah. Great." He smirked then leaned in again, pressing a fast kiss against my lips, and then pulled away with a wink. I took Liv's food and hopped down from the truck, giving Elliot my best smile as I shut the door. I turned, walking back to my dorm, hoping Liv hadn't died of starvation, thinking about how excited I was to spend the summer getting to know Elliot.

Chapter Six

Present Day

"Ruby, Jax, come on, time to wake up."

It had taken every ounce of strength I had to muster up the courage to come back to Devon's house the next morning. Every time I closed my eyes, I saw the image of Devon's hand sliding over my belly, felt his lips on me, felt my body react to him in both lust and shock. I hated that my body liked his hands on me, wanted to feel them again, had secretly been longing for them for years. But I felt anger and guilt most, anger toward myself for feeling these things for my dead best friend's husband.

The children hadn't stirred. "Ruby, Jax, time to get ready for school." My voice sounded harsh and angry, even to me. Ruby stirred, groaning, but I had to shake Jax awake, gently moving his shoulder back and forth. "Come on, kiddo, let's go."

"Auntie Evie?" I heard Ruby ask, her voice thick and gravelly with sleep.

"Yeah?"

"Last night you left before we finished my mummy."

My pulse thrummed through my veins, beating hard in my ears. "Yeah, sorry, Ruby. I had to go home." I walked to Jax's dresser, opening drawers, pulling clothes out for him, trying to keep myself busy so I didn't have to look into the eyes of my best friend's daughter.

"Daddy said you weren't feeling well. Do you feel better today?"

"Yeah, baby." I lied to a child.

"Daddy wasn't very good at making my mummy. He didn't really know what he was doing."

"I'm sure it's fine, Ruby. Come on, time to get dressed. Jax, you awake?"

"Yeah," his tiny voice rang out.

"Okay, get up, kids. I'll go get breakfast ready."

I walked down the stairs, hands trembling, heartbeat racing, knowing that in just minutes I'd be seeing Devon. I'd tossed and turned all night trying to come up with a good way to play this situation. Avoidance? Should I stay away forever? Denial? Should I pretend like nothing happened? The direct approach? Should I confront Devon and force us to talk about it?

None of the options I came up with sounded like a good solid plan so, in the end, I decided just to follow his lead. Minutes later, as I was placing bowls of cereal on the table, I heard his footsteps on the stairs and I froze. Something that felt perfectly akin to fear ran through my veins like ice. I was petrified. Absolutely terrified to face him. I heard him make it all the way to the kitchen, then his footfalls stopped, and I knew he was stalled in the entrance, could feel his eyes on me.

"Evelyn." The fact that he used my full name might as well have been a knife right through my back. He *never* used my full name. Well, not usually. "I wasn't expecting you to be here this morning." The proverbial knife twisted counter-clockwise.

"Well," I managed, my voice only trembling slightly, "It's a good thing I came, otherwise your children would probably have been late."

"Evie," he sighed, and I heard two footsteps bring him closer. "I didn't mean that to sound like I didn't want you here."

"All you have to do is tell me not to be here anymore, and I won't be. I told Liv I'd help take care of her family, but I won't stay some place I'm not wanted."

"Please, Ev—" he said, stepping toward me, but I turned around and held up my hand to stop him.

"No. No apologies. I couldn't take it if you apologized again."

His hands dropped to his sides, his face fallen in defeat. "Please, tell me how to fix this."

I turned around and moved toward the kitchen island, inwardly cringing, knowing I'd moved to the exact spot I was standing the night before when he'd touched me. I started to mindlessly make the kids' lunches, trying to keep my eyes on *anything* besides him.

"There's nothing to fix. Let's just move on and pretend it never happened."

Devon never responded, just stood in the doorway for a few moments, then sighed, and moved further into the kitchen, prepared his coffee, then walked out the door.

I'd never sighed as loudly or heavily as I did moments after he left. Never, not even when Liv passed away, had I had such stinging tears burning in my eyes. I couldn't help but hate myself a little more for that fact. Hands braced against the counter, head bowed, breaths heaving, I fought hard to keep the tears at bay, to keep them inside me where they mattered less than splattered on my dead best friend's countertop.

And, as if I couldn't hate myself any more in that moment, I realized I was angry with Liv for being dead. If she were alive, this never would have happened.

I couldn't keep the cries in anymore. They fell out of me, clawing to get free, until I heard the voices of Ruby and Jax coming down the stairs. With strength I never knew I possessed, I harnessed my sobs and reined in my emotions. I was in control just enough so that when the children entered, they were only slightly convinced I wasn't upset. Children, no matter how often we try to tell ourselves otherwise, are observant and smart. They just lack tact.

"Are you crying?" Ruby asked as soon as she saw my face.

"I stubbed my toe." More lies to a child.

"But you're wearing shoes," she questioned. See? Smart. Observant.

"I stubbed it really hard. Here. Sit down and eat your breakfast."

The children did as they were asked, and didn't question my splotchy face.

"Jaxy, today is a half day at preschool, so I'll be there to pick you up, okay?"

"M'kay," he answered, his mouth full of the kind of sugary crap their mother would never have fed them. Liv would have gotten up early and made sure her children had a well-balanced breakfast before they went to school.

"Ruby, I'm gonna go take a look at your mummy. Where did your daddy put it?"

"It's in the laundry room. Daddy said he could turn the fan on in there and it would dry faster."

"Well, that was pretty smart." I walked away from the kitchen table and headed toward the laundry room. When I peeked inside, I nearly got whiplash from the rapid change in emotion. One second, I was morose and riddled with guilt. The next, I could hardly hold myself up from laughing so hard. Sitting atop a collapsible drying rack was, what looked to be, a mummy that had been completely disfigured and then put back together in the wrong order; kind of like a Mr. Potato head if it had been put together by someone who had lost all feeling in their hands. And was blind. And possibly drunk. Nothing about the mummy looked great. But it was dry, so not all was lost.

I walked back to the kitchen, examining the poor mummy, still smiling at the mental image of Devon, still in his work clothes, sleeves rolled up, attempting to papier-mâché a tiny person.

"Rubster, I'm sorry, but this mummy is going to have to do. Just tell your teacher you were trying to portray the people as they're drawn in the hieroglyphics."

"The what?" The wideness of her eyes indicated she had no idea what hieroglyphics were.

"What kind of education are you getting where you're studying Egypt, but not hieroglyphics?"

"Uh, the kind where they teach speaking English," she answered, with more snark than I'd like to hear from a seven-year-old.

"Touché, kid."

"Why do you keep using words we don't understand?" Jaxy asked, just before he shoveled more cereal into his mouth.

"Hieroglyphics were drawings people made in ancient Egypt that told stories. They were kind of like the first stick-people drawings. And sometimes the people they drew looked a little funny."

"Like my mummy?"

"Exactly."

"What does too-shay mean?" Jaxy's asked and I smiled at his pronunciation.

"It's the same as saying 'good point.'"

"So, why didn't you just say 'good point?'" Ruby asked, again with the snark.

"Because then we wouldn't have had this enlightening conversation." Both kids looked at me with a question in their eyes, probably wondering what enlightening meant, but then they both smiled at the same time, with the same smile, and I couldn't help but smile back. They had their mother's smile. Two tiny Liv's were smiling at me, and I couldn't find a way to be upset in that moment.

All the anger and guilt washed away when those children smiled. Liv knew I wasn't perfect, and she didn't expect me to be the perfect fill-in for her. She just wanted me to be here and love her kids. I was doing the best I could.

And so was Devon.

Suddenly, I felt terrible about the way I'd treated him. The last thing he needed was someone making him feel worse about a mistake he already felt terrible about. Even the instant it occurred, I knew he was sorry, knew it wasn't intentional, and I shouldn't have made him feel worse. I had no idea what it felt like to lose a spouse.

I continued to smile because I was glad I'd resolved the situation in my mind, but I knew I still had to resolve it with Devon. I sighed, resigning to get the kids to their respective schools, complete my work for the day, and hopefully come up with a solution by the time he returned home that evening.

With Ruby on the school bus and Jax safely delivered to preschool, I headed toward my tiny studio. I paid more for rent on my tiny studio space than I did for my apartment, but it was my most favorite place to be.

I unlocked the deadbolt and reached to my right, flipping on the lights. They flickered on, brightening up the small space. I walked to the left side of the open room to where my desk was, which only served as a catch all most of the time. Hanging on the wall above my mess of a desk were some of my most favorite photos I'd ever taken. Liv's face was there, along with the faces of her children. A picture of Liv and Devon on their wedding day. There was also a black and white photo, shot downward, framing a man and woman's legs, tangled in bed, a sheet covering them until the knees, then just feet. It was intimate, yet tasteful. Elliot had been asleep when I'd snapped the photo. I'd always just loved the way our bodies fit together – even our legs. Every time I saw the photo, my heart ached a little. I missed Elliot, or I missed having someone to be with. Elliot and I were never built to last; we wanted different things. But he was a good man and I was lucky to spend the years with him that I did. Every time I saw that picture I thought about taking it down, but in the end, it gave me more warm and happy feelings than sad.

I jumped when the phone rang, then took in a deep breath to calm my nerves.

"Evelyn Reynolds photography, Evelyn speaking."

Thus began my day of running my own business. Three new clients made appointments for shoots, and I scheduled two more appointments to proof photos with existing clients. I was deep in editing the photos of Shelby I'd taken the day before when I heard the alarm on my phone go off, signaling it was time to leave to pick up Jaxy.

My mind was swirling with thoughts of the conversation I'd had with Shelby, the fight I'd had with Devon, and the memories I'd shared with Elliot. The drive to Jaxy's school seemed to fly by, and truthfully, I didn't even remember it when I arrived. I tried not to drink too much coffee, but it was apparent I needed something to snap my mind out of its funk.

Jaxy came bounding out of his preschool, his usual enthusiasm shooting him along like a rocket aimed right for the backseat of my car.

"Hey," I said with a smile as he settled into his booster seat. "How was school today?"

"Great! I colored a picture of a tiger. But I wanted a purple one, so I made it purple."

"Very creative," I said with pride, hoping that perhaps some of my creativity had rubbed off on him.

"My teacher told me tigers weren't purple and she made me color another one black and orange."

"Really?" I didn't like the idea of preschool teachers stifling his natural instincts to be different. "What did you do?"

"I colored the new one every color of the rainbow."

"That's my boy!" I turned and held my hand up, smiling as his little palm slapped against mine in an epic high five. I watched as he leaned back into his seat, pulling his seatbelt over his chest, clicking it into place. "I made my teacher mad a lot today."

"What do you mean?" I asked, finding his face in the rear view mirror as I pulled out onto the street.

"Well, earlier, we were supposed to draw a picture of our family. My teacher said my picture was wrong."

"Wrong?"

"Yeah. I drew Daddy and Ruby, and Mommy with a yellow circle over her head. One of those hollow thingies."

"You mean a halo?" I asked, my voice thick with emotion at the thought of tiny Jax drawing his angel mommy.

"Yeah, a halo. Then I drew you standing next to us and when I showed my teacher, she said you weren't a part of our family. I told her you were, but she just shook her head at me and told me I was wrong."

"She what?" Surely there must have been some mistake. "She told you I wasn't a part of your family?"

"She said that unless my daddy was married to you that you weren't family."

Before I could rein in my emotions, the car was pulling a U-turn, heading back in the direction of Jaxy's preschool. I parked in the parking lot and then opened Jaxy's door, holding his hand as we walked into the building. I headed straight for his classroom, but stopped outside the door, kneeling down to look in Jax's eyes.

"I want you to stay out here in the hallway, okay?"

"Are you gonna punch her?" His eyes were wide and worried.

"No, I'm not going to punch her," I said as I rolled my eyes. "No more action movies for you, buddy." I rubbed my hand up and down his arm, trying to comfort him. "I'm just going to talk to her for a minute. But I need you to stay out here." He nodded his head, still looking worried, so I ruffled his hair as I walked past him and into his classroom.

I saw his teacher sitting at her desk, stacking some papers into a neat pile. She heard me walking across the room and her eyes came up to meet mine. She looked perplexed for a moment, but then I saw the recognition come over them. She stood, a tight smile pulled across her face.

"Hello, Ms. Reynolds," she said, folding her hands in front of her.

"Please, call me Evelyn."

"What can I do for you?"

"I was just taking Jaxy home and he told me he was having some trouble in class today. Something about a purple tiger and a picture he drew. He said you told him I wasn't a part of his *family*." I used my fingers to make air quotes around the word, trying to emphasize the ridiculousness of her assertion. She opened her mouth to speak, but I was amped up on adrenaline and not willing to let her stop my rant. "I know you're aware of the tragedy his family has been through this year, but what you might not know is that I have been in that boy's life since before he was even conceived. I held his mother's hand when she took the pregnancy test. I was in the room when he was born. I was the very first person his mother trusted to babysit him when he was just three weeks old. I have loved that child every single day of his life." I paused, trying to take in a breath, but it shuddered on the way in, and I felt tears threatening.

"Evelyn, please, let's sit down." She motioned toward the tiny chairs built for four-year-olds.

"No!" I hadn't meant to yell, but I could feel the emotions flowing through me like lava; slow and smoldering, getting hotter and hotter as more anger piled up on top of itself. "Jax lost his mother. His *only* mother. She was my best friend and I promised her I would take care of him and his sister." I took one more step toward her desk, which she was still standing behind, drawing my hand up, my index finger pointing at her.

"Who the hell do you think you are telling him I'm not a part of his family? You don't get to make those decisions. You don't get to tell him things like that. Luckily, he's a smart boy and he knew you were full of it, but the fact remains that you had no right. You had no right to tell him that."

"I never meant to imply-"

"No, I'm sure you didn't, but maybe next time you open your mouth, you'll think about everything he's lost. He lost a lifetime of love. He lost his *mother*. Don't try to take more love from him. As far as I'm concerned, he could use all the love he can get. I can give him so much love. Don't ever try to tell him I'm not a part of his family."

"You're right. I'm sorry." Her tone, contrite and remorseful, caught me off guard. Then she was silent, obviously waiting for more verbal abuse from me. I was suddenly exceedingly tired.

"Okay then," I sighed, my fingers coming up to rub my forehead. "I didn't mean to be such a bitch." I cringed at my own words. I was in a preschool classroom, swearing at Jax's teacher.

"No apologies needed. Really. Jax is lucky to have you."

"Okay. One more thing?"

"Hmm?"'

"Please don't tell him tigers can't be purple. He's four. Let him believe in purple tigers for a little while. It won't hurt anyone."

She gave me a sad yet friendly smile, and then nodded in agreement.

"Okay, I'm going to go."

"Have a good rest of your day." Her voice sounded full of pity and concern.

"You too."

I turned and walked out of the classroom to find Jax right where I had left him. He looked sad and bewildered.

"Hey, buddy," I said kneeling down to his level again. "I'm sorry if you heard me yelling. I didn't mean to. I shouldn't have. Yelling doesn't solve anything." I felt terrible; obviously, I was the worst role model ever.

"You really love me that much?" His small voice soaked into the tiny cracks of my heart, like water flooding an engine, and my heart just stopped. My hand came up to caress the side of his round, little face.

"Sweetie, I love you more than I could ever put into words."

"More than my mommy loved me?"

"No, Jax," I said with tears welling in my eyes. "No one will ever love you as much as your mommy loves you. But I still love you more than you could ever imagine."

"I miss her sometimes."

"I know, baby."

"But I like that you're around. You help with stuff that only mommies know."

My heart started sputtering back to life, aching like it might explode. I wasn't a mommy, but somehow, I'd picked up on some secret mommy things. Perhaps I had a maternal bone in my body after all. "I like being around. And I'll be around until you tell me to go away, okay?"

"Okay," he said, sniffling and wiping a tear away that had escaped down his cheek.

"Your sister won't be home for a few hours. Should we go get super-secret ice cream cones?" My voice was full of forced excitement, trying to convince this little boy that an ice cream cone was a sufficient replacement for the love of his mother, at least temporarily.

"Really? I haven't had lunch yet."

"Listen, sometimes life calls for super-secret ice cream cones for lunch."

"Can I get swirl?"

"Sweetie, you can get whatever kind of ice cream you want."

"Cool!" he said, all previous sadness erased from his gorgeous face.

"Very cool. Let's go." Before I could take even two steps, his little hand found its way into mine and my heart nearly stopped again.

I was exhausted. Not physically, but emotionally. I felt as if I could collapse on a bed and fall asleep instantly, and perhaps not wake up for days, just to make up for all the emotional upheaval Jaxy and I had been through that day. The worst part was, it wasn't over yet. Devon would be home later and we needed to talk.

I had fed the children dinner, bathed them, and they were upstairs in their bedroom watching a movie I was sure they'd seen no less than one thousand times. When I heard the door just off the kitchen open and close, I knew Devon was home, and my heart rate spiked. He walked into the kitchen, looking just as exhausted as I felt. When he saw me waiting for him, his expression changed to surprise. That hurt me a little, made me feel terrible, that my waiting for him without a scowl or anger radiating from me would surprise him. I immediately felt like shit for everything that had transpired in the last twenty-four hours.

"Hi," I said, knowing it was my responsibility to open the lines of communication between us. "How was your day?"

"Honestly? It sucked."

"I'm sorry."

He set his briefcase down on a kitchen chair and ran his hand through his hair, which was longer than he normally kept it. "It's not your fault."

"No, I mean, I'm sorry. For everything. Last night. This morning. I'm sorry. I blew everything out of proportion, and I shouldn't have flipped out on you."

"Evie, we need to talk about what happened."

"Um," I said, turning away from him, trying to hide the fact that I was uncomfortable. "I don't need to talk about it. I'm okay. I understand. I get it. Really. It's fine."

When he spoke next, he was right behind me. "What if I want to talk about it?"

I swallowed hard, trying not to follow my natural instinct to run away. "What do you feel like you need to say?"

"When I came up behind you yesterday evening, when I wrapped my arm around you, I thought you were Liv. I don't know why, it's never happened before, but some part of my brain forgot she was gone for a moment, and I couldn't stop myself."

"It's okay, Dev. She hasn't been gone long and you're still healing."

"Yeah. You're right. But when I realized it was you, that you were in my arms and I had kissed you, I wasn't sorry it was you."

"*Devon...*" I whispered, unable to say anything more.

"I was sad it wasn't Liv, but I wasn't sad it was you. Does that make sense?"

There were so many things in the world I wished I were doing, rather than having that conversation. His words had so much power: the power to save me, the power to kill me, the power to render me completely broken, unable to put myself back together.

"Losing her was the worst thing that ever happened to me, the worst thing that ever happened to my kids. But, if you were to go away too, I have no idea what I'd do, Evie. I didn't think I could live without her, but somehow it's happening. Life is moving on, going forward. It sucks without her, but only in a blunt kind of way now. The pain is duller, not so sharp. But, if we were to lose you too, because of something so stupid and instantaneous and *stupid*, I don't think I could handle that."

A part of me was hurt he'd called what happened 'stupid.' It was stupid. But it was so much more than that.

"I got into a fight with Jaxy's teacher today," I said suddenly, trying desperately to keep myself from saying something I'd regret, something that might alter our relationship in an irrevocable way.

"What?" he asked, his voice louder and a little concerned.

"Not really a fight. I just kind of went into her classroom and yelled at her. She took it really well."

"What happened?"

"Jax drew a picture of his family that included me, and his teacher told him I wasn't really a part of his family. It upset him." I stepped away from him, pretending as if the dishes in the sink needed to be rinsed at that exact moment.

"And you yelled at her?"

"It was wrong of her. Imagine, poor Jaxy, after losing his mother, some person telling him it was wrong to love someone, wrong to be loved by someone else. The last thing he needs is someone taking more love from him. I was upset."

He was behind me again, closer than he was before, and his hands came to rest on top of my shoulders. He gave me a gentle squeeze and my breath stopped, my heart halted. "He's lucky to have you, Evie. And you've always been a part of this family. Regardless of whether Liv is here or not, you're a part of us."

His confirmation should have made me feel better, but all I heard was him alluding to the fact that nothing had changed between us. I was the same to him, with or without his wife. All the feelings about Devon and our argument and Jaxy were swirling in my brain and making my whole world hazy. I didn't want to be confused anymore. Didn't want to be unsure. But then his hands squeezed my shoulders again and the swirling got more intense.

"I just wanted to let you know, in case he said something about it. And I wanted to tell you that I was sorry about everything. Really."

"Can we just go back to normal now?"

Normal? His normal could turn out to be my ruin. "Sure."

"Great."

"Great."

Then we were drenched in silence. Uncomfortable silence. Luckily, Jax and Ruby chose that moment to reappear and the room was filled with the noises of children welcoming their father home. After a few moments, Devon ended up on the couch in the family room, Ruby on his right and Jaxy on his knee, listening to stories of disfigured mummies and super-secret ice cream cones.

I grabbed my purse and slowly snuck out of the house, glad to see the three of them thriving, but also grateful to have some time to myself to lick my wounds.

Chapter Seven

Summer between Freshman and Sophomore Year

I tried to ignore the butterflies swarming in my stomach. I wanted to look like the cool, calm, and collected person I wished I was, but I probably resembled the bumbling fool I felt like. I was about to leave my house, with a boy, to stay for the weekend in a cabin. The whole weekend. With a boy. Well, a guy.

Elliot had told me his parents had a cabin near the mountain and said we should go there for a weekend sometime. I said, 'sounds like fun.' The next thing I knew, he was making plans for us. *Us.* I was still surprised there was an us. School had been over for a month, and true to his word, he'd driven to my town to see me twice, both times making it seem like the nearly four-hour trip was no big deal. I knew it was. I felt it. And although I appreciated that he wanted to see me and had driven all that way to do so, it was a lot of pressure. Pressure I'd never really dealt with before.

I saw his red pickup truck turn the corner onto my street and the butterflies not only multiplied, but they grew larger. I was trying to convince myself I wasn't going to throw up.

The two times he'd come to visit, he'd been a perfect gentleman. He'd shown up, taken me out, done everything by the book: insisted on paying, pulled out my chair for me, made sure we had my favorite snack at the movies. Perfect. He held my hand, and I felt the tingles. Those telltale shivers, which only came on when special people showed you affection. I wanted to hold his hand, and when he brought me home, I'd purposefully instructed him to park down the block from my house so my parents couldn't spy on us.

His kisses were incredible. He tasted like summer, sunshine, and spearmint. He'd pulled me to his side of the bench in the cab of his truck and kissed me until I was breathless. Kissed me on the lips, on the neck, on the shoulder, but never pressured me for anything more. I knew he'd wanted to take things further, but he was letting me lead, and I appreciated that more than I could ever tell him.

Now, I was to spend an entire weekend with him. Surely, something would happen between us. I just wasn't sure I was ready for it. I wasn't normally a nail biter, but I'd chewed my nails to the quick just thinking about how I would tell him I wasn't ready to sleep with him.

From my bedroom window on the second floor, I watched him park his truck and then walk to my front door. He was wearing khaki cargo shorts and a blue cotton t-shirt that only made his blond hair look more sun-streaked. He reached forward and I heard my doorbell ring. This was it. I walked as smoothly as I could down the stairs, not wanting to appear at the door too soon and seem too eager. I didn't want him to think I'd been sitting in my bedroom waiting for him.

I opened the door and his smile assaulted me, left me feeling a bit like Jell-O.

"Hey, babe," he said as he stepped into my house and gave me a chaste kiss on the mouth. Apparently, I'd been upgraded to a pet name. "Are your parents home? I wouldn't mind saying hello."

"Uh, no. They have a dinner thing they do once a week with their friends. Kind of like a kid-free, we-want-to-pretend-like-we're-teenagers-again thing. It's a little pathetic. They drink and then my mom usually falls on her way up the stairs, giggling loudly then shushing my dad. Then I have to pretend like I don't hear them."

He laughed at my description. "Oh, okay. Maybe when I drop you off then."

I was a little suspicious that he was so concerned with wanting to see my parents, but I chalked it up to his reputation of perfection. Perfect boyfriends would have a good relationship with parents. But he wasn't my boyfriend, was he?

"Are you my boyfriend?" I spat out before my mind had even processed the words.

He laughed again, louder this time, his arm wrapping around my waist and pulling me toward him. "We haven't really talked about it," he said, leaning down so our eyes were level. "Do you want me to be your boyfriend?"

I thought about his question. Did I want him to be my boyfriend? I wasn't sure. I had boyfriends in the past, and they'd only turned out to be disasters. Possessive and overbearing. But nothing about Elliot made me feel like he could be possessive or overbearing if he tried. I felt like if Elliot were my boyfriend, he'd only be sweet and attentive, chivalrous, playful. I also thought he'd kiss me a lot, which I wasn't opposed to – he was an excellent kisser.

"I'm not opposed to you being my boyfriend."

"Well, that's a convincing response." His words indicated I might have hurt his feelings, but his face was still smiling, those damned blue eyes sparkling. He leaned forward again and pressed his lips to mine. This time, the kiss wasn't chaste. It was hot. And wet. His eager tongue barged into my mouth, took control, tasted every part of me, and left me panting when he pulled away. "Tell you what. You hang on to your answer for now. When I drop you off on Sunday, I'll ask you again, and maybe you'll have a more convincing answer."

"Okay," I breathed, literally unable to form any words besides the one. He picked my backpack up off the floor and then motioned for me to leave the house ahead of him – ever the gentleman. He helped me into his truck, hands on my waist, which I was becoming accustomed to, even started looking forward to. When he was in the driver's seat, he turned his head my way and crooked a finger at me. I smiled and moved to the middle so our shoulders were touching.

"I'm not driving for two hours without being able to touch you."

"You've already driven so much today. I could have met you at the cabin, you know."

"But then I wouldn't be able to drive you home. And trust me when I say, Evie, taking you home, saying goodbye, those are some of my favorite times with you."

I blushed because I knew he was thinking about all the making out we'd done in his truck down the street from my house. I couldn't argue with him. Those were some of my favorite times with him as well.

For two hours we drove, listening to the radio, telling each other memories the songs brought up, learning a little more about one another. Either his hand was on my thigh, my knee, or wrapped around mine, his fingers threaded through my own. I'd lost track of where we were as we headed into parts of the state I was unfamiliar with.

When we pulled off the main highway onto a gravel road, my nervousness spiked. I was comfortable being alone in his truck with him, but we were venturing into new territory. Would he assume we were staying in the same room? Did I want to stay in his room? If I stayed in his room, would he expect sex? I shook my head at the thought. Of course, he wouldn't *expect* sex. Elliot was, and had always been, exceedingly respectful.

Perhaps I was just nervous that I would *want* to have sex with him.

He gave my hand a squeeze, but then released it, needing both hands to mind the steering wheel as he navigated the unpaved and pothole-riddled road. The shaking of our bodies as we drove over the road hid the trembling of my hands, which I was grateful for. The truck pulled around one last bend in the road and I saw two things immediately. The first was a gorgeous and rustic-looking log cabin. It only appeared rustic though, because I could tell by looking at it that it was pretty new. Exposed logs on the outside made it look like every log cabin I'd ever seen in movies or books. It was almost too perfect.

The second thing I noticed was we pulled up right next to another car parked in front of the house. I looked at Elliot and he was wearing a sneaky grin, but before I could ask him who the car belonged to, Olivia came bounding out the front door, yelling "Surprise!" She launched herself toward the truck, but I quickly turned to Elliot.

"How did you...? What is she doing here?"

He didn't have time to answer before my door was pried open and I was yanked out. Olivia had her arms around me in a tight hug. "Are you surprised?"

"Yes," I managed, even though she was depriving me of oxygen. As she loosened her grip on me, I saw the front door open again and Devon came out, walking toward us with a smile. I tried not to notice how the sunlight brought out the lighter brown highlights of his hair. I hadn't seen him all summer, so the difference in him physically was a little startling. He was bigger, if that was even possible.

When we'd met in the spring, he'd already been one of the biggest guys I'd ever met. But, he was bulkier now. More imposing.

"Evie." Devon said my name with such ease, as if I was one of his best friends. "Glad to see you're surprised, and that this one here didn't blab to you that we'd be here," he said as he wrapped his arm around Liv's shoulders.

"I don't blab," she said, insulted.

"Babe, you keep secrets for shit."

"That's not true," I jumped in, ready to defend her. "When it really counts, she keeps a good secret. It's gossip you're thinking about. She spills gossip faster than butter melts in a hot pan."

"Thank you, Evie. I think." She stepped out of Devon's arm as the two boys did that typical male handshake, back-pound ritual.

"I'm glad you guys could make it up. I think it's gonna be a fun weekend." With that, Elliot took my bag from the truck, as well as his own, and then nodded his head in a way that said I was to follow.

We walked into the foyer and I tried to keep my mouth closed, but I felt it drop open in awe. The cabin looked like it could have been staged for a photo shoot in some home journal magazine about the filthy rich's vacation homes.

"Wow," I breathed. I was used to my family's humble split-level home. We weren't poor, not by a long shot, but I was not familiar with that kind of luxury. "This place is really nice."

"Thanks. I've only been here once before. My parents bought it while I was at college, so I never really got a chance to use it."

"Wait, this is *your* house?" My head snapped to look at him. In the back of my mind, I knew it was his. We'd planned all along to go to *his* cabin, but I'd never imagined something like this.

"I don't think I'd fare well in jail, Evie. I'm not into B&E."

"Of course not, uh, I just didn't know..."

"That my family has money?" I nodded, feeling any words I might have been able to conjure up getting stuck in my throat. "Don't go all weird on me now. My parents have money. Not me. I'm the same guy you've been talking to all summer." He shrugged. "Sometimes I take advantage of the fact that my parents are well off," he said, moving his arm to motion to the great expanse of the beautiful house we were standing in. "But most of the time, you'd never be able to tell."

"You're right. I'm sorry," I whispered. "I think I was just caught off guard."

He smiled his relaxed, happy smile. "Follow me." I let him lead me through the house as he pointed out the important features. Bathrooms, kitchen, family room. I tried to be nonchalant about the movie theatre room, the hot tub, and the infinity pool. When he led me into one of the bedrooms, my pulse started thundering through my ears.

"So, this is the room I'm staying in," he said as he placed his bag on the bed. Then he turned back to me, his eyes gentle and warm, with a tiny smile playing across his face. "I'd really like you to stay here with me, but I understand if it's too soon. I promise I'll keep my hands to myself, if that's what you want, but I have imagined waking up next to you all summer."

His words both melted and frightened me.

"I've never shared a bed with anyone before. Well, anyone besides Liv."

"How is that possible?" he asked, stepping closer to me very slowly, almost as if he thought I would spook and run away.

"The only serious boyfriend I had was in high school and neither one of our parents was the cool kind that allowed sleepovers." As I spoke, he started toward me and when I finished, he was right in front of me, our toes nearly touching. I lifted my chin to keep my eyes on his, so when his gentle fingertips grazed the underside of my jaw, I startled in surprise. But the shock quickly gave way to goose bumps as he trailed his knuckles down both sides of my neck.

"You have no idea how much my need to sleep in the same bed with you has multiplied knowing I'd be the first."

"Oh," I said, feeling my face turn an as-of-yet-undiscovered shade of red with my blushing. "I'm not a virgin. I mean, I haven't slept around, but, you see, my high school boyfriend-"

"Evie," he said laughing, and then shushed me further by pressing his lips to mine in a soft and non-pushy kiss. He pulled away, his thumbs grazing over my cheeks. "I'm not talking about sex."

"Oh," I replied, sheepishly.

"Will you stay with me?"

All I could do was nod. I did want to stay in the room with him. I wanted to know what it felt like to be held by someone as I fell asleep. He kissed me again, only that kiss was hungrier, more urgent. More like the times in his truck outside my house when we didn't want to say goodbye to one another. When our mouths eventually parted, I was panting, gripping his shirt with clenched fists.

"Okay," he breathed, pulling away, just as worked up as I was. "First step to not rushing into anything is no making out in view of a bed."

I laughed, glad that he was finding the situation just as painfully delectable as I was.

"Maybe we should go find Liv and Devon. Hey," I said, suddenly remembering my shock at seeing them. "Was it your idea to invite them along?"

Elliot's hands started at my shoulders and gently moved down my arms to link each of his hands with mine. "I just thought that maybe you'd be a little more comfortable if it wasn't just you and me here."

"That was really thoughtful of you," I said as I looked down at our joined hands. "You're always doing sweet things. It kind of ruins the 'cool guy' persona you try to put off."

"Is that how I come off? Like I'm trying to be cool?" He shrugged then brought our linked hands between us, resting them between our bodies against his chest. "This isn't a game, Evelyn. I'm honestly just trying to make all the right moves so you'll let me in. I'm trying really hard to prove to you I'm not just some guy looking to score."

The sudden serious tone of his voice and the way our bodies were intertwined in that moment sent a flash of panic through me, causing my defense mechanism to activate – deflection. "But you are looking to score eventually, right?" I asked with a sly smile.

He laughed, but seemed to see through my attempt at distraction. "Eventually. But not any time soon." Then, before one of us could say anything to bury ourselves any deeper, he kissed the knuckles on one of my hands and led me out of the room.

The kitchen table was littered with empty beer bottles, snacks, and rejected playing cards. I'd never been one to gamble before, but when Elliot had told me we were playing for pretzels, I decided it couldn't hurt. So far, my pile of pretzels was the largest. Elliot was running a close second, Devon third, and Liv was completely out because she kept eating hers and losing terribly when she managed to play.

All four of us were drinking, playing cards, and having a great time.

"I think you lied when you said you'd never played poker before," Elliot said to me, but keeping his eyes on his cards.

I scoffed loudly, feigning insult. "I never lie, and it's rude of you to imply I would."

"Oh, I'm not trying to imply that you lied, I'm calling you out as a liar. There's no way anyone could have this much beginner's luck."

I shrugged. "Some people are just luckier than others, I guess. Or perhaps I have more good karma saved up than you." I picked up one of my many pretzels and tossed it in my mouth, not glancing his way. However, I could see out of the corner of my eye that he was smiling. I picked up my beer and took a long pull, loving the way the saltiness of the pretzels mixed roughly with the wheat beer.

"You guys are killing me. This is officially boring." Olivia's words were a little slurred, but her eyes suddenly got wide. "Let's go in the hot tub!"

"I don't know," I said carefully, glancing up at Devon. "Won't sitting in the hot water just make us more drunk?"

"What's wrong with *more* drunk? I'm only halfway drunk anyway. Come on, Evie. Don't be a buzzkill."

"I'm not a buzzkill, Liv. I just don't want to spend the night taking care of you." Her eyes widened a bit and it looked as though I'd offended her, but just as quickly, she put on her party-girl, no-worries mask and waved me away with her hand.

"You won't have to take care of me. That's why I brought my boyfriend, here," she said patting Devon playfully on the arm. Devon didn't move, didn't give one single physical clue that her words had affected him, but I could feel the air around us grow thick with tension.

"I'm up for the hot tub," Elliot said, also oblivious to Devon's change in mood.

"Great!" Olivia jumped up from her chair. "I'll go get my suit on." She ran down the hallway, only swaying a little on her feet.

"I'll go get the jets started," Elliot said as he stood, but before he left he turned to me. "Did you pack a suit?"

"Yeah," I said with a forced smile, not liking the way the evening was progressing.

"Great. See you out there," he said, leaning down and pressing a kiss to my forehead. He walked away toward the French doors, which I'd learned on my tour led to the veranda. Devon and I sat at the table for a few seconds in silence. I knew he was upset, but didn't really know how to broach the subject. As my best friend, my loyalty should have always been with Olivia. However, in this situation, I couldn't help but feel sorry for Devon.

"I think Olivia has gotten into the habit of confusing having fun with being drunk," I said cautiously, not sure if Devon would be offended for Olivia by my words. I raised my eyes to look at him, only to find him looking directly at me. We didn't speak for a few moments, but then he sighed, brought both of his hands up, and rubbed them down his face, groaning.

"Has she always been like this?" he asked, his elbows coming to rest on the table with his forehead resting in his hands.

"No," I said thoughtfully. "She didn't start drinking heavily and often until a few months ago."

"You mean, until she met me."

I hadn't thought about it that way. "I guess. But I don't think it's you who's making her this way. I think if she were seriously involved with *anyone*, she would have a hard time dealing with it. It's always kind of been against her MO to be exclusive with someone. Maybe she's using alcohol to deal with things she's had buried that are being brought up by your relationship."

"Hmm." Now he sounded angry. Irritated. "Maybe one of these days she'll open up enough for me to figure out what's bothering her."

"She hasn't talked to you about it yet?"

"No. Every time our conversation turns serious, she changes the subject or suddenly remembers she needs to be somewhere and bails."

Without thinking about it, I reached out and covered one of his hands with my own. "She really is a great girl, Devon. You just have to break through the tough exterior she puts up." He heard my words and then turned his hand upward and his fingers closed around mine.

"The funny thing is, Evie, before I met Olivia, there was this one girl who I'd been thinking about for weeks." His fingers squeezed mine a little harder and my throat went dry. "If only I'd been brave enough to ask you out that first day we met, things might be different right now."

"Devon," I whispered, my voice betraying me and saying his name like a curse. I shook my head and pulled my hand free from his, both afraid of the words coming from his mouth and the way they made my heart tumble in my chest. I was panicking. Panicking because even though Devon had made small remarks to me over the last few months about caring for me, I had never chosen to believe they were meant in any more than a friendly capacity. Not only out of respect for my friend, but also out of preservation of my heart. I'd fallen for him that first day too, but learned to live with the regret of letting him walk away. Learned to tamp down the longing I felt whenever he was near – and even when he was nowhere in sight. But his words, his acknowledgment that I wasn't alone in those feelings, was dangerous.

Before I could say anything more, even if I could think of the words that were supposed to come next, Olivia came out of the hallway clad in a pink bikini that left little to the imagination. She came right up behind Devon and leaned down, wrapping her arms around his chest, putting her lips to the skin of his neck that I had imagined to be soft and smell of him. She kissed him there, tenderly, as his eyes bore into mine.

"Come on, baby. Let's go get in the hot tub. I bought this new bikini just for you." His fingers came up to pat her hands that were clasped together over his chest.

"I'll be out there in just a minute."

"All right," she said with an easy smile while standing up. "I'll just go make sure it's extra warm for you." She strolled away, opened the French doors, then closed them not so gently behind her, and disappeared into the darkness.

I was frozen in place. Stuck in what seemed like an important moment. I didn't know what to say, how to move forward, or if I should even acknowledge what Devon had said. Then, making my decision for me, he stood up from the table and walked down the hallway toward his room.

I exhaled as soon as he was out of sight, feeling a tremendous weight lift from my shoulders. For the rest of the weekend Devon made obvious efforts not to be alone with me – not obvious to everyone, but plain enough to me. And I tried to convince myself he hadn't meant what he'd said, and I didn't feel what I felt.

Chapter Eight

Present Day

"Evie, I'm really sorry, but there's another late meeting I've got to attend. If you can't stay late with the kids, could you maybe see if Mrs. Welner from next door could sit with them? I don't have her phone number handy. Thanks, Evie. Let me know what's up."

I swiped the screen of my phone to the left, deleting Devon's voicemail. "Sure," I said to no one since I was in my car all alone. "I'll just leave your children with the woman next door who is so old she can't even walk from room to room without assistance. That sounds safe." I flung my car in reverse, taking all my frustration out on my poor gearshift. "How in the hell did your wife live with you all these years?" My own breath caught at my words. Liv hadn't lived with it. In fact, she'd died. But I knew she'd give anything to be here with him, being the one he called when he was going to be running late home from work.

I took in a deep breath trying to push away the sadness I felt at the thought of Liv, and the disgust I felt with myself as I took everything I'd been given for granted. Liv, in essence, had given me a family. I loved Ruby and Jax, and I needed to recognize that Devon could very well have hired a nanny, and I'd be stuck with weekend visits to the children I loved dearly.

I sighed as I merged into traffic, pulling my sunglasses down to cover my eyes. Knowing full well I'd be going to his house to be there when his daughter got out of school, then going to get his son, I silently cursed Devon for having such wonderful children who would always have a hold on my heart.

After I'd wrangled both kids, we walked up the driveway as I tried to text Devon to tell him the kids and I would wait at his house for him – no need to bother his elderly neighbor.

Ruby unlocked the door and Jaxy ran in ahead of us. As usual, the kids headed for the kitchen because they hadn't eaten in over forty-five minutes so, obviously, they were starving.

"I'm hungry," I heard Jax yell from the kitchen at the same time I heard the sound of the refrigerator opening. I heard the hum of the freezer, but something else was catching my ear. I put my purse down on the table and stood still, trying to figure out what was making me uneasy. I looked around and nothing looked out of place, and then I zeroed in on the noise coming from the laundry room.

I walked down the hallway and immediately knew something was wrong. Halfway down the hall, my feet were met with water. Standing water. Water that was slowly making its way toward the kitchen.

"Oh, my God," I whispered, trying to make my way through the lake that used to be the hallway. When I opened the door to the laundry room, I couldn't stay calm anymore. "Holy shit!" My yells were heard by the children and somewhere in the back if my mind I registered they were coming toward me, but couldn't think past the sight of water spraying out of the wall behind the washing machine. The water was freezing cold and ankle deep by the time I'd made it into the laundry room. The water was spraying out from behind the machine, sending water *everywhere*. It was coming straight at me. It was falling from the ceiling, and it was running down the walls. And I could tell it was coming out fast and I knew soon it would be flooding the whole bottom floor of Devon's house.

"Yay! We're going swimming!" I heard Jaxy's excited yells from behind me and could see him jumping up and down near the door. I brought my hand up to shield my eyes from the water coming at me from all angles and shouted to Ruby.

"Get your brother and go upstairs! I've got to find the valve to shut this off." Ruby followed my instructions and I noticed Jaxy's face fall in disappointment, realizing it wasn't a fun event. I waded through the water toward the washer, trying to find where the water was coming from. I pulled on the back corner, trying to move it away from the wall, but it only gave an inch. I squatted and pulled harder, trying to leverage my weight against the machine.

Water was still spraying everywhere, and all of my clothes were drenched and sticking to my skin. My shoes were completely filled with freezing water, and my fingers and toes were starting to go numb.

I adjusted my hold on the backside of the washer, now able to squeeze my arms between the two machines, and pulled hard. It took at least ten tries. Me tugging on the machine as hard as I could, feeling it barely budge, but move enough to motivate me to try again. Eventually, the machine was pulled far enough away from the wall that the plume of water spraying out was smaller and there was enough room between the machine and the wall to fit my body. I hopped on top of the machine and then squeezed my body down, feet first, still trying to assess where the water was coming from.

I was not familiar with anything I was looking at, made only more foreign to me by the water spraying everywhere, but I did spy a turn dial that looked just like the ones I'd usually seen outside of houses to turn hoses on and off. I reached for it and started turning furiously. After what seemed like a million rotations, the volume of water flowing from the hole in the wall finally tapered off and eventually turned into a trickle.

I was standing up to my calves in freezing water, drenched from head to toe, with absolutely no idea what I was supposed to do next. I climbed back on top of the washer and then hopped off again, heading back to the kitchen. The water had made its way into the dining room. I saw my purse sitting on the kitchen island and I grabbed it, searching for my phone. I called Devon, but I went straight to voicemail.

"Devon, some sort of pipe burst in your laundry room. There's water everywhere. I have no idea what to do. Call me ASAP."

I walked out of the kitchen and went up the stairs, heading toward the master bedroom. When I passed the kids' room and saw them sitting silently on Ruby's bed, so I halted in their doorway.

"Hey guys. Everything's okay. Just a little leak." Ruby's eyebrows went up as if to say, "Little? Really?"

"Can we go downstairs?" Jax asked.

"Tell you what, gather up all the towels in the house and meet me in the kitchen, but don't go into the water, okay?"

"Got it!" Jaxy yelled as he hopped off the bed and ran past me into the hallway, opening up the linen closet, on a mission.

"Help your brother, please? I'm gonna go try to find some dry clothes?"

"You're going to wear Mommy's clothes?" Ruby's voice was both surprised and sad. I knew they hadn't gotten rid of anything of Olivia's, I knew it was all just sitting in her closet and dresser. None of them were ready to remove her from the house, and I wasn't ready either. But it hadn't occurred to me that wearing her clothes would upset Ruby or Jax. In fact, I hadn't really thought about how *I* would feel wearing her clothes. The emptiness is my gut told me it was a bad idea.

"No, baby. I'll find something else." I saw the relief float over her features, tension obviously leaving her shoulders as she exhaled. "Don't worry, sweetie," I added, knowing that if there weren't a lake currently residing on the bottom floor of her house, I would sit down next to her, hug her to me, and tell her all the ways her mother loved her. But in that moment, I couldn't take the time to give that to her. *Later*, I thought. "Can you go make sure your brother doesn't try to swim in your laundry room?"

"Yeah," she said, her normal sassiness gone. She walked past me and I kissed the top of her head, wanting so much just to make all her pain go away. When she disappeared down the stairs, I continued on my way to the master bedroom.

When Olivia had been alive, I'd spent a good amount of time in her bedroom. Not a lot, but enough that I was familiar with it. We'd dye her hair in her attached bathroom, try new facial masques in there. When she'd gone to fancy dinners for Devon's work, I'd sit on her bed and watch her try on dresses, always jealous of her amazing body and natural beauty. Even when she'd been hugely pregnant, she'd been slim and seemed to grow only in the belly.

When she'd brought Jaxy home, I'd spent hours in this room, watching her nurse her newborn, helping her in any way I could. When she'd been sick, I'd also spent hours in this room trying to help take care of her. It hadn't ever occurred to me before, but in that moment, I was glad she hadn't died at home. It was painful enough to stand in the doorway of the room I'd avoided since she passed. I don't know if I could have gone in knowing I'd see the last place she'd been alive, or the place she spoke such soft and sullen words to me.

Her side of the room, the side farthest from the door, seemed untouched. Her satin robe still laid across the back of her big reading chair by her favorite bay window. There was still a glass on her bedside table with a stack of paperbacks next to it, as if she were going to lay down that night, pick one up, and start reading it. Everything seemed to be waiting for her return.

My heart started beating faster and I knew if I didn't leave the room, soon the tears would come. Being in that room was too much for me to handle. The room still had so much Liv in it, I could only think of how much Liv I *didn't* have.

I moved quickly to Devon's dresser and pulled open drawers frantically, sighing in relief when I found a drawer with jogging shorts and t-shirts. I pulled one of each out quickly, nearly ran to the bedroom door, and then slammed it behind me as I left. I leaned against the closed door, sucking in deep breaths, trying to calm myself down. After a few moments, I felt the control of my emotions come back to me, and moved to the kids' bathroom to get out of my soaked and frigid clothing.

I went back downstairs wearing Devon's clothes. It was impossible not to smell him on them, but I tried my hardest not to hold the collar of his shirt purposefully to my nose and inhale. I'd smelled him plenty of times in my life and, as sad as I knew it was, I could pick out his particular scent over any other. It was clean and spicy. All male.

I found Ruby and Jax standing in front of a pile of towels that were all soaked and doing nothing to help the standing water problem.

"Thanks for getting the towels guys." They smiled at me, but then just continued to look at me as if I knew what was supposed to happen next. "I've got no idea how to deal with this."

I pulled up a browser on my phone and Googled, "How to deal with standing water." None of the pages that popped up looked as though they'd be of any immediate help, and the only thing I could think of was to get the water out any way I could. So I grabbed a big mixing bowl from a cupboard, and started bailing water out the French doors. The kids grabbed cups and helped, but I told them to stay out of the water, as it was still intensely cold.

We'd been working for a while, not making much progress, when I heard Devon's voice.

"Oh, my God," he said, and I looked up to see him placing his briefcase on the island, eyes wide, taking in all the chaos.

"What are you doing here? Did you miss your work thing?" I immediately felt terrible, as if I was causing so many problems. My feet were freezing, I was wearing clothes that smelled fabulous and were too big for me. My hair was a disaster from the earlier incident with the storm inside the laundry room, and all I really wanted to do was take a warm bath. "I'm sorry," I cried, dropping my hands to my side, making the giant mixing bowl I held onto slap against the side of my leg. "I didn't know what to do. Google wasn't any help. The thing in the laundry room was spewing water when we got home and I was just trying to get the water out." I was rambling and on the verge of tears, no longer able to keep my composure together when Devon walked straight to me, through the freezing cold water, dress shoes and slacks still on, and wrapped his arms around me.

I was startled at first because, well, we never really touched except when it was accidental and detrimental. So, to have him wrap his arms around me, knowing it was me, in an effort to comfort me, well, I lost it. I cried into his suit jacket, dropped the bowl, and moved my arms around his waist, pressing my face further into his chest.

I was crying out the stress of the last few months, crying for every time I'd held it in since Olivia passed, crying for all the times I wasn't enough for her children or her husband. But I was holding on to him for entirely different reasons. I was pulling his body closer to mine because I could, when I never could have in the past. I was feeling all the muscles in his back as my hands ran up to his shoulder blades because I just couldn't stop myself. I was reveling in the knowledge that his hands were on me and paying excruciatingly close attention to the fact that I *liked* his hands on my body. I loved everything about being in his arms, but hated myself for loving it so damn much.

"Ruby, Jax, why don't you guys go upstairs and put on some pajamas," he whispered softly to his children, and I couldn't imagine the scene I was making in their kitchen.

After a moment, he pulled away slightly, his hands coming to frame my face, feeling very warm against my exceedingly cold skin.

"Are you okay?" he asked, the sincerity in his voice breaking me open just a little bit more.

"I'm c-cold."

"Yeah, your lips are a little blue." His eyes kept darting between my lips and my eyes. He hadn't moved his hands and I wasn't about to pull away from his touch. "Let's get you to the living room and warm you up a bit, all right?"

"Ok-kay."

He turned from me, but reached for my hand at the same time, and pulled me into the living room. My feet started to tingle as soon as they were out of the water, and I made my way to the couch. When I sat, he knelt in front of me, just between my parted knees, one of his hands on each of my thighs. His finger hit the mesh of his basketball shorts and realization came over his face.

"Are you wearing my clothes?"

"Yes-s," I stammered, teeth still chattering. He leaned forward until his face was exactly a hair's breadth from mine and my lungs seized up with his proximity. A blush crept over my face when I realized he was only reaching for the throw blanket draped over the back of the couch. He pulled it around my shoulders, wrapping it around the top half of my body. "I got s-soaked while I t-turned off the valve. I w-went upstairs but c-couldn't bring myself to p-put on Liv's clothes."

"Shhhh," he said as he rubbed his hands up and down my arms, trying to build some heat between his hands and my skin. It seemed like I'd been waiting years for him to use his heat on me, but thinking about it in that moment made me feel shameful.

"What are we going to do about the water?" I whispered, unable or unwilling to use my full voice to ruin the moment.

"Um, well, I'm not sure."

"Google isn't much help."

His mouth quirked up in an adorable grin and I couldn't help it when mine did the exact same thing. "Really? Well, I guess we'll have to use some good old fashioned ingenuity then." He thought for a moment, his hands still torturously kneading into my arms. I had to admit though, I wasn't feeling the cold anymore. I was only feeling the slow burn building deep inside me. "You stay here, warm up. I'll be right back."

I didn't have time to answer before he disappeared down the flooded hallway. But I did hear the splashing and figured he must have gone right into the lake that used to be the laundry room. I cringed, thinking about his shoes again. There was a lot of noise coming from down the hall and I couldn't help but stare at the entrance, waiting for him to come back.

When he finally reappeared, he was carrying a large round machine that had a hose like a vacuum. "What is that?"

"It's a shop-vac. It can suck up almost anything. We'll have this place cleaned up in no time."

"Auntie Evie, we're hungry." Ruby appeared at the bottom of the stairs with new, dry pajamas, looking exhausted. I immediately felt terrible. Amidst the flooding crisis and my emotional breakdown, I'd forgotten to feed the children.

"Okay, Ruby, go upstairs and put on a movie for you and your brother. I'll bring up a picnic for you to eat in the TV room on a blanket."

"Really?" Some of her exhaustion left and was replaced with excitement. They were never allowed to eat anywhere except the table.

"Really. But you have to promise to keep an eye on your brother for me while I help your daddy clean this up."

"Okay," she yelled happily, as she skipped back up the stairs.

Three hours passed, in which I'd made sandwiches for the kids and brought them up with grapes, crackers, and juice boxes, calling it a 'picnic'. They'd eaten and watched their movie while Devon and I worked together to suck up the standing water. Once most of the water was gone, all we could do was use towels to try to dry the floor and the walls. After inspection, Devon concluded that the hose that hooked up to the back of the washer had broken, causing all the water to flow out onto his beautiful hardwood floors.

"We've got a few fans in the attic, I'll go get them."

I heard his footsteps go up the stairs and I focused all my mental energy on his use of the word 'we.' He'd meant him and Liv. The *we* he thought he'd be using for fifty or sixty more years. He wasn't a *we* anymore, but, to me, he always would be. Liv and Devon. My best friend's husband, regardless of whether or not she was alive. For a reason I only assumed was for my personal torture, I'd been totally fine with Devon and Liv as a *we* when she'd been alive, but now that she was gone, the fact that he still attached himself to her in that way made me feel sad and heavy.

When I heard him clear his throat a minute later, I turned to see him looking at me with soft eyes. "There were so many times when we were younger, before life really happened, when I'd imagined you in my clothes. I'd have these fantasies of coming home from my big important job to find you in one of my button up shirts, or just in one of my ties." I could feel my cheeks burning at his words, but couldn't move my gaze from him, didn't want to shatter whatever was happening between us, because I knew it was fragile, like spun sugar.

"Then things got serious with Liv and me and the fantasies sort of turned into forbidden thoughts. Thoughts I knew I shouldn't have, and managed to turn off all together for the most part, aside from the few moments when you were absolutely too beautiful to push to the back of my mind. Just little snapshots of heaven I tucked away and only thought about when I was really happy, because thinking of you when things weren't going well with Liv was too close to infidelity. I couldn't think about you when, perhaps, I wanted to most because I was afraid of what that would do to my marriage. So, I tried not to. And it worked, for the most part. I still got to see you often. Still had you in my life, *our* lives. Still got to tell you that you looked nice, or that I liked your new hair style, still got to know you were safe and close by."

I could remember practically every compliment he'd given me in the last nine years. I'd tucked them away too. Tried not to read too much into them, because it felt too much like I was betraying my best friend.

"And then I come home one night and there you are, in my kitchen, wearing my basketball shorts, and Liv is nowhere to be found."

The air in the room crackled with his words, filled with the regret of the enormity of the thought. Olivia was nowhere to be found, but she was still everywhere.

"And the mind boggling part is you're even more unavailable to me now than you were before. Olivia's absence took you so much farther away from me. Even though you're here, in my house, every day. You're *here*, but you've never been more out of reach."

"Devon," I managed to whisper, not really even knowing what I wanted to say, just needing to stop his words.

"Unless-"

"Devon, no."

"Unless it's you who's keeping yourself away for her sake."

"I'm here, Devon, but we can't-"

"There's no reason we can't-"

"Yes, there is. Olivia-"

"Is dead."

His words hurt for so many reasons I couldn't even begin to count them. Olivia *was* dead; there was no reason to deny him that fact. I stood up, finally finding some feeling in my body besides the pounding of my heart. I walked to him, stopping just far enough away so that he didn't get any ideas about reaching out and touching me. Surely, that would break me.

"Olivia being dead isn't the reason we can't be together. But, it can never be the reason we are."

Chapter Nine

Summer between Sophomore
and Junior Year of College

"So, when you decided to get an apartment on the third floor, was it always your master plan to make me do all the heavy lifting?" Elliot's voice rang out through the semi-empty apartment, and I smiled automatically as I always did around him.

"Well, first of all, it wasn't my *plan* to get an apartment on the third floor, that's just what was available. But, yeah," I said, turning and leaning my backside up against the kitchen counter, "I kinda knew you wouldn't let me haul my stuff up two flights of stairs." I watched, a little breathless, as he dropped a box full of textbooks on the floor of my soon-to-be living room, then turned toward me. His t-shirt was beginning to stick to his body, just slightly damp from working up a sweat carrying boxes upstairs. I knew from personal experience what the landscape of his chest looked like, but something about it being covered in cloth but still visible had my heart rate pounding.

I'd found over the last year of dating Elliot that you could grow to love someone, grow to trust them, build something with them. We'd started out a little rocky, mostly my insecurity and wariness to start a relationship at all, but Elliot had been a steady and constant presence in my life, and made being with him easy, made loving him easy. He was one of the best people I'd ever known.

He was also terribly handsome and sexy, as demonstrated in that moment as he strode toward me with determination and heat in his eyes.

"Every time I have to haul your belongings up those stairs, I'm going to take a kiss from you," he said, trying to sound threatening, but the idea was anything but unpleasant.

"That will surely add time to the move," I said, trying to sound as if I couldn't care less, as if giving in to him was a nuisance rather than a thrill. I turned to put a cup in the new place I'd just deemed my "cup place," and felt the tingles shoot up my spine as he came closer.

"What if I told you," he said, his body coming to press up against mine, deliciously warm and firm, his hand brushing my blonde hair off my shoulder, "that every time I kiss you." His breath was warm on my neck as my breath stalled in my lungs. "I'll kiss you in a different place?" His lips pressed against my neck, just barely, but then he added pressure and a hint of tongue, and my knees went weak. I gripped the countertop, both trying to hold myself up but also because I simply needed to hold on to something.

I swallowed thickly, and then took in a sharp breath at the feeling of his teeth nipping at me. "I'd tell you," I rasped, not able to hide the arousal in my voice, "that there are *a lot* of boxes to be moved."

"You think I can't find enough places on your body to put my mouth?"

My hand reached behind me and found its natural place at the nape of his neck. "I think you'd do just fine." With that, he spun me around, quickly fitting his mouth over mine, hands gripping my backside. I loved kissing Elliot. He was an expert kisser, always passionate. He didn't kiss as a means to an end, he genuinely enjoyed kissing and therefore, so did I. When his fingers found the hem of my tank top and slid up my back toward the clasp of my bra, I knew if I didn't stop him, we'd add a half hour to our moving time.

"Hey now, no one said anything about second base," I said as I gently pushed him away, my hands on his chest. He gave me a smirk, but then backed away, making his way to my front door.

"We'll see what you have to say about bases after about twenty boxes," he said with a wink.

"Keep talking, Elliot. I don't see any more boxes making their way up the stairs on their own."

He clutched his chest, mimicking pain. "You wound me. I knew you only wanted me for my brute strength." I raised his arm and kissed his, admittedly, impressive biceps.

"Get out of here," I said through a happy laugh. He winked again, but then disappeared out through my door. I turned back to the work of unpacking my kitchen. I was still smiling a minute later when my door burst open again, only this time I didn't hear Elliot's beautiful voice, I heard Olivia's melodic one.

"Look at this awesome bachelorette pad!" Her voice was soft and friendly. I leaned back from the counter to see her turning circles in my living room, taking in my new and mostly empty apartment. She dropped her purse on the floor against the wall, and then joined me in the kitchen.

"Hey you," I said, smiling even harder because she was there. "I didn't know you were coming over. I'm glad to see you."

"Devon and I got all our stuff moved in yesterday and then this morning we were just sitting around, twiddling our thumbs, and realized that living together wasn't much different than what we were doing. So, I wanted to come see your place."

Liv and I had lived on campus for our sophomore year. We'd gotten a dorm room which we shared with two other girls that had a private bathroom. It was sort of like an apartment, but came with a meal plan and was within walking distance of all our classes. I loved living there and building friendships with the other two girls, but as Devon and Liv grew closer, she had wanted to take their relationship to the next level.

Devon had been good for Liv, but he'd also been good *to* Liv. He'd been nothing but steady and reliable and, eventually, once she'd finally realized he wasn't going to rip her heart to shreds as it had been in the past, she calmed down. She stopped drinking excessively, stopped partying often, and became the Liv I'd known all along. She was back to being the sweet, funny, caring friend I'd had for years. When she'd told me they had decided to move in together, I was happy for her, but a little disappointed. I'd imagined living with her throughout our college experience. Not to mention that since I'd been dating Elliot for the same amount of time they'd been together, I'd felt the pressure to make the same move with him.

"Well, I'm glad you're here," I said sincerely. "Where's Devon?" I tried to ignore the familiar nervousness that shot through me like the crack of a gunshot whenever I said his name. I was always afraid that when I said his name she'd be able to hear it in my voice, hear the way I said his name and know. Know that, of everyone I'd ever met in my whole life, I felt more connected to him, felt more like we were always trying to ignore the pull that existed between us. Because of that, I tried desperately to never say his name aloud. But sometimes it was necessary.

"Someone say my name?"

The panic I felt letting his name pass through my lips was immediately smothered by the low and thick roll of electricity that moved like a wave through me with the sound of his voice. His eyes met mine and we shared our usual moment of unified uncomfortableness. We both felt it and we both acknowledged it, but we never spoke of it. It was the strangest relationship I had with anyone, but possibly the most important.

"Hey," I said with a genuine smile. It was weird to be around him, to feel the pull to him that I did, knowing he was the love of my best friend's life, but none of that changed the fact that he was genuinely a nice guy. It was natural to be nice to him, as he was nice to everyone.

"Hey," he replied with an equally friendly smile, carefully setting the box in his hands down on the floor. "I would have come and helped Elliot move in your stuff, Evie. You should have asked."

I shrugged. "You guys have your own things going on."

He let out a small chuckle. "It took twenty minutes to move Liv in, since most of her belongings came in suitcases with wheels." We all laughed because it was true. Liv had more clothes than anything else. Moving in to Devon's apartment had been more like switching bedrooms. She didn't have an apartment to furnish whereas I'd been collecting belongings over the last few months in anticipation of living on my own.

"Well, thank you. I'm sure Elliot would appreciate some help." He smiled at me then turned and walked out of the door, passing Elliot as he came in with another box. He dropped it on the floor and then walked straight toward me, not stopping until his lips were on mine, kissing me again until I was breathless. When he finally pulled away, after succeeding in making me forget anyone else was in the room with us, he tucked a lock of hair behind my ear.

"That was for all the kisses I can't give you now that we've got company."

"Oh," I said, still a little off kilter.

Then he unceremoniously slapped my ass and walked out the door again.

"Something tells me Devon and I might have interrupted a terrifically sexy game you had going on with your boyfriend."

"Yeah, well, something tells *me* that he'll find a way to make up for it later."

"My goodness, Evie. I never knew you had it in you."

I looked at her for a beat and we both lost our composure in a fit of laughter at her unintended euphemism.

A minute later, both guys came back with boxes and just stared at the two of us as we lay giggling on the living room floor.

"They're doing that weird *girl* thing again," Elliot said, his voice teasing and friendly.

"Yeah, we better just keep moving heavy boxes so we don't catch it."

Their remarks only made us laugh harder and soon enough we'd laughed until tears had sprung from our eyes and the guys had moved all my boxes. I allowed Liv to boss the boys around and arrange my furniture in the living room as I kept chipping away at organizing my kitchen. When my love seat, coffee table, lamp, and TV stand with small television were all arranged, the boys started grumbling about food.

"I could have pizza delivered," I called out.

"Pizza is the moving food of choice," Elliot remarked.

"But if we have it delivered, it will take so long. Plus, they can't deliver beer. Boys," she said, turning her pretty face toward them, batting her eyelashes, "won't you please go get beer and pizza for us?"

"Wait, wait, wait," Elliot said loudly, waving a hand in the air, "you want the people who did all the moving to be the ones to go get the reward-for-helping-her-move food? That makes no sense."

"Well, Evie and I aren't old enough to buy beer yet," she replied, fluttering her eyelashes even more. She was right, we were both a few months from being legal. "Besides, I'm sure she'll give you your reward for helping her move later," she said, adding a wink. He groaned in annoyance.

"Come on, man. Let's just go," Devon said, grabbing Elliot's arm. "They won't stop whining until we relent anyway."

"Ah, the wise words of a man who's learned the hard way," Liv joked. Devon walked to her and bent down to kiss her.

"Stop being annoying," he said the words with a smile so I knew he was kidding. Then he kissed her again, quickly, before turning toward the door. "Any special requests?"

"None. But let me give you some money," I reached for my purse, but Elliot snagged it from me before I could open it, then grabbed my wrist and hauled me into his chest.

"You're not paying for pizza and beer, babe." His words were said quietly, his mouth hovering barely above mine.

"But you moved all my stuff," I said, confused but also a little breathless from all the grabbing.

"And I'll take my payment from you later." And with that, he brushed his lips against mine so softly and slowly, completely in opposition to the harshness his words promised. When he pulled away, he left me dazed, but I watched the two guys leave my apartment, not missing the way Devon's eyes stayed on me until the very last second possible. I stood in place for a few moments, trying to piece together what Elliot had said, how he'd handled me, and what he'd meant by his words.

"Sounds like you're in for it tonight." Liv's voice pulled me from my thoughts and I turned to see her sitting on my love seat.

"Yeah," I replied. "I'm not sure how I feel about it though."

"Well, I don't want to miss an opportunity to evaluate your relationship, but we've only got a small window of boy-less time, and I kind of need your help with something."

"Okay," I said instantly, not missing the way her voice, which had been happy and carefree since she'd arrived, was now serious and sullen.

She reached into her purse and pulled out a small paper sack. She didn't even have to open it for me to know what was inside. There were only two reasons a girl in college had anything in a small paper sack, and this wasn't an occasion for condoms.

"You think you're pregnant?"

"I'm pretty sure I'm pregnant. This test is a formality, really." She said those words with not one bit of emotion, which was worrisome. If I thought I was pregnant, with any semblance of conviction, you could bet I would be hysterical.

"How late are you?"

"About four weeks."

"You're a *month* late?"

She nodded. I moved to sit next to her on the love seat. "Why haven't you told me? Or taken the test sooner? If you're four weeks late, that means you're eight weeks pregnant, Liv. That's, like, *really* pregnant."

"I know. I guess I was just hoping... ugh, this sounds terrible. I was hoping that I would become *un*pregnant." I thought about her words for a moment and completely sympathized with her. "I didn't, like, do anything to try and end the pregnancy, I guess I was just hoping it would go away on its own."

I reached up and rubbed my hand down her back.

"I'm guessing you haven't told Devon?"

"Nope."

I wanted to ask her why not, but it didn't matter. The only thing that mattered was that she truly believed she was pregnant with his baby. "Well, do you want to get it over with?"

She let out the longest and loudest sigh I'd ever heard, but then popped up off the couch and headed toward the bathroom.

"Do you want me to come with you?" I wasn't sure what best friend protocol was in this situation. Was I supposed to be in the room with her? Hold the stick? Hold her hair back? I didn't know, but I'd do anything she wanted.

"I can pee by myself, but if you could just be here when I come out, that'd be great."

"Of course."

Minutes ticked by and I was about ready to beat the door down when, finally, it opened. She came out, holding a little white stick in her hand any woman over the age of sixteen could identify from twenty feet away. She was only two feet out of the door when she lifted her eyes and found mine across the room, a depressingly sad smile across her face, as if she were trying to appear like she was happy.

"Can my kid call you Auntie?"

I rushed to her just in time to feel her body start to shake with sobs. We stood in my new apartment, a pee stick between us, and I held her as she came to realize her life would never be the same.

Thankfully, the guys made the longest beer and pizza run known to man, and by the time they returned, Liv was able to put on a good game face. She didn't know when or how she was going to tell Devon, and I couldn't offer her any advice. Had not one word of encouragement. I knew if I was pregnant, I would be completely broken. Devon and Liv had only been together a year, and now, a baby. We ate pizza, I declined beer as a sign of solidarity with Liv, and after we'd watched a movie, Liv and Devon left.

I exhaled loudly as I rested my back against the door. I felt terrible for Liv, but couldn't help but be thankful it wasn't me. And that thought proved me to be a horrible friend.

"Okay, what's going on?" Elliot asked, still sitting on the couch, one ankle resting on his other knee.

"What do you mean?" I replied, standing up straight and walking past him into the kitchen.

"I mean," he said as he stood, following me, "the two of you were acting weird ever since we got back. What's up?"

I was torn. I wasn't used to keeping secrets from Elliot, but this was huge and not just normal gossip. "I don't think I can tell you yet." I picked up a dishtowel and started worrying it between my hands.

"Babe, you can definitely tell me. Whatever is wrong, I'll help you however I can."

His concern was evident and that only made me feel even guiltier for worrying him. "It's not me; it's Liv."

He frowned and his brow furrowed, and I knew he'd figure it out. When he did, I saw the shock come over his face. "She's not..."

"Yeah. Pregnant. Took the test while you guys were out getting pizza," I sighed and tossed the dishtowel on the counter, dropping my head into my hands and massaging my temples. When I felt his body right in front of mine, I instinctively leaned into him, resting my forehead on his chest. His fingers found a soothing rhythm up and down my arms. I gripped his shirt and tipped my head up to look him in the eyes. "You *cannot* tell anyone, especially Devon. Promise."

"Of course," he said before kissing my forehead. "Are you all right? This changes pretty much everything."

"I'm trying not to think about that."

He was quiet for a moment, steadily running his hands along my skin. "How did they even let this happen? Didn't they use protection?"

I steeled a little at his question, my best friend defense system kicking on, but then I realized that it was a valid question. "She missed a few days of her pill."

"And they weren't using anything else?"

I shook my head.

"Damn," he whispered.

"What do you think Devon will do?"

Elliot was quiet for a few moments, and then he sighed. "Honestly? I think he'll marry her."

The ground dropped out from beneath me. The air simply vanished from my lungs. Every part of my body froze in panic. Never had five words ever caused so much of a physical reaction in me before. "Marry her?" The panic in my voice matched that of my body.

"Whoa, babe, calm down."

I couldn't breathe. "He can't marry her."

"Hey," he said as his hands gripped the sides of my face, bringing our eyes to the same level. "Breathe, Evie. Breathe."

I did breathe, but only because I started to cry. He wrapped his arms around me, holding me while I cried, and little by little, I could feel everything about my life unraveling. Eventually, after I'd completely broken down and tried to put myself back together, he took me into my bedroom and put my sheets on my mattress that was resting on the floor while I took a shower. When I lay down, he lay down with me, but I couldn't touch him. He didn't kiss every part of me like he'd promised, and I didn't turn to him either.

Chapter Ten

Present Day

I opened the door to the house and was surprised to hear voices coming from the kitchen. Usually, when I came in the mornings, the house was quiet because the children were still asleep. But from what I could hear, they were definitely awake.

Laughter floated through the foyer along with the unmistakable scent of pancakes and bacon. When I stepped into the kitchen, I couldn't help the surprised look on my face. The kids were dressed and sitting at the table. Devon was at the stove cooking. I stood there for just a moment, taking it all in, soaking in the sight of Devon with his children, all happy and smiling, together. It was a sight I hadn't seen since before Olivia passed.

Eventually, Ruby noticed my presence and alerted the other two.

"Auntie Evie! Daddy's making pancakes!"

"I can see that," I said, trying to force a smile on my face. When Devon turned to look at me, I saw the surprise come over his face too. Apparently, we were both caught off guard by each other that morning.

"Evie," he said, sounding as if he was seeing me after years of being gone.

"You know how to make pancakes?" I couldn't remember a time when he'd made a breakfast besides cereal or toast.

"I never have before," he said carefully, and I could see he was trying to figure out what to say next. "I didn't expect you here today. Didn't think you'd come. So I got the kids up and decided to try my hand at a real breakfast."

I knew why he didn't expect me. Hell, when I woke up that morning I didn't think I was going over there either. But then the guilt showed up and I imagined the kids' faces when they realized I wasn't there, and I decided any uncomfortableness I faced would be worth it if it saved the kids some sadness. Besides, I'd been pretending for nine years that everything was fine between Devon and me, why should that day be any different?

"Don't look in the trash though," he said, his voice lighter, turning back to the stove. "It's like a burnt pancake graveyard."

"Daddy made icky, black ones," Jax said from his chair, his mouth half full of what I assumed wasn't an icky black pancake.

"Yeah, they smelled really bad," Ruby added.

"Well, in your daddy's defense, the first pancake always burns. That's just the way of pancakes."

"Yeah, but Daddy threw away, like, fifteen pancakes."

"Icky, black ones," Jax added.

"How's the laundry room?" I asked, trying to avoid any conversation that would cause tension between us.

"Well, the floor's ruined and I think the bottom portion of the walls too. I have to go to the hardware store soon and rent some industrial fans to try to dry the place out a little more. My insurance company is sending over a contractor to look at the damage."

"Wow. You've accomplished a lot this morning," I said, peeking down the hallway.

"I couldn't really sleep," he said, his voice thicker, full of meaning. I tamped down the urge I felt to turn and look at him, to see if his eyes were full of longing. It was a masochistic urge and I was done torturing myself. "The insurance company said I needed to take pictures of the damage. I was going to do it myself, but since you're here and all, do you think you could?"

"Definitely." Could I pick up a camera and use it as a shield against all my emotions? I was actually, very good at that.

"Actually, if you could get the kids ready for school, I could drop Jaxy off at preschool and run to the store to get the fan real quick before the contractor gets here."

"I'm here to help," I said, plastering a fake smile on my face.

"And my mom said I'd never use my visual arts degree," I said to myself as I snapped pictures of Devon's waterlogged walls. Everything was damp. The floor was soft and the entire area that had been flooded looked terrible. I moved out of the laundry room and down the hall, taking pictures of anything and everything that looked affected by the water. Minutes later, when the doorbell rang, I thought I'd gotten all the pictures I needed. I placed my camera on the kitchen island as I walked past and opened the door with a smile.

My smile froze a little when I saw the man standing on the porch.

"Hi, good morning," he said, his voice deep. "I was sent here to look at some flooding damage." He stood there, smiling at me, and I couldn't find a way to make my mouth work. "Um, do I have the right house?" His smile broadened as if he were used to women being slack jawed around him. I managed to bring myself out of my stupor.

"Oh, yes. Please, come in." I opened the door wider and stepped back, allowing him in to the foyer. Even though my mouth had started functioning, I couldn't stop my eyes from taking him all in. It was almost unbelievable, the way he looked. Almost as if cheesy music was going to start playing and he would peel off his tool belt. He was, quite nearly, a perfect male specimen. I shook my head, trying to clear the images from my mind. I shut the door and tried to form a normal sentence. "The laundry room flooded yesterday. You can follow me." I walked past him and started toward the kitchen, trying not to think about how hot the back of my neck felt with him behind me, how acutely aware I was of my body in that moment. I kept walking until I approached the laundry room door. I motioned into the room and he inched past me with a killer smile.

"I'm Nate, by the way," he said as he passed me, holding out his hand. I took it, even though we were too close to actually shake hands comfortably. For a moment we stood, squeezed close to one another, just holding each other's hand, smiling at each other. When he pulled away, I took my hand back and pushed it through my hair, trying to convince myself it hadn't been a severely intense moment.

"My name's Evelyn."

"Evelyn, huh?" he asked as he knelt next to the washing machine, moving the handle of his hammer out of the way of his thigh like he did it one million times a day, without even looking. "Were you named after a relative or something?"

I laughed a little because it wasn't the first time someone had insinuated I had an old-fashioned name. "Nope. My mom just thought it was pretty."

"Well, she was right," he said, reaching behind the machine, his smile making my face heat and heart flutter. "Looks like the line to your washer split."

"Huh?" I asked, confused, then I caught on to the change of subject, now blushing from embarrassment. "Oh, yeah. Right. I came home and there was water spraying everywhere. It was a mess."

"I can imagine." He stood and moved around the room, then came back into the hallway, looking at the floor, then kneeling low again to look at the walls. "You're gonna need new floors and new drywall." He looked back at me without standing up. "You're lucky you caught it when you did. If the water had gotten into the kitchen, it could have hit electrical and then you'd really be in a mess. This shouldn't take more than a few weeks to fix."

"A few weeks? That's a good estimate?" I asked, laughing a little. "That seems like a long time."

"That's kind of how it works. We gotta tear it all out before we put the new stuff in. But we have to dry it out first."

"Oh, right! The fans. Devon is out getting fans right now."

He stood at my words and a little bit of light was gone from his eyes. "Fans'll be good. Once it's all dried out, we can start working."

With impeccable timing, I heard the front door open and turned my head to see Devon walking through the kitchen with two strange looking contraptions in his arms. The two men saw each other and a frost came over the room. I watched as Devon eyed Nate, and even though I couldn't see him, I knew Nate was doing the same thing. It was tense and strange, and I was painfully uncomfortable.

"Devon, this is the contractor the insurance company sent over to look at the damage."

"I gathered that," he said, catching me off guard by his short and sharp words. He put the things that I assumed were fans down, and then reached his hand out toward Nate. "Thanks for coming out on such short notice," he said, his tone not any nicer. Nate grabbed his hand and I winced watching their forearm muscles bulge. It was obvious they were both squeezing the hell out of the other's hand.

"That's my job," Nate replied, smiling at Devon, but not the friendly smile I'd gotten. No, he gave Devon a smirk. They shook hands for way too long, neither one of them seeming to want to give up first, but when they finally let each other go, it was with a sharp thrust. "As I was telling Evelyn here, you'll need new flooring and new drywall. It'll take a few weeks. I can probably start once everything is dried out."

"Well, are those the fans you needed?" asked Devon, motioning toward the ones he'd brought in with him. They looked kind of like snails, rounded with a lip at the bottom. I'd imagined the kind of fans you'd use in your window on a hot day.

"Those'll work, if it's all you've got," Nate said to Devon.

"I don't usually keep a supply of industrial strength fans on hand," he replied.

"Well, why would you?"

"Okay, boys, let's calm down a little. Let's get the fans set up, and get the drying process started. I'm sure we all have places to be." I'd never had to defuse testosterone before. I reached for one of the fans, surprised by its weight.

"Here, Evelyn, let me do that." Nate took the fan from me and turned to walk back to the laundry room.

"Her name's Evie," Devon said, the coldness of his words sending shivers down my back.

"Not what she told me," Nate called from the laundry room.

"Devon, stop it," I whispered, hoping Nate couldn't hear me. "You're acting like a child."

Nate walked back into the kitchen, grabbed the other fan, and left again, his eyes darting back and forth between us. I kept staring at Devon, willing him to stop acting like an asshole. A moment later, the loudest fans I'd ever heard started up and I almost had to cover my ears. Nate came back in the kitchen and stopped just short of the dining table.

"Leave those fans on twenty-four-seven. I'll come back in two days to check on the progress."

"They're really loud," I said, still fighting the urge to cover my ears.

"Industrial," Nate said in response.

"How are the kids supposed to sleep through that?"

"You've got kids?" he asked, his eyes boring into mine, and I could have sworn he sounded a little disappointed. Before I could clarify, Devon butted in.

"Two kids. Small ones. Need their sleep." Great. Now he wasn't even using complete sentences.

"You can turn it off when you're sleeping if you need to, but it might take an extra day to dry in that case." He looked at me, and then his eyes moved back to Devon, hardening. "I'll be back Monday morning." With that, he walked to the front door and left. I had an unfamiliar urge to stop him before he made it to the door, to explain everything that Devon had so conveniently left out, but it didn't matter. I did, however, turn to Devon with daggers in my eyes.

"What the hell was that?" I asked, yelling partly because of the fans, but mostly because I was irritated by his behavior.

"What?" he answered, yelling back, obviously irritated as well.

"You totally made that guy think we had kids together!"

Devon rolled his eyes and walked out of the kitchen into the living room. He went to the front windows and pulled the curtains over, watching as a truck drove by that I assumed belonged to Nate. "I didn't do anything of the sort, Evie. That guy was a douchebag."

"What exactly did he do that made him a douchebag?"

"You didn't see the way he was looking at you."

"What?" I exclaimed, my voice shriller than I'd ever heard it before. "You're insane. And even if he *was* looking at me, you don't get to be all assholey to people for that. I've never seen you act like this."

"I come home to find some stranger in my house, ogling you, nearly fucking you with his eyes, and I'm just supposed to sit back and act like nothing's happening?"

"YES!" I screamed, my breath panting, heart pounding, hands shaking. "You've got no right doing anything about it! Besides, he was perfectly respectful. Nice, even. You didn't have to go all Neanderthal on him. He thinks we're married for Christ's sake!"

"You're upset because I chased off the contractor? Were you going to date him, Evie? You don't date, ever."

"I date."

"Not since Elliot."

His words sliced through me and my mouth fell open at his. He knew I didn't like talking about Elliot.

"I talk with him sometimes," he continued, his eyes mean, purposefully trying to hurt me. "He hates you. Hates what you did to him. You're the reason he left the country, you know. He couldn't even stand to be on the same continent as you."

"Shut up," I whispered, shocked at the acid dripping from his voice, the anger I'd never heard from him before.

"Why should I? I think it's time we talked, got everything out in the open. You and I have been silent for too long."

I shook my head. "I'm not talking to you while you're like this, while you're hurtful. I don't know who you are right now."

"This is me, Evie. This is me after years of torture. You think a person isn't changed after going through what I did? Watching my wife die? Watching someone I thought I could protect be taken right out from under me? There was no order in her death. No reason. Nothing I could piece together to make any sense. So I just had to watch." He took an angry step toward me. "And then, there's you. Always pretending to be something you're not."

I gasped. "I'm not pretending to be anything," I whispered. "You're upset, Devon. I get that, but don't take it out on me. I haven't done anything."

"That's exactly the problem. You haven't done anything. Ever. Besides pretend. You've been pretending since the first day we met. Pretending there wasn't this *thing* between us. Pretending it didn't cloud every single time we've ever been in the same room. It's exhausting pretending not to be drawn to you."

"I'm not pretending," I said, my voice thick with the cries I was holding back. He came closer.

"You are. All the time. Even now. And I'm tired of it." He kept walking toward me and I kept retreating, until I was backed into the refrigerator, only to watch as his hands pressed flat against it right next to my ears, blocking me in.

"Elliot won't tell me what you did to him that made him hate you. Says it's not his secret to tell. But I can hear in his voice how much you hurt him." His eyes were darting back and forth between mine, and his face was so close. I wasn't afraid he'd hurt me, but I was afraid that whatever was happening in that moment was going to change everything forever. "But I know your secret. It's the same secret I've kept all these years."

"Please, Devon. Don't…"

"Don't what? Be honest for once? Be real? What are you afraid of? Elliot's gone. Olivia's gone. It's only us now. We're the only ones we can hurt anymore. We can only damage each other."

"I don't want to hurt anymore," I pleaded with him, begged him with my eyes to let whatever tirade he was on go, to let us slip back into that place of un-acknowledgement, where we let our problems lie just under the surface and fester.

"We've been hurting each other for years, Evie."

I nodded. "I know," I whispered. His forehead came to rest gently against mine, his breath passing over my face. I reached forward tentatively and gripped his t-shirt in my fingers, wanting to touch him but afraid of how hard it would be to eventually let go.

"We were both trying to be the better person for so long, and then Ruby came along, and life happened. And I swear to you, with everything that I am, I loved Olivia. I loved her and the family we made together. Not once did I think I'd made the wrong choice, Evie. I still don't think I made the wrong choice. But I'd be lying if I said I didn't ever think about what my other option was. Didn't wonder how life would have been with you. If only…"

"Please, don't do this. We can't do this."

"If only I hadn't walked away from you that first day."

I finally let out the cry I'd been holding in for what seemed like days. Years even. I dropped my forehead to his chest, pulled his t-shirt closer, and cried. I'd cried a lot in prior months, losing a best friend would cause that to happen. But those tears might have been the most gut wrenching I'd felt in a while. How many times, in that first year of knowing Devon, had I wished for the exact same thing? Wished he'd asked for my number, made an effort, and pursued me, done *anything* that would have given me a claim to him over Olivia. Given me even one sliver of hope that what I'd felt for him was real.

I cried against him and I felt his hands cradle the back of my head, holding me close to him. I felt his lips press against my hair, heard him whisper soothing words to me, telling me it was going to be all right. When the tears finally stopped, it wasn't because I felt like I'd exorcized all the feelings I'd held inside for so long. No. The crying stopped because I was able to close the door that had been holding them in again. I felt the wall go back up, brick by brick, I tucked my heart away just like I had so many years ago. It was the only thing to do – the only way everything could remain the same – and I wouldn't end up losing anything more.

I slid away from him quickly, my hand coming up to wipe the tears his shirt hadn't caught, as I grabbed my purse and left the house. I walked out the door listening to him calling my name, chasing after me. I slammed the door behind me, hoping that would be enough to deter him from following me. I made it to my car, but then realized I was crying too hard, making it difficult to find my keys in my purse. When I finally did, I started the engine and pulled away from the street, speeding one mile down the road before I pulled over. The tears were so thick I could hardly see the road, so I pulled into a gas station parking lot and cried until I was too exhausted to cry any more.

When I finally pulled up to my studio, hoping to salvage the day and get a little bit of work done, I realized I'd left my camera sitting on the kitchen island at Devon's house. So I cried all over again.

Chapter Eleven

Evening of Olivia's Bachelorette Party

"Well, I hope you're satisfied," I grunted, carrying most of Olivia's weight, her arm wrapped around my shoulder, unable to walk on her own. I'd worn a short, black, cocktail dress, and impossibly high heels, per Olivia's dress code for her bachelorette party. Of course, I'd complied; I didn't want to be the only woman at the party who stood out like a sore thumb. However, now that I was practically carrying Olivia and contemplating trying to launch her onto my shoulder like a sack of potatoes, the outfit choice was looking like a poor one.

"I am very satizzfied," she replied, her speech slurred and sloppy. "Between the pregnancy and having a small baby at home, I haven't been able to get drunk in a very long time, Evelyn." She said my name like I'd done something wrong, like somehow her getting pregnant was my fault.

"Well, I'm glad you were able to have fun," I said in response, not really sure what I was supposed to say. As far as Olivia's new life went, I understood it was a very sharp contrast to her old life – new baby, new fiancé – but in general, I found it hard to feel sorry for her. I was unable to deliver the sympathy she longed for from me. Sure, I put on a guise of feeling sorry for her because otherwise, it would cause a ripple in our relationship, but her life was a product of her choices and behavior. In addition, Devon had proposed to her, wanting to give her and their daughter a normal, family life. Well, I could find nothing terrible about that. So, my sympathy was reserved for people who actually needed it.

I made it to the door of the apartment she shared with Devon. They were planning to buy a house soon, but for now, the two of them lived in the same one-bedroom apartment Olivia had moved into last summer, only now they had a baby. Little

Ruby. The sweetest, tiniest, and loveliest little baby girl I'd ever known. She was perfect. And I never thought of Olivia as particularly maternal, but watching her with her baby made even my ovaries squirm a little. Olivia was a natural mother and Devon was a nervous, but doting father. I could tell he wanted to do everything he could, be a good father and also a good provider, but it was sweet to see him hold his daughter with a little bit of fear in him, not wanting to hurt her.

Not surprisingly, I could also tell there was strain on their relationship. It was only natural to expect some issues when you got pregnant one year into your relationship, only being twenty-ish. They became engaged during her pregnancy for two reasons: because they loved each other, but more so, because they both felt like it was expected of them. I didn't feel like they should be getting married, didn't feel like it was a good idea to enter into marriage simply because of the baby. However, I never found the nerve to express that to Olivia. I knew, on some level, if I told Olivia I thought the timing of her marriage was a mistake, it would be the beginning of the end of our friendship. I knew she'd see past my reasoning, even though it was sound, and pick out the bigger reason I might object; because of Devon. Because even watching him promise to be with her forever, even after watching him hold their baby, tears in his eyes, smiling at his fiancée – my best friend – there was still no absence of my feelings for him. Even though I *loved* my boyfriend. Even though…

I leaned Olivia against the wall next to her door, took her purse from her shoulder, and found her keys. I opened her door and was not surprised to find it dark and empty inside. Devon was out for his bachelor party and the baby was with his parents. I knew the boys would be bringing him home eventually, but I wasn't surprised we'd beat them. I took her by the arm and led her into the apartment, heading straight for the bedroom.

She flopped down on the bed, lying straight back, arms flailed out to the sides.

"That was an epic night," she said, not really sounding like she was speaking to me directly, but throwing it out into the universe.

"I'm glad you had a good time," I said sincerely. I might not agree with her marriage, but she was still my best friend and I still wanted her to be happy. "I don't think you'll think it was so epic come tomorrow morning."

"I never get hangovers," she slurred.

"That's a lie. Plus, it's been over a year since you've been drunk. Maybe all the baby hormones have made you more susceptible to hangovers," I said without much thought as I tried to undo the buckles on her high heels.

"You'd like that wouldn't you?" Her tone was less playful, serious even.

I let my hands fall away from her feet. "Excuse me?" I whispered quietly, more than a little surprised by her comment.

"You'd love it if I woke up miserable. Face it, Evie, you want everything I have and the idea of me waking up with a hangover would put a smile on your face." She sat up a little, surprising me with a smile on her face. "You'd think it served me right to wake up miserable."

In the two years since I'd met Devon, since he'd started dating her and they'd been together, never had Olivia and I discussed the tension that existed between us all. I was at a loss for what to say in response to her. I never imagined she would call me out, confront me about it.

"Liv," I said softly, not wanting to hurt her or do irrevocable damage to our friendship.

"It's okay, Evie," she said as she flopped back down on the bed. "I don't blame you. Devon is the best and he wants to marry me. I'd be jealous if I were you too. I had his baby, so now I have a claim on him forever. No one else will ever be the mother of his first baby. I gave him something sacred."

I tried not to focus on the fact that her statement made it sound like she expected Devon to have another baby momma at some point, as if she was admitting her relationship was temporary. I knew Devon didn't think of it as such, but was surprised to hear it from Olivia.

"You're drunk, Olivia." That was the only thing I could think to say to her. I couldn't deny what she was saying – I was jealous. But not in a hateful way, not in a way that made me angry with her. I was happy for her and Devon. Them having a baby and getting married changed nothing about our predicament. Devon had been, from the start, out of my reach. Not within my grasp. The minute he linked himself to Liv, it was over for us, and it had never really began. I'd made peace with that long ago, but it never made the connection go away, the awareness that I loved him in a way I hadn't ever loved anyone. Loved him enough to let him be with her, to step back and watch him be happy with someone else – with my best friend.

"I'm *really* drunk," she said with a giggle, which morphed into a huge belly laugh. She laughed for five minutes, making it nearly impossible to get her shoes off. When her laughter tapered off, I guided her into the bathroom.

"Here's a nightgown," I said, placing it on the counter. "Go to the bathroom and change. I'll get some Advil and water for you."

"You're the best," she said, with words I barely understood because they were so mushed together, and all tension from our earlier conversation dissolved away.

"I'm glad you think so, Liv. You're pretty awesome yourself." I shut the door as she ambled toward the toilet, glad to be done with the nerve-wracking conversation she'd started. I sat on her bed, dropped my head into my hands, and took in a deep breath. As her maid of honor, my responsibility included making sure she was safe and taken care of, which meant getting her home. Therefore, I'd consumed far less alcohol than she had. And in that moment, I was regretting that fact immensely. I scrubbed my hands down my face, breathing out a large sigh. After a quiet moment, I heard more giggles coming from the bathroom and let my lips form the smile that came naturally. Despite what drunk Olivia thought, I would never want her to be uncomfortable just to make myself feel better. I loved her. I treasured our friendship. It was a little more complicated than I ever would have imagined, but only for me. I'd never make my feelings for her fiancé affect anything. Ever.

I walked out to her kitchen, finding the drawer I knew they kept their medicine in, and opened the Advil. As I was filling a glass from the faucet, I heard the front door open and then watched as Elliot and Devon came inside. Only, in exact opposition to me helping Olivia home, Elliot had his drunken arm draped over Devon's shoulders.

"Evie!" Elliot yelled, removing his arm from around Devon, and nearly falling forward to get to me. I put the glass down before he made contact, but was promptly wrapped up in his arms, being held close to him, smelling the alcohol wafting off his skin. His hands wandered, smoothing down my back to cup my ass, at which point I felt his scruffy face against the skin of my neck. "Damn, Evie. You're hot." He continued to paw at me, but I managed to push him far enough away so that his hands were only able to reach my shoulders.

"Babe, you're drunk," I said with a laugh. "This was Devon's night. You were supposed to let him get hammered. Some best man you are."

His eyes narrowed a little. "Devon doesn't mind."

My eyes found Devon standing by the dining room table, hands in his pockets, just watching us. His eyes were on Elliot and he didn't look completely happy with the situation.

"Olivia is in the bathroom. She's pretty wasted too. I was going to bring her some water and Advil." My eyes darted to the cup and pills on the counter.

He nodded, took the pills and water, and then walked toward the bedroom.

I moved my hands from Elliot's shoulders up to cup his cheeks. His eyes were glassy, hooded by his eyelids that looked like they weighed a million pounds. "Are you ready to go home?"

"Unless you had other plans," he replied, his tone not particularly friendly.

I tilted my head to the side, unsure of where he was trying to take the conversation. "I've got no plans. I'm here. You're here. I'm sober. Let's get you home."

"If we lived together, you'd only have to go to one place," he slurred, turning from me once the words had left his mouth. I felt the verbal punch to my gut, but tried not to react immediately. He was drunk, after all.

"Well, I was planning on staying with you, so I'd only have one stop anyway. Unless you had other plans…" I couldn't hold back the snark as I threw his own words back at him.

"Why are you always pushing me away when he's around?"

I let out an exasperated sigh. "I push you away when you're being inappropriate."

"I'm not allowed to touch you? You're my girlfriend. For two years."

"Being my boyfriend doesn't give you the right to put your hands on me whenever you'd like. Come on," I said, my voice becoming a little softer. "Let's just get you home."

His hands reached out for me again, but this time they ended up on my hips so I didn't move them. I just looked him in the eye. "Will you still stay with me? I didn't mean to upset you."

He sounded sincerely sorry, and I knew he'd probably pass out in the car on the way to his apartment anyway. "Yeah, I'll stay. Come on, let's go." I grabbed his hand and pulled him toward the door. I stopped at the door and called out softly, "Bye guys, we're headed home." I didn't get a response, but figured Devon had his hands full with Liv.

We made it all the way to my car before I realized I'd left my purse behind. I leaned him up against my car. "I'll be right back, I left the keys inside." He grumbled but didn't argue, so I ran back to the apartment as fast as I could in my stupid heels.

I inched the door open, not wanting to alarm anyone, and saw my purse on the dining table. I tried to tiptoe through the apartment, but nearly screamed when Devon walked out of his bedroom, startling me. I jumped, but managed to keep quiet. When my brain registered that Devon was only wearing a pair of cotton lounge pants, I kept my hand over my mouth, but for an entirely different reason. I was no longer trying to stifle a scream, I was attempting to hide that my mouth was gaping open at the sight of his naked, chiseled, glorious chest. I'd seen it before – the first time we'd met, for one – but usually there were other people around. We were at the lake, for example, and everyone was showing skin. But I had never seen Devon in an intimate way, never seen him only visible by the dim light coming from the bathroom, wearing the very thing I imagined he would go to bed in, looking at me like if I didn't leave, didn't get out of his reach, he might devour me.

I slipped past him, grabbed my purse, and left without a word. Lord knew, if either one of us spoke right then, our worlds might come crumbling down.

When I'd gotten Elliot safely into his apartment, I finally reached down to take off my godforsaken heels. He wandered drunkenly through his apartment and into the bedroom. I sighed, still reeling from the tense interaction I'd had with Devon, wanting desperately to just fall asleep and start a new day with a clean slate. Suddenly, I heard Elliot's voice, deep, gravelly, and drunk, ring out through his apartment.

"You'd tell me if you'd fallen out of love with me, right?"

My heart lurched at his question, ached inside my chest. He was drunk, but I knew he was asking me a serious question. The truth was I wasn't *in love* with Elliot. I loved him, in the way one would love a wonderful guy after dating him for two years. But I'd never been *in love* with him. I didn't know if it was something I was capable of with Elliot. I loved him. I cared about him. I didn't regret being with him.

I walked back to his bedroom and saw him lying on his back on the bed, much like Olivia had been – arms sprawled out, eyes glued to the ceiling. I crawled onto his bed, my dress inching up my thighs as I made my way to him, and found my usual spot, my cheek on his chest, his arm coming to naturally curl around me, holding me close.

"Nothing's changed," I whispered, pressing my face in closer to him, unable to say the words with any kind of conviction. I couldn't shout them, couldn't plead with him to believe me; all I could do was whisper my half-truth to him. When he rolled toward me, his hand finding the side of my face, eyes level with mine, all I could do was lean forward and press my mouth to his to stop any words he had for me. He didn't push me away, didn't try to say anything more to me. And even though he was drunk, and we'd had a tumultuous past hour, I let him make love to me – it was the least I could do.

Chapter Twelve

Present Day

It was Monday morning and Devon had left the house without saying one word to me. He also went out of his way to leave the house in a way in which he wouldn't have to walk past me. Which meant he walked through the backyard, opened the back gate, and climbed over the pile of firewood kept at the side of his house in order to go to work without having to see me. It was ridiculous, but most of me was glad he'd gone the extra mile.

I had no idea what I would have said to him if he'd had big enough balls to face me. I was certain, however, that I would more than likely pretend as if nothing had ever happened between us, just like I'd been doing for ten years now.

After I'd snuck back into his house on Friday to get my camera, after I was certain he'd left and the house was empty, I'd spent the weekend in my car, driving until something caught my eye. I'd stopped when I wanted to, photographed my temporary muse, then pack up and move along. I drove all day Saturday until it was dark and my eyes were tired. I stopped at a run-down motel, slept on top of the scratchy covers, and woke up on Sunday ready for another day. I took a different route back home, stopping again whenever I felt like it.

I knew I had to be home in time to get to Devon's house Monday morning. I knew, even though there were a million other places I'd rather be than there, the kids needed me and my conscience would be shouting at me if I'd abandoned them. Liv asked me to do one thing – to help take care of her family. So, no matter how upset I was with Devon and myself, I would be there for the kids.

The kids hadn't mentioned anything unusual and didn't seem like they knew anything was off between Devon and me, so I tried to act as normal as possible.

I was herding both kids toward the door, mentally counting backpacks and lunch boxes, making sure they both had everything they needed for their day. I heard the door open just as I grabbed my purse, but was surprised to hear Jaxy's voice say, "Hello, there. You must build stuff. Bob the Builder wears the same belt."

My head snapped toward the door, heart pounding, but then a wave of relief rolled through me when I saw Nate on the other side of the door, tool belt and all.

"I do build stuff. I tear stuff down too." Nate's voice was soft and gentle, his words said with a smile. "In fact, I'm here to look at your house where all the water was."

"You mean the room that flooded? It's kind of smelly in there," Jaxy said, scrunching up his nose. "And we've had loud fans on all weekend."

"I'm here to fix that too," he said, laughing. "Good morning, Evelyn." His eyes found mine as he spoke, his eyes a little more cautious with me than they were with Jax. "Is now a bad time to take a look at the damage?"

"We're going to school," Ruby supplied, her tone a little unfriendly, which caused me to frown.

"We are, actually, headed out the door to get them to school." I said, a little surprised by my own disappointment. "But," I said, hoping to stall him, "I could be back in a half hour. Any chance you can come back then?"

A smile spread over his face slowly as he nodded. "Sure. I'll just go grab a coffee." He paused then, and I saw indecision sweep across his face. Moments later, it changed to a more hopeful expression. "Can I bring you anything?"

There was no way for him to know that it had been months, possibly years, since someone had asked me if they could do something for me. It shouldn't have mattered that much, shouldn't have shifted something inside of me as significantly as it did, but I couldn't help the emotions his simple question evoked.

"That would be great. Just an iced coffee, please." My voice was slight and tiny, all I could muster without letting more show in my words than I would have liked.

"Got it. See you in a half hour." He nodded slightly, then backed away before turning and heading toward the big truck parked at the curb which I assumed was his.

"Let's go guys," I said to the kids, urging them through the door.

"Who was that?" Ruby asked.

"The man who's going to fix your house," I replied as I shut the door behind me.

"He looked at you funny," Ruby said with her usual snarky tone.

"He did not."

"He was cool. I like all his tools," Jax remarked, doing his typical skip-walk down the path toward the sidewalk. We all turned, heading toward the corner where the bus would pick up Ruby. As we waited, the kids seemed to forget about Nate, talking instead about their exciting plans for summer vacation, which was coming up quickly. I silently wondered what Devon had planned for the summer. I certainly couldn't spend all day with the kids. Spending the mornings and evenings with them was stretching my abilities as it was. My job was already suffering; I couldn't stay with the kids full time without giving up my career completely.

I felt the panic rising up, but did my best to tamp it down. Surely, Devon wasn't expecting me to stay with them. He'd probably already signed them up for daycare or summer camp. I wouldn't mind continuing the morning and evening routine, but anything more than what I was giving them now would cause a lot of issues. I pushed the stressful thoughts out of my mind, trying not to give in to the urge to overthink and panic.

I kept the radio on as I drove Jax to preschool, trying to keep my mind occupied by the voices of the DJs, or the songs they played. When I pulled out of the parking lot and headed back to Devon's house, my pulse picked up and the blood pumped through me with such force I could hear it in my ears.

I pulled into the driveway, trying not to stare at the attractive man standing on the porch, two coffee cups in his hands, elbows bent, and biceps stretching the cotton of his sleeves beautifully. His skin was tanned, which I imagined was only natural for a man who probably worked outdoors a lot.

His eyes tracked me as I got out of my car and I couldn't help but notice the way his smile started on one side of his mouth and then spread across widely.

"You're like a full service contractor, bringing me coffee and everything." I said the words with mocked confidence, as if I were totally comfortable with attractive men doing nice things for me.

"On my good days, I can be terribly accommodating."

"Well, thank you," I said, trying to look him in the eyes, but finding his gaze too intense. I looked away before the blush creeping over my cheeks became too prominent. I put my key in the door and unlocked it, pushing it open and welcoming him in with a sweep of my arm.

He walked past me and held my coffee out, still smiling. "Shall we get a look at your laundry room?"

"Sure," I said, watching him walk toward the kitchen. I took in a deep breath, tore my gaze from the broadness that was his back, and shut the door. I followed him through the house, noticing he placed his cup on the kitchen counter as he walked by, not stopping on his way to the laundry room. When I came into the laundry room, he was stooped down low touching a portion of the wall near the floor that had been under water.

"The fans did a good job of drying all this out," he said, not looking away from the wall. "Like I said last week, the work should take a couple of weeks." At that point his eyes looked up at me as I stood in the doorway. "Do you work from home?"

I was caught a little off guard by his question, trying to find the link between his previous statement and the question he'd asked me, trying to formulate an answer. He must have noticed my confusion and tried to explain.

"Most people work during the day, so they give me a key and I do the work while they're out of the house. But this was twice now you've been home so I assumed..." His voice trailed off and he was obviously looking for me to fill in some of the blanks.

"I don't live here. This isn't my house."

"Not your house?"

"No. This is Devon's house. He lives here with his children."

"I guess I kind of figured you were-"

"No." I was compelled to tell him everything, but also afraid to tell him anything. He was, after all, a stranger. But for some reason, I wanted to tell him who I was, who Devon was, how it came to be that his children were a part of my life.

"Do you think he will be all right giving me a key then?"

I shrugged. Honestly, after their testosterone battle the week before, I wasn't sure what he'd be okay with. "I can ask him."

Nate stood, shaking his head, wiping his hands on his jeans. "No, it's fine. I can ask. He's the homeowner." He looked at me, his eyes piercing, brows furrowed. Suddenly, he sighed loudly and ran a hand through his hair. "This is going to be totally inappropriate of me, but I'm really confused, so I'm just going to ask." He didn't give me enough time to respond before he asked his question, words spilling quickly from his mouth as if he were afraid he'd lose his nerve. "What are you to him? I mean, what's your relationship?"

If he'd been anyone else, any other man on the planet, I'd find his question rude and intrusive. I'd tell him it was none of his business. I'd ask him to leave, tell Devon to find another contractor. I'd push him away, along with all the feelings his question brought up. I'd push it down all in an effort to avoid the answer. The answer was – I was nobody. *We* were nobody to each other. And I'd worked hard for ten years to make it that way. But this was the first time in ten years when I had reason to be *glad* Devon wasn't anyone to me.

"Devon was married to my best friend. She died earlier this year. I help him take care of their kids. That's all." That's all. Two words, so full of meaning. That's all. A dismissive phrase. Words used to indicate unimportance. That's *all*. All. Everything. That's what Devon and his children had been to me since Liv passed. Devon had been my *all* for years, but standing in his house, looking at the man who was supposed to repair its walls, suddenly my all, my everything, seemed to shift.

"I'm really sorry to hear that," he said with so much sincerity, all I could do was smile.

"She was a great mom. I'm just here to get them to school on time and be here when they come home. He's still trying to figure out how to do it all without her."

"Seems like he's trying to figure out how to do it all with you."

I had no words to say to that, so I turned and walked back toward the kitchen. "When do you think you'll be able to start the work?"

"Not until next week. We have to finish up a project first. But I can order the supplies we need now, that way it'll all be ready to go." He paused and I looked back at him, waiting for him to finish, but he looked indecisive. "Never mind," he said, running his hand through his hair again. I watched as the brown locks slid through his fingers effortlessly. His hair looked soft and I found myself wanting to touch it. "I'll tell all this to Devon. I probably shouldn't even be here right now. I thought you lived here."

"Nope," I said on a sigh. "But I'm here most mornings, during the week anyway."

"But you do work, right?"

I laughed a little at his question. "Yeah, but I'm my own boss, so I can work whenever I want to. I'm a photographer."

His eyes lit up a little with recognition. "I did see a fancy camera on the counter when I was here last time."

"Yeah. I was taking pictures of the damage for Devon's insurance."

"But that's not what you do for a living, right? Take pictures of water damage?"

"Not usually," I said, laughing again. "I take all kinds of photos, but right now I make a living doing weddings and events. You know, portraits, family sessions, and stuff like that." As I spoke, he picked up his coffee cup and leaned back against the counter, as if he were settling in to listen. "But I really enjoy landscape and nature photography, mixing in a little bit of beauty," I said, putting my coffee down so I could use my hands, finding myself excited to talk about my job and my love of photography. "Like, finding a really beautiful landscape to take pictures and adding a really beautiful model. When I can capture a moment when the model looks like she's a part of the landscape, man…" I sigh, smiling widely. "There's nothing better than that."

"Why don't you do that instead of weddings?" he asked, sounding genuinely curious.

"Well, the work I do now, people pay me to take the pictures they want. If I were doing the type photography I wanted to for a living, I'd have to take the pictures and then hope people wanted to pay for them." I shrugged. "Call me crazy, but I'd rather go for the guaranteed paycheck."

He laughed, and the deep rumble sent every nerve ending in my body singing. I had never considered anyone's laugh to be sexy before, but I had images of him laughing, his mouth against my neck, the stubble growing on his jaw scraping along my sensitive skin, and I nearly grabbed the edge of the counter to hold myself upright. "Well, that's a good point," he said through the tail end of his laughter. "I'd love to see some of your photos." He lifted his coffee cup and took a sip, staring at me over the edge, and I felt the heat of a blush creep over my neck again, making its way to my cheeks.

"I don't have any with me, but some are on display at my studio."

"You have a studio?" He sounded impressed, which caused me to laugh.

"I imagine you have some sort of office or place you do business," I said, smiling.

"Touché," he said, laughing again.

"I thought I was the only person in the world who said touché."

"It's one of my favorite words," he replied, taking another sip from his cup. "But I was being serious. I'd really like to see your work."

His eyes held my gaze for a moment and I could see he was being sincere. It had been a while since someone outside of my paying customers was interested in looking at my photos. "Okay," I said as I walked to where my purse was sitting. I reached in and took a business card from my wallet. I placed it on the island and slid it across the granite toward him. "The address to my studio is on there. Feel free to stop by any time."

He reached forward and I didn't even bother trying to hide the fact that I watched his muscled forearm as his fingers found the card. His eyes were on it, so I took a few more moments to let my eyes wander up and down the contours of his impressive arm. Suddenly, I had wildly vivid images in my head of Nate with no shirt, pounding a hammer, sweat glistening on his skin in the sunlight. And for once, having those images in my mind, feeling a hint of arousal at the sight of him, didn't cause heavy layers of guilt to rest on my shoulders.

"I'll be sure to contact Devon about the work that needs to be done."

His voice snapped me from my daydream and when my gaze flickered back to him, I saw the smug grin on his face. He'd caught me staring and, surprisingly, I wasn't embarrassed. I felt a wave of entitlement. I was a single woman admiring a man. It hadn't occurred to me he might be involved. My eyes immediately darted to his ring finger and I let out a small, relieved sigh as I saw it was naked. There also didn't appear to be a tan line where a wedding ring might have been.

"Okay, sounds good," I said lamely, still trying to recover from letting myself be unabashedly attracted to someone without wanting to cry afterward.

He smiled that sexy smile that started at one side and swept across his lips entirely as he pulled away from the counter and started walking toward the front door. He walked past me, not stopping, but flipping my business card at me, and said, "I'll be seeing you soon."

I swallowed hard, tried to smile, but then succumbed to the roll of shivers sent through me at the sound of his deep and throaty promise to see me again. I didn't even follow him to the door, which was rude, but I couldn't bring myself to move. I just wanted the entire encounter to wash over me, make me believe that there was something more than the prison I'd been living in for the last ten years.

"I think it would look incredible in an antique frame. You know, something shabby chic."

Shelby and I were standing in my studio, both looking at an immensely large print of a photograph I'd taken of her in front of a small waterfall a few weeks before. The canvas had come in and I wanted to display it, but I was torn about what kind of frame to use.

"So, white?" I asked, crinkling my nose up, not liking the visual I conjured up in my mind.

"It doesn't have to be white. But something light. Maybe a very pale mint green."

I imagined the photo hanging on the wall with a nearly white, mint green frame and I smiled. The hint of green would complement the foliage surrounding Shelby, and the airiness of the hue would lend itself to the almost mystical feeling of the photo.

"You're a genius," I said, turning to her and smiling.

She shrugged. "Colors are kind of my thing."

I laughed and moved to my desk. I pulled open the bottom drawer and then pulled out a giant catalogue from my favorite framer. I could order a frame in the correct size and have it shipped, then mount the photo myself. I sat in the desk chair I'd splurged on. It had been an expensive purchase, but I knew the horror of sitting in an uncomfortable chair while editing photos, and when I opened my own studio, I knew I needed a great chair. It was like sitting on a cloud, only a cloud that had great back support. I loved it. Shelby came to stand behind me, peering over my shoulder at the pages and pages of available frames.

Like two kids in a candy store, we flipped pages, pointing to frames we loved and frames we hated, debating with each other when we didn't agree. We were so engrossed in our task, neither of us noticed when the door opened, and we both startled at the sound of a deep voice.

"You're a difficult woman to get ahold of." The voice was playful and gravelly. Entirely sexy. My eyes snapped toward the door where I saw Nate standing right inside. His frame filled the doorway and my eyes struggled to stay locked on one part of him, roaming over his body, too greedy to focus on one single aspect.

"I'm actually pretty easy to get ahold of. Just a few drinks really..." Shelby said, not missing a single beat. Before I could contain my reaction, I gasped and turned to her, a little mortified that she'd say something so brazen to a complete stranger. I saw the way she was looking at him, her eyes hazy, a lazy but sexy smile on her face. Immediately I was moving.

"Nate, hi," I said lamely as I stood, walking around my desk. "Wow. You actually came."

"I said I would. When I say I'm going to do something, I always follow through."

"Okay," I said, my voice breathier than I would have liked, but something about his words had my lungs working overtime. I watched as his eyes left me and started moving around my studio. I looked around, trying to see what he might see, wondering what he would think of my little corner, a studio that meant more to me than brick and mortar should.

"You took all these?" he said as he walked by a wall displaying my work. Usually, I would mentally roll my eyes at this question. Why would I hang someone else's work in my studio? But when he asked, the question made me nervous, as I desperately needed him to like my photos, to connect with him in that way.

"Yeah."

He looked at me, with one side of his mouth quirked up, and then looked back to another photo. "They're amazing." He stopped as he approached the large print Shelby and I were discussing. He peered down at it and then turned his head to look at me again. "You took this photo?"

I made it all the way around the desk and went to stand next to him, my eyes taking the photo in, wondering again what it might look like to him. "I did. And that's Shelby in the photo." I motioned back to Shelby, noticing she was standing behind my desk, still looking at us.

"It looks like something out of a fairy tale," he remarked, his eyes looking wistful. I turned back to the photo and tilted my head while I contemplated his words. "The way she kind of looks like she's part of the water, like, rising from it. It's remarkable."

Wow. Okay. He got it.

"Thank you," I managed, turning an obvious and embarrassing shade of red.

"You're really talented," he added, facing me.

"It's a mixture of luck and knowhow."

"Are you trying to be humble?" he laughed. "It's cute, but it's not going to work. You're really good at what you do. You shouldn't brush off your abilities like that."

"Hello there," I heard from behind us. Turning, I saw Shelby with her hand stretched out toward Nate. "Since Evelyn here is being rude, I'll introduce myself. I'm Shelby," she said the words in a playful way, but I could tell she was irritated I'd forgotten about her altogether.

"I'm sorry. Nate, this is Shelby. She's one of my favorite models and is also a great beautician."

He smiled a friendly smile as he reached out and shook her hand. "Nice to meet you, I'm Nate."

"Are you a friend of Evelyn's?" Shelby asked, not releasing his hand.

His eyes shot to me and his smile changed to something a little sexier. "Something like that," he replied.

"He is the one doing the work on Devon's house. He's fixing all the water damage."

"Ah ha," she said slowly, as if an elusive puzzle piece had just fallen into place. But she still didn't let go of his hand, she just kept slowly shaking it, her eyes narrowed at him. "Are you single?"

"Shelby!"

"What?" she asked innocently, finally letting go of his hand. He didn't look rattled by her question, but he did look slightly uncomfortable.

"You don't have to answer her," I said to him, quickly shaking my head.

"It's okay," he said with a nervous laugh. "I don't mind. I'm not dating anyone right now."

I tried to hide the wave of excitement that swept through me at his words, but the wave crashed when I heard Shelby's next question.

"Ever been married?"

"Oh, my God, really?" I cried, now exasperated by her behavior.

"Never been married," Nate said, now full on laughing, which also sent excitement shooting through me.

"See?" Shelby said, looking at me. "You've got something in common. Discuss amongst yourselves." She snatched her purse from a chair by the door and made her grand exit, leaving Nate and me in an uncomfortable silence. I gave him an apologetic smile, and he turned back to look at the print.

"That was the model in the photo?"

"Yeah, we took that a couple weeks ago."

"Is that somewhere up the Gorge?"

"Bridal Veil Falls," I said. "Have you been there?"

"I used to go hiking quite a bit up there."

"Ah."

"Do you hike?"

It shouldn't have, but his question caught me off guard.

"You mean, like, for fun?"

He laughed loudly and for a long time at my completely serious question, but then answered, "Yes, I mean for fun."

I shrugged. "Not really," I started, but when I saw his happy expression fade away, looking a little disappointed, I recovered with, "but, I mean, I've always wanted to." A big fat lie.

"Yeah? I haven't gone in a while, but your pictures make me want to get out there again. Maybe you'd like to go with me?"

"Hiking?" I swallowed down a lump of nervousness. I wasn't really an outdoorsy type. I liked taking photos outdoors, loved nature, but hadn't ever purposefully climbed mountains to get the pictures.

"Yeah," he said through another laugh. "It's the perfect time of year. Not super cold, but not too hot, either. Come on, it'll be fun."

My pulse sped at the thought of spending time alone with him. It exhilarated me even more to think it would be on purpose, instead of both the times I'd seen him at Devon's house. This would be the two of us, alone, intentionally. I was scared to say yes, but knew it would be a mistake to turn him down. Some part of me, on a very base level, wanted to go with him, to talk to him, to get to know more about him. So I agreed before I could mentally talk myself out of it.

"Sure. Why not?"

"Well, there's the answer every guy wants to hear when he asks a woman out on a date." He laughed again then ran a hand through his soft-looking brown hair, not sounding offended, but more like he was teasing me.

"Sorry." I smiled, and then tried again. "I'd really like to go hiking with you."

"How about tomorrow? Do you have any plans?"

"I was going to work…"

"So bring your camera, call it work. I'm sure I'd make a great model." He said it as a joke, but he wasn't wrong. He would make a fantastic model. For someone else in another life. I don't think I could look at him objectively if I tried. No, I would lose focus if I tried to work him into a shot. But, he didn't have a bad idea. I could bring my camera and that might alleviate some of the guilt I would feel taking a day off completely when I really should be working.

"You won't mind stopping when I find something I want to photograph?"

"Not at all. I think it will be interesting to watch you work."

"Okay then." I had a ridiculous smile on my face and he had his sexy gorgeous smile on his, and we just stood there for a moment, staring at each other, smiling. Finally, he broke the trance when his hand came up to rub the stubble growing on his chin.

"Can I pick you up? Around nine?"

"Sure. I'll probably be working, so if you don't mind, you can pick me up here."

"You'll be working at nine a.m. on a Sunday?"

"Unfortunately."

"Well, I'll be here to get you, but you have to promise you'll take some time tomorrow to relax while we're out. You can work, but not the whole time."

"You've got a deal." We both continued to stare at each other, our lips turned up in matching grins, but after a few moments, he broke the silence.

"Well, I guess I better go."

"Do I need anything specific for tomorrow?"

"Nope. Just some good shoes, a bottle of water, and sunscreen."

"Okay, I can manage that."

"Great. I'll see you at nine." He ran his hand through his hair again, as if he knew I liked it so much, then pushed the door open and disappeared through it. I watched him leave but then sagged in relief when he was gone. It took a lot of energy to be in a constant state of awareness, to be completely in tune to the fact that your heart was beating quickly, that there was a strange tingling sensation in your belly, to know at all times where your hands were, because all you wanted to do was run them through his soft, brown hair. However, before I could relax for too long the door opened again. Luckily, for my nerves, it was only Shelby.

"That didn't take long," she said as she waltzed into the gallery portion of the space.

"What didn't? And where did you go? I thought you left."

"I went and sat in my car. I was trying to give you some privacy. I was hoping you two would go at each other after I left. But, judging on how quickly he left after me, I'm guessing nothing exciting happened."

"Are you for real?"

Shelby raised one perfectly sculpted eyebrow at me. "Evelyn, when is the last time you were with a man?"

I scoffed at her, pretending to be offended by her question when, in reality, I was a little embarrassed. "First of all, that's none of your business. Second, even if it had been a while, that doesn't mean I'm just going to throw myself at the first man I'm left alone with."

"Hey, I'm not trying to offend you. He was obviously here because he's attracted to you."

"He was not."

"Did he ask you out?"

"Maybe."

"See. He likes you. There's nothing to be ashamed of here, Evie." Her tone took on a sympathetic, softer timbre. "It's okay to be attracted to someone, to be interested in someone. This is the natural progression of life. You need to start living again."

Her words were meant to be friendly, to help alleviate some of the fears she'd picked up on, but the word *living* only made me remember Olivia was *dead*. Those moments, when her loss of life crept up on me, when all of a sudden the loss was so deep and dark, in those moments, I felt as if I were drowning. How do we all just *go on*? How do I move past her death without leaving her behind? There were so many questions to which the only answer was sadness. The only possible outcome of the questions running through my head was devastation.

"Hey," Shelby said, moving toward me, putting a comforting hand on my shoulder. "Olivia would love for you to find someone to be happy with."

I knew she was right – mostly. Olivia would have enjoyed watching me date again, would have taken great joy in helping me get ready for a date, listening to me recount the entire date over the phone when it was over, dissecting every detail until we were both crazy with anticipation. Unless, of course, the person I was with was her husband. I shook my head, trying to erase that particular thought from it.

"Sometimes," I said softly, trying to ignore the pinching in my throat and the stinging in my eyes, "moving on with my life only reminds me that she lost hers."

Shelby's hand moved up and down my arm, trying her hardest to make me feel better, but nothing she could say or do would ease that particular pain. I'd been told time would be the ultimate healer, but I was still waiting.

"I'll be okay," I said with as much conviction as I could muster. "Let's go pick out a frame for this beast," I said, motioning toward the large print.

Chapter Thirteen

Present Day

The next morning, I sat at my desk, trying not to glance at my phone every twenty seconds for the time. I took in a deep breath and tried to calm my nerves. *It's just a hike, Evelyn. He's just a man, and it's just a hike.* At three minutes past nine, my knee was bouncing and my heart was racing. Oh God, my palms were sweaty. I heard the door open and glanced over to see Nate walking through it. My heart, which was used to speeding up in his presence, decided in that moment, it was necessary to stop altogether. His soft-looking brown hair was mussed and sexy, pushed back away from his face, which only made his prominent jaw that much more attractive. The gray of his t-shirt brought out the golden flecks in his brown eyes. He was wearing khaki colored cargo shorts and I'd never taken a moment to consider men's calves sexy, but damn, his were. Every single thing about him, on its own, was attractive, but when put all together in the whole package, he was sinful.

To top it all off, he held out a cup of what appeared to be iced coffee.

"I brought this for you," he said, smiling his crooked smile that immediately restarted my heart. "I figured you had to have gotten up early if you were planning on working before our hike. Thought you could use a little caffeinating."

I stood and walked toward him, took the cold cup of coffee, and smiled – as if I could have stopped myself. "Thank you. That was thoughtful."

He shrugged and then I could have sworn I saw a tiny blush creep over his face. "It was nothing." *God, he was cute.* "Are you ready to go?"

"Yup, all ready." I grabbed my water bottle and camera, then we walked out and I locked the door behind me. He'd driven his work truck, and I wondered if it was the only vehicle he had. Once we'd settled and he'd started the engine, I asked him a question to avoid falling into awkward silence.

"So, is this just a work truck, or do they let you drive it all the time?"

He chuckled. "They let me drive it all the time. They don't really have a choice. It's my company."

"Oh, really? I hadn't realized. I'm sorry."

"No, don't be sorry. There's no way you could have known. I worked for about ten years with my dad, but when he retired, he sold me the business, so it's mine now."

"That must have been fun, working with your father."

"It was all right most of the time. My Dad is from Boston, so he kind of has a tough shell. He loves really hard, but he's also a little rough around the edges. So, as long as I was in agreement with him, it was fun. When I disagreed, or wanted to go in a different direction, things could get tense. But my mom never let us disagree for long," he laughed, which only made me smile again, listening to the sound of his laughter float through the cab of the truck.

"Do your parents live around here?" I asked because I was curious. Also, I wanted to listen to him talk forever. His voice was on a wavelength that made a new and familiar connection with something inside of me.

"Yeah, about twenty minutes from my house. My whole family is local. We're pretty big."

"Siblings?"

"Two brothers and two sisters. I'm right smack dab in the middle."

"Wow. I can't even imagine. I'm an only child and my parents had me later in life, so it was almost like growing up with grandparents." I thought about how, and not for the first time, my life might have been different had I had a brother or sister. Then again, growing up that way made me comfortable being lonely, so it wasn't all bad. I was used to being by myself. "Do you see your family often?"

"There's a dinner at my parents' house every Saturday. Everyone is welcome every week, but not everyone goes all the time. If you've got other stuff going on, it's not a big deal. It's kind of just like an open door dinner. Come if you can, and if you can't, maybe we'll see you next week." He shrugged and as his shoulders moved up and down. I couldn't help but think of how comfortable he seemed talking about his family, how easy it must have been to have the kind of relationship where you knew every week you could go and be with people who would accept you just as you were and love you regardless.

"Are you close with your family?"

"Yeah, I guess. My mom and dad are enjoying their retirement and keep busy. They're not around too much, but I see them every now and then."

"What was it like growing up an only child?"

"Lonely, I guess. But I did have the undivided attention of both my parents, which, in hindsight, was nice. I thought it a little oppressive as a teenager, but looking back, I know my parents loved me tremendously and did their absolute best. But I never had that built-in friendship I imagine other people had with their brothers and sisters."

"There were times it would have been nice to have the undivided attention from my parents though." He was quiet for a moment, and then added, "The grass is always greener, ya know?"

I laughed quietly, "You're right."

"Have you ever been to Oneonta Gorge?"

"I can't say that I have," I turned my head toward him and smiled, a little relieved he was changing the topic.

"It's a pretty easy hike, right between all the falls, but when you get to the end of the trail, it's pretty amazing." He looked at me quickly, his smile so bright and perfect, then looked back at the road. His excitement over his chosen hiking trail was almost adorable.

"I can't wait," I responded honestly. We spent the next thirty minutes falling into easy conversation. He was so easy to talk to, and more than a few times made me laugh. I found his unrestrained laugh hypnotic and I, also, found myself wanting to make him laugh often. I wanted to be the reason his loud and happy laughter filled the cab of his truck, sending prickles along my skin, watching his mouth turn up into the sexiest smile.

He pulled into a small parking lot right off the highway and the trailhead was just south of us. He wore a large backpack, but wouldn't let me take anything when I offered.

"You just carry your water bottle and we'll be square. It's not as heavy as it looks," he said, tilting his head back to indicate he was talking about his backpack. Then he winked at me, and everything except him and his beautiful face faded away. Every trouble I'd dealt with in the last year, every sad moment, every tear was washed away and replaced by warmth. Then, the warmth was replaced immediately with fear. Surely, if this man had the ability to wipe away my sadness with only one wink, he could cause much more heartache than I was ready to endure.

"Okay," I said breathily, still trying to recover from his beautiful eye winking at me and the way it made me want to hold on to him and push him away all at the same time.

It was still early in the day, but the hikers were out in full force. There were young adults hiking in groups, teenagers taking advantage of the nice weather, young couples taking their children on a hike, which admittedly, made me feel like I could handle it. If toddlers were on the trail, surely I could make it through.

"I wish I would have had the forethought in high school to take a date hiking," Nate said quietly, nodding his head toward a couple a few feet in front of us. They looked like they were probably just finishing high school or near the end. "It seems like a much better alternative to sitting in a dark theatre watching a movie. At least outside you get to actually see the other person." I looked ahead, watching as the young man reached out and took the young girl's hand. She turned to look at him and gave him a shy smile as a blush spread across her face, obviously pleased with the contact. It was sweet and innocent.

"I have to admit, I've never been hiking on a date before. It would have been a welcomed idea."

"Well, I'm glad I could be a first." I heard his words and then looked at him, giving him a shy smile much like the young girl had just given her date. He didn't try to hold my hand, but the implication was the same. He wanted me to know I was his date, that he wanted me there in that capacity.

We continued down the path and every once in a while I stopped to take a few photos of something that caught my eye.

He was exceedingly patient and even seemed interested in the process, asking a few questions about my camera or how the natural light affected the photo. Then, a few times, I'd finish taking a photo and find him looking at me with affection.

"It's inspiring to watch you work," he said with a smile. "Your face is cute when you're concentrating. I mean," he said, his smile widening, "you're cute all the time. But when you're concentrating, you get this little crinkle between your eyebrows." His hand came up and his thumb gently brushed my face there. After a moment of reverently caressing me, he dropped his hand and wore a bashful smile. "Come on, the best part is coming up."

I couldn't answer him. I could only concentrate on trying to breathe normally, drawing air into my lungs and forcing it back out at a regular pace, so he didn't pick up on the fact that my heart was pounding and palms were sweating. I'd been touched by a man before, been on the receiving end of a tender caress, but nothing had felt like that. No one had made time stop like Nate's skin against mine.

After another thirty minutes of wandering along the path, winding through trees, and following a small stream through a narrow gorge, eventually we came to a place where the path ended.

"This is where the hike gets fun," he said, his eyes lit up with excitement. I looked around, trying to find the next portion of trail to follow.

"Uh," I said hesitantly. "Where exactly are we supposed to go?"

"Right through there," he said, pointing straight ahead. I followed his finger and was still confused. The small stream we'd been following continued through a narrow crevasse. It looked like two strikingly tall rock walls with about ten feet between them. No path. No land. Only water between rock walls.

"Through the water?"

"Yeah. It's only about waist-deep." He said this as if wading through waist-deep water wasn't a big deal.

"It's only spring. That water has got to be freezing," I said, my voice steadily climbing an octave. "And my camera..."

"Give it to me, I'll keep it dry."

"You want me to trust you with my *camera*? No one holds my camera." I didn't care if we were on a date or not, I wasn't about to hand him my camera. He could have been the second coming of Christ; he wasn't going to carry my camera.

He held up his hands but still wore a friendly smile. "No problem. I just thought I'd offer. I'm at least eight inches taller than you." Then he shrugged and started to walk backward toward the stream.

"You're serious about this?" I asked, still a little surprised it was happening.

"Come on, it'll be fun. Promise." He held his hand out to me, waiting for me to take it, his signature half-smile making him irresistible.

I sighed loudly, then reached out and took his hand, trying to ignore the zing of electricity I felt shoot through my body at his touch. "I wish you would have mentioned this beforehand. I might have worn a swimsuit or something."

"Seriously?" he asked, his hand still gripping mine, paused mid-step. "Damn," he sighed, hanging his head in mocked disappointment. "Opportunity missed," he said, sounding distraught, making me giggle. "I'll remember that for next time."

"Yeah. Okay," I said sarcastically through my laughter. "Oh, holy shit," I said as I stepped into the frigid water, soaking the athletic shoes he'd told me to wear. "Oh, my God, that's cold."

"It's not that cold," he said, laughing as he held onto my hand and pulled me farther into the water, inch by inch. I was hissing with each step, hating the feeling of the cold water creeping up my calves, inching toward my thighs. Luckily, there were other people there making fools of themselves in the cold water as well, complaining just as I was at the glacial temperature.

Suddenly, a terrifying thought flitted through my mind. "Do you think there are fish in this water?"

He shrugged. "Probably."

My eyes darted to the water and I tried to see through it, looking for indications of any creatures moving under the surface. I started to panic, thinking I was feeling something brush up against my skin under the water. "I swear to God, if my leg touches a fish, I'm gonna flip out." The water wasn't murky, but as was the way with the Pacific Northwest, the riverbed was full of rocks and dirt, making everything under the water look brown. I could see my feet, but it was hazy and unclear.

Nate, still holding my hand and leading me through the water, stopped and let out a loud laugh. His happiness made me temporarily forget I was, possibly, surrounded by fish, and I smiled along with him. When his laughter died down, he gave my hand a gentle squeeze, which somehow shot all the way to my heart, making it clench in my chest.

"Don't worry, Evelyn. I'll protect you from all the fish in the stream."

We continued to wade through the water, my skin finally becoming used to the temperature, and my body slowly submerging as the depth rose from my ankles to mid-thigh. He hadn't dropped my hand since he first took it, and I didn't try to pull away; I liked the way it felt to have a man hold my hand. I liked being just half a step behind him and took every opportunity to admire him from my vantage point.

The sun had come out and although it wasn't terribly hot, the direct sunlight offered a beautiful light to his form. The most interesting part of him, as far as I could tell in that moment, was the way the muscles in his upper arms stretched the fabric of his t-shirt. With every step he took and every sway of his free hand, his biceps and triceps gave a delicious show of contracting and relaxing. A few times, he'd reached up to point out something overhead, and the sleeve would creep just a little further up, displaying even more tanned skin and taut muscle.

"Hmmm," I heard him murmur right before I walked into the back of him. I let out a surprised oof as my front hit the side of his arm, and I looked up at him to see him smiling down at me, as if he could tell I'd been staring at him.

"Something distracting you back there?" he asked with a knowing grin.

"Perhaps," I said, not admitting to anything. "Why'd you stop?" I looked around his formidable body to see what had caused his abrupt halt.

"Looks like we might be in a bit of a situation," he said, raising his free hand to point ahead of us. I saw people wading, or actually swimming, through water that was much deeper than "waist-deep."

"I thought it only went waist-deep?" I asked, horrified at the thought of putting my nipples in the frigid water. Every woman could attest to the fact that cold water and nipples didn't mesh well. "Well, this has been fun, Nate," I said, turning away from him and heading back the way we came. A sharp tug on my hand brought me right back to his side, my breasts pressed against the hardness of the biceps I was just previously admiring.

"Don't give up on me now," he said, his eyes peering down into mine with such intensity, I found my breath sneaking away from me. "I've got you. Don't worry." His free hand came forward and his fingers pushed the wisps of hair that had escaped my ponytail back behind my ear, and every hair follicle on my neck came to attention. He held my gaze for a long moment, his fingers resting at the base of my neck, my pulse pounding through my veins, and all I could think was, 'please, God, kiss me this very instant.'

But he didn't, and instead of breathing Nate in, I had to take in actual oxygen, inhaling sharply as the presence of his fingers disappeared from my skin.

"Here's the plan. I'm gonna go through first, and then I'll come back and help you through. I'll take your camera and my backpack and put it on the other side."

"I'm not going to give you my camera." My voice was still a little breathy from all the non-kissing that was happening, but I still wasn't giving him my camera.

He rolled his eyes, which should have pissed me off, but for some reason it only made me smile. "I promise I won't get it wet. I'll hold it above my head. It'll be dry as a bone when it reaches the other side."

"And what if you trip? What if you get bitten by a giant river monster and my camera falls to the floor of this godforsaken stream? Then what?"

"There is no river monster and I'm not going to trip. Come on, Evelyn. You're going to have to learn to trust me eventually. This just speeds up the process."

My head instinctively tilted to the side as I contemplated his words. I was going to have to learn to trust him eventually? This was a foregone conclusion, already? I'd only trusted a handful of people in my lifetime and for some reason, Nate assumed he was going to make the short list. I couldn't figure out if I thought it was sweet that he wanted to gain my trust, or if I should be running in the opposite direction.

"If you drop my camera in the water, you have to replace it," I said by way of relenting, my voice still full of air, obviously affected by our close proximity.

"Done," he said confidently.

"It's really expensive," I threw back at him, only slightly annoyed by his confidence. Honestly, his cockiness was more arousing than annoying, but I knew it was imperative to the survival of my tough exterior to remain impassive to all his charms.

"I think I can handle it," he replied, his voice dropping lower and tinted with a gravelly rumble. My mind immediately started thinking about everything he could handle, including me, and I felt my pulse in profoundly private places.

Since it was impossible for me to speak without saying, "Take me now," I simply nodded in response. He smiled, all sexy and rugged, then released my hand and lifted my camera from around my neck. Before he could take it away from me fully, I grabbed it and opened the compartment that held the SD card and took it out. If he was going to ruin my camera, I wasn't going to let him ruin all the pictures I'd taken. I kept my gaze on him as I slipped the card into my bra. His eyes widened and mouth dropped open.

"That was just cruel," he groaned.

I gave him half a smile and lifted one shoulder in a shrug. He narrowed his eyes and gave another groan. Then proceeded to put my camera inside his backpack. Once it was all zipped up he turned back to me. "I'll be right back."

"Okay," I managed. He stepped away from me, heading toward the narrow passage where brave hikers were up to their armpits in water. Some laughing, some cursing. I looked behind me and found a large rock to sit on while I watched him navigate the water. He held the backpack above his head and even from a distance, I could see his knuckles turning white from gripping it so tightly. Eventually he disappeared around a bend and I could no longer see him or his backpack, so my eyes wandered and I took in the beautiful imagery around me. I laughed to myself, wishing I had my camera to take some photos.

After a few minutes of sitting on the rock and watching people navigate the stream, going in and out of the gorge it created, I finally saw Nate return, his shirt completely wet. As he got closer, I noticed his neck was wet as well. But his hands, which were still up above his head, were dry.

"Your camera is safe and dry on the other side. I left it with a responsible-looking group of hoodlums spraying graffiti on the pine trees."

"Shut up," I said, narrowing my eyes at him, but still grinning, unable to stop my lips from turning up at his words. I immediately regretted saying that to him, afraid he'd find my retort offensive. I didn't know him well enough to be telling him to shut up in a playful way – not everyone understood my sarcasm. Thankfully, his smile broadened at my words and, surprisingly, he only seemed to enjoy my sass.

"I'm kidding. It's nestled safely at the trunk of a tree about ten yards away from the water. Come on, I'll take you." He held out his hand to me again, but that time, I didn't try to talk myself out of the butterflies I was feeling. I felt them, and I acknowledged them for what they were – a budding attraction. A crush. Nate was a man I wanted to let lead me.

He walked me out into the freezing water until it was barely above my knees, but then stopped short and turned to face me.

"I'm gonna take you out until the water is about to your belly button," he said, pressing a hand against my stomach, making my breath stop and my heart pound. "Then I'm gonna go under completely and you're gonna get on my shoulders. Then I'll walk through and you'll stay mostly dry."

"You are not," I scoffed. "I can see the water came up to your neck. You can't walk through there with me on your shoulders; you'll drown."

He laughed. "I'm not going to drown. Are you always this dramatic?" He lifted a hand to motion toward the gorge. "I might have slipped a little going through the first time and went under a little, but I kept your precious camera dry – I promise."

My eyes went wide at his admission. He *had* fallen in the godforsaken river. But I reminded myself that my camera was fine, that he was only trying to help me.

"You think you can really carry me on your shoulders through there?"

He raised one eyebrow at me and pulled his chin back in surprise. "Are you serious? Shut up."

I immediately laughed at his words, and then continued to laugh because it felt so good to do so. With one *shut up* from Nate, I'd lowered a wall I'd had built for years. Granted, it was still pretty much up and surrounding the most vulnerable part of me, but those few bricks that had just collapsed weighed a ton. I'd never felt this light before.

He tugged me farther into the water and I kept my yelps silent as the water encroached on the apex of my thighs, the icy water causing all kinds of nerves to fire haphazardly. True to his word, when the water had reached my belly button, he stopped and faced me.

"Okay, I'm gonna go under and you just hop onto my shoulders. When I stand up, hang on tight. If you fall in, this will be all for naught."

It was my turn to raise an eyebrow at him. "Did you really just say *all for naught?*"

He only winked at me in response, then turned his back to me, and proceeded to dunk himself under the water.

"Oh, shit, he was serious," I said to myself as I clamored to climb up onto his shoulders. I managed to get my legs over his shoulders, trying not to think about the jolt of electricity that shot up my spine when his hands wrapped around my thighs, holding me tightly. Once I was situated, he started to rise out of the water. As more of my body left the cold water, it became apparent his body was taking on more and more of my weight, and I started to feel badly for the poor guy.

When he was standing straight again, I heard him take in a deep breath trying to compensate for the oxygen he missed while underwater. I leaned forward a little, my hands plastered against his forehead. "Am I too heavy?" I asked, but before I could get the last word out, I lost my balance and started to fall forward. Instinctively, my feet wrapped around the back of Nate's waist, and my hands gripped him below his chin, trying desperately not to fall in the mountain-cold water.

"Whoa, I got you," he said, his hands gripping me tighter on my thighs, his big arms squeezing my legs, keeping me in place. "You all right?" I heard him ask, noticing the garbled sound of his voice. It was then I decided to loosen the death grip I had on his face.

"This was a dumb idea. Just put me down, I'll swim through."

"Evelyn, trust me. I've got you."

"Okay," I whispered, knowing he couldn't hear me.

I felt him take the first step with me atop his shoulders and I felt my face pull back in excitement and fear. I hadn't been on anyone's shoulders since spring break in Cancun my senior year of college when Elliot, Liv, Devon, and I were playing drunken chicken during one of our late-night pool excursions. This was different. Nate's body was unfamiliar and, any way you looked at it, my most private and sensitive areas were pressed against him. For someone who I didn't really know that well, it was an unusually familiar situation to be in. But regardless of what my head was telling me about what was appropriate or inappropriate, I liked feeling Nate that close to me, with his strong arms snaked around my legs. It had never been this exciting on Elliot's shoulders.

He walked through the canal created by the water and at its deepest, I saw the water ripple from his heavy breathing. He was scarily close to being underwater and I tried not to panic. Surely, my dry shirt wasn't worth his dying. But then the water line started to lower, and more and more of his body was out of the water. When we'd made it through the deepest part and the water had receded to his waist again, he tapped my thigh with his large hand. Again, I ignored my body's immediate response to the feeling of his hand and the primal sound it made against the wet skin of my leg.

"I'm gonna dunk down again so you can climb off, all right?"

I nodded, still gripping his forehead tightly.

"Evelyn? You good up there?"

"Sorry," I said, realizing he couldn't hear me nod my head. "I'm fine. Go ahead." He slowly slipped down into the water, and when it was deep enough, I pushed off his shoulders and found my footing on the riverbed below. He stood up and even if I'd tried, I couldn't have kept my eyes from watching the water cascade down his back, his arms lifting to run his hands through his wet hair. It was, possibly, the sexiest thing I'd ever seen in person.

He turned back to face me, eyes wide as cold water rushed down his face. A hand came down and brushed the water away, and then his eyes focused on me. His gaze darted from my eyes, to my shirt, then back up again.

"You're dry," he said with a smirk.

"Relatively," I responded quickly, before I thought much about it. I realized what I'd implied, blushed, and then watched as his smirk grew into a smug grin. "Okay," I groaned, embarrassed, "where's my camera?"

Chapter Fourteen

Present Day

True to his word, my camera was safely deposited under a tree, dry as a bone. We continued our *wade* through the water, and when we came to our next obstacle, I couldn't hold in my laughter.

"This is the weirdest hike I've ever been on," I mumbled. Before us, blocking the stream was a naturally made stack of logs. A pile of downed trees had obviously fallen from the tops of the ravine and landed in the gorge. A legitimate logjam. I watched as people climbed over the wooden obstacle course. The image of the logs alone was breathtaking. It was a little amazing to think nature had made something so intricate and beautiful.

"Hey, I never said it was going to be boring. In fact," he said, turning to look me in the eyes, "I can pretty much promise it'll never be boring with me."

"Noted," I breathed. His smiled changed, grew a little warmer, but then his eyes swung back to the mound of logs.

"It doesn't look difficult. See, children are climbing over it." He pointed toward a group of teenagers climbing up the crazy log pile with gusto.

"I never said I wasn't going to do it."

"Well, all right then. Let's see what you've got." He winked at me and then started toward our next adventure.

Not one to ever back down from a challenge, I followed him. Approaching the naturally made ladder of sorts, I tried to think objectively about how best to get to the top. I placed my foot on one log, but then changed my mind and tried another tactic.

Nothing felt natural. No step I took felt like the right way to tackle the problem.

"Lyn," I heard Nate call out, and then I heard him say it again before I realized he was talking to me. I looked up and caught his gaze. "Sorry," he said, his eyes smiling so brightly at me. "It just kind of slipped out. I know other people call you Evie, but Lyn seems to fit you so much better."

I shook my head, breathlessly. "You can call me Lyn. That's fine." I wasn't sure how I'd managed to use real words. He was right. Everyone did call me Evie and I'd never thought much about it. But thinking about Nate calling me something different, something he liked, something he had come up with, made every part of me ache in a delicious way. Even more, knowing he was the only one who would call me that made it even sweeter.

He smiled as his shoulders relaxed a little, looking as though they were sagging with relief. "Don't overthink it, Lyn. Just go for it."

It took me only a moment to realize he'd been talking about the log obstacle. He waved a hand at me, urging me to join him. He was easily ten feet up the giant log ladder. I let out a deep breath and decided to try it his way and just wing it.

Hand over foot, I slowly made my way up, log by log. Some were cramped tightly together, others were farther apart and caused me to take longer strides to make it up. I stole a glance at Nate after a few successful steps and was happy to see him smiling down at me. It took about ten minutes of climbing and strategizing on the fly until I reached the summit of the logs, and was happy to see Nate standing on the tallest log, looking a little like Captain Morgan with one leg propped up higher than the other, hands on his hips.

"You made it," he said, a genuine smile spreading over his face. I couldn't help but blush when he reached a hand out to me, helping me up the very last log, and then continued to hold it, threading his fingers through my own. I was closer to thirty than I'd like to admit, but I was holding a guy's hand and blushing about it.

"That was fun," I managed, smiling up at him, hoping the blush of my cheeks could pass for a healthy glow from the climb.

"Wanna sit up here and have lunch?"

I shrugged. "Sure." He gave my hand a gentle squeeze, and then released it as he pulled off his backpack. He walked toward the edge of the logs and I followed, understanding that he wanted to be out of the way of the rest of the hikers trying to make their way over the pile.

He straddled a log, sitting with his backpack in front of him and I copied his stance.

"So," he said, unzipping his backpack and bringing out what I immediately recognized as Subway sandwiches. "I have turkey with American cheese, or roast beef with cheddar. Your choice. And if you don't like either of those I might dive off this log mountain."

"I'll take turkey," I said through laughter. He handed me a wrapped sandwich, then reached back into his bag and opened his palm toward me.

"Mayo? Mustard?" He had little packets of condiments in his hand, offering them to me.

"You think of everything, don't you?" I asked, taking a little mayo packet from his hand, noticing the zing that shot through me when our skin touched, but trying not to react to it.

"Listen, I never hold back on a date. I'm here to impress. I had to ask the sandwich artist especially for the to-go packets."

I laughed even harder as I imagined Nate, the masculine, imposing person he was physically, asking a teenage girl for mayo packets.

"I appreciate it. There's nothing worse than a dry sandwich."

"See? I knew you were perfect for me." His tone was light and playful, but his words made my heart pound in my chest. Partly because it had been years since someone had said anything romantic to me, but more so, because I wanted the words to be true. I wanted to be perfect for someone. I'd spent the majority of my life feeling like the only person who was perfect for me, had already found his perfect match. "You took the mayo and I took the mustard. You're the yin to my yang."

I blushed even harder, made speechless by his almost childish yet adorable mushiness. It was quite ridiculous. I'd always told myself I didn't need flowers and romance, but his condiment comparisons were enough to make my heart skip a beat.

"So, tell me about your life." He made the request just before he took the first bite of his sandwich, looking at me as if my answer was going to be the most interesting thing he'd ever hear. I watched as his Adam's apple bobbed with his swallow and found myself mimicking him, swallowing down the need that grew in my belly with that one stupid yet ridiculously sexy movement on his neck.

"My life?" I finally asked, needing a little more clarification.

"Yeah. You know, what you do for fun, your hobbies, your likes, dislikes, murderous tendencies – anything interesting."

"I have never murdered anyone," I said through a laugh.

"See? That's useful information. Continue." He took another bite and I looked down at my own sandwich, refusing to watch the man eat a sandwich to satisfy my own twisted attraction.

"For the most part, I'm kind of a hybrid between a single gal in my late twenties and an old cat lady in my late fifties."

"Do you have many cats?" One of his eyebrows was raised and his sandwich was paused halfway up to his mouth. He looked concerned.

"No," I giggled. "I actually don't have any pets. But, I fit the profile. I *should* have cats. But I'm too busy working, and now taking care of Ruby and Jax, I don't even have time for a cat, let alone the twenty minimum I'd need to reach cat lady status."

"Yeah. Ruby and Jax. They seem like great kids. Their mom must have been pretty special."

I fought past the lump that formed in my throat at his words. "She was the best," I managed, but my voice was strained and my eyes were down again. Suddenly, I felt Nate's warm hand on the top of my knee.

"I'm sorry for your loss," he said quietly, rubbing his hand gently over my bare skin. "How long ago did she pass?"

"It's been a few months. But it feels like days or hours." I let out a loud sigh. "Those kids though, they're tough. Some days you can't even tell they've lost their mother, which I'm glad for. That's a blessing. The days when they're laughing and smiling like nothing ever happened, I live for those days. But then there are days when there aren't enough tissues in the world to dry their tears." I paused, trying to push the images of those two kids crying out of my mind. "Ruby's eight, so she feels the loss more. She knows what she's missing a little deeper than Jax. But Jax is a little momma's boy with no momma. Some days, he seems lost and that's hard."

I was quiet for a few moments, not really knowing where to take the conversation from there.

"And what about their dad?" Nate's voice was like velvet draped over hard steel. It was rough, but I could tell he was trying to ease it up. He didn't like asking the question, but wanted too badly to know the answer to let it be.

I shrugged. "Devon is a man who lost his wife, the mother of his children. He struggles daily, but is trying hard to be the pillar of his family. He's still trying to figure it all out."

"Does it bother you to talk about him?"

"No," I answered immediately and truthfully. I'd much rather talk about him than be with him. Being around Devon was becoming confusing and tiring. Things were tense between us.

"It just seems like there's more going on than a friend helping out a friend."

"It's a little more complicated than that."

"How complicated?"

I paused, searching for words, searching for truth. I wasn't sure how complicated it was. The relationship between Devon and I had always been so much more than what lay on the surface, even if we never spoke about it or acknowledged it. Finally, I shrugged, not having any words for Nate.

"Complicated enough that I should stop pursuing you?" My eyes snapped up to meet his gaze and I felt the intensity of his question, his eyes holding mine with a force I'd never experienced before.

I shook my head gently and whispered, "No." The only thing stronger than the strange connection I'd always felt with Devon was the way Nate's eyes were locked on me in that moment. His gaze said more to me and made me feel more than any passing touch from Devon had caused.

I'd always thought Devon was the end-all and be-all to my being. I'd always assumed he would be the pinnacle of emotions for me, thought he'd been the yin to my yang. And I'd stupidly been all right with letting my other half spend a lifetime with someone else. Suddenly, atop a pile of logs in the middle of the forest in the Columbia River Valley, I came to realize that, perhaps, I'd been wrong. Perhaps, Devon wasn't my other half.

I felt my mind take a mental snapshot of that moment. Nate across from me, tanned skin glistening in the sun, legs straddling a formidable log, brown hair shining in the sunlight, eyes trained on me, expression serious yet compassionate. I wanted to remember the moment when I realized life wasn't as bleak as I'd made it out to be, and I wanted to remember the person who'd reminded me that I was still worth pursuing.

"No," I repeated, my voice a little sturdier than before. "You shouldn't stop pursuing me."

The smile that spread across his face was award winning. Bright, genuine, relieved. "Great. I didn't plan on it anyway."

We finished our sandwiches, drank our water, and sat atop those logs for an hour, talking about everything and nothing. Nate collected comic books. This did not surprise me in the least. He'd shown some boyish tendencies all day, but it wasn't unattractive; it was sweet. And it took the pressure off a little. Picturing him perusing a comic book store, purchasing plastic wrapped picture books somehow made him less threatening.

How dangerous could a man who read comic books be, after all?

Any ideas I had about him being boyish, however, were thrust to the back of my mind as we climbed down the logs, trying to make our way toward the end of the 'trail'. I was slowly stepping down the logs when my foot hit a wet spot and I stumbled. I was going down, my hands splayed out in front of me, trying to break my fall, when I felt his strong hands grip my shoulders. My eyes snapped up and I realized he'd caught me. He'd simply reached out and gripped my shoulders, stopping me from tumbling down a hill of logs.

"Whoa. You all right?" he asked with concern lacing his voice as I found my footing again.

"Yeah, thanks."

"I knew I'd get you to fall head over heels for me, but I don't want you to break a limb doing it." His screen-worthy smile was back and his hands were not letting me go. In fact, he just moved down my arms and wrapped his hands around both of mine. I was standing on a log above him, so my eyes were level with his beautiful brown ones, and I felt my breath hitch at his words and the playful yet sexy look he was giving me. His confidence was on full blast again, and just like before, I was eating it up.

My eyes darted down to his lips, for one brief stolen moment, without my permission, and I saw his reaction. His sexy smile morphed into a cocky one, which, for the record, wasn't any less sexy. Quite the opposite, in fact. In the split second I was staring at his lips, his tongue darted out and wet the tip of his top lip, and my knees almost buckled again. Reluctantly, I brought my eyes back to his.

"Maybe you'll be the one to fall for me," I said, unsure of where my bravado suddenly came from.

He laughed. "Lyn, baby, I'm pretty sure that was a foregone conclusion."

"Oh," was all I could say in response. My heart was thundering in my chest at his use of the word *baby*. Had we progressed all the way to the pet-name stage of our relationship already? Not only was I unsure of when and how you were supposed to start calling people things like baby and honey, I also didn't care. He could call me whatever he wanted as long as he used that particular timbre of his voice, which made every inch of my skin crawl with anticipation.

He gave my hands a squeeze, broadened his smile, then let one of my hands go, keeping one, and leading me down the ladder of logs.

We walked in companionable silence, never letting go of each other's hand, soaking in the sights and sounds of our surroundings. The water, which continued past the log graveyard, never went more than waist deep again. After about thirty minutes of wading and walking, we came to the climax of the trail, the place which was responsible for the people risking their lives on the enormous logjam. Obviously, someone had leaked what waited past it, because otherwise, fewer people would traverse it.

I was looking at the most beautiful waterfall. Without thinking, I dropped his hand and started snapping photos furiously. I very truthfully forgot he was there for a few minutes, finding perfect shots and lining them up in my viewfinder, snapping away. I started to back up, trying to get more of the falls in the shot, when suddenly he was in my screen. He was facing away from me, one leg bent more than the other, hands resting at his sides, his face angled toward the sky trying to see where the water was falling from. The sun was bursting above him, rays raining down on his gorgeous hair, and I was captivated.

I captured the image in my camera, in my mind, and more deeply, in my heart. He was burnt in it, forever plastered against its walls, leaving a permanent mark. I knew the photo would be immaculate, but it wouldn't do the moment justice. Not even close.

He turned and caught me taking his picture, but only smiled at me, allowing me to take one last perfect picture of his gorgeous smile with sunlight radiating around him, mist from the falls clouding the air around him. He held his hand out to me and said, "Come on."

I let my camera drape from my neck and took his hand, unable to hide or smother the smile I wore.

He walked along the edge of the water, leading me around the pool that formed at the bottom of the falls. He continued to hold my hand as he led me up a rocky ledge that led to a manmade path that brought us back behind the falls. It was, compared to other falls in the area, a relatively small waterfall, but the cavern behind the falls was large and dark. Water dripped from the cavern roof and a cold breeze blew through, making me shiver. Nate stopped when we were deep in the cave and sat on a large rock. My voice caught in my throat when he pulled me into his lap, leaving me sitting sideways on his large thighs. He wrapped his big, warm arms around me, his hands moving over the exposed skin of my arms.

"You're freezing," he said softly.

I'd been extremely cold only seconds before, but then he pulled me to him, and put his hands on me, and suddenly, I couldn't remember ever being warmer. His hands moved up and down my bare arms and my eyes stayed locked on his. Slowly, on each pass upward, his hands moved farther up until finally they caressed my shoulders, rubbing gently, kneading just enough to make my eyelids flutter. After a few moments, his rough yet tender hands moved to grasp each side of my neck, thumbs gently stroking me there, and his eyes were silently asking for permission.

I nodded, ever so slightly, and watched as his eyes, which looked almost pained, moved closer to me until finally his lips feathered over mine. I took in a shuddering breath, not prepared for the enormity of what I would feel with his mouth against mine. Kissing Nate was like coming home. It was like coming in from a rainstorm to sit in front of a roaring fire. Like the first sunny day after months of clouds. It was simply everything. And as if he knew I would be lost with his mouth pressing against mine, knew I'd be drowning in feeling, he wasted no time taking control.

His hands came up to cradle my face, holding me to him, his lips moving over mine with purpose. His lips parted slightly and I let out a breathy gasp as he took my lower lip into his mouth, sucking gently. He may as well have been sucking on a few other parts of my body for what it made me feel. I was instantly hot and buzzing, imagining his mouth doing that exact same thing in other places. I groaned slightly when his teeth came to nip at me, and at my noises, he seemed to lose a bit of his control.

Instantly, his arm was around my waist and I yelped as he stood, holding me to him, but swinging me so that my legs wrapped around him, then sat again with my legs straddling him. He reached up and wrapped his fingers around the neck strap of my camera, then paused, silently asking permission to take it off. I bent my head forward and felt him lift it over, then watched as he placed it gently on top of his backpack, keeping it off the wet cavern floor.

When he turned back to me, each of his hands landed on one of my knees, and then slowly slid up my thighs, to the side of my hips and up my ribcage. His large, warm palms slid over my back and he pulled me closer to him, my breasts pressing up against his hard chest, and then he kissed me again. This time, though, the kiss was hungry. He wasted no time parting my lips with his tongue. Then, he just took.

I'd never submitted to anyone like I did in that moment. I was happily giving control over to him, finally glad to feel like I was allowed to give someone whatever he wanted. Excited not to feel shame or guilt for kissing someone, for feeling *whatever* I was feeling. And, at that moment, I was feeling hungry too.

My hands wandered over his chest, my tongue pressed against his, and I reveled in the feeling of being so close to him, of letting him get that close to begin with. This was no at-arms-length encounter; he wasn't someone I was trying to keep at a safe distance. He was in it with me, entirely present, fully pressed against me, and his body was asking for more.

His hands raked down my back then came around my waist and while one hand rested on my hip, the other floated up my belly then came to cup my breast, gently palming me over my shirt. The contact was maddening and I wished we weren't just yards away from other hikers. The brief brush of his hand over my breast was enough to light a fire, but now I had no way to put out the flame.

His mouth pulled away from mine roughly, but then landed on my neck, kissing down the sensitive skin there until his tongue met the hollow part at the base. I was panting, my hands threaded through his soft hair, practically holding his mouth to me, hoping he never stopped using it on me.

"God, Lyn, I can't get enough." His mouth dragged back up my throat, moving over my jaw, then took my mouth again. I rocked forward, trying to get as close to him as I possibly could, trying to, Jesus, I didn't know. I wanted to climb inside of him, wanted to be a part of him, and to have him be a part of me. I wanted to somehow bind myself to him, mark him, leave some sort of proof I had been there, on his lap, writhing against him, and his mouth had been on my skin. I wanted all kinds of things that didn't seem possible. I wanted things I'd never *thought* possible. I wanted him. Even if it was just once, just one time to feel that connection to him, I'd give anything.

"*Nate*," I groaned against his mouth, loving the way he growled when he heard his name come from my lips. If we'd been anywhere else even remotely more private I'd be peeling my shirt off, hoping he'd take me and never look back. But we were outdoors with plenty of people right on the other side of the falls. Anyone could walk back there and find us.

I pulled away from his mouth again, but he wouldn't let me go far. His hands gripped my face, gently holding me to him, our foreheads pressed together. I felt his fast and fevered breaths pant across my face. My hands rested on his chest feeling his heart beat rapidly.

"I'm sorry," he finally whispered.

"You're sorry?" I asked, afraid he regretted the whole exchange. Afraid he thought he'd made a mistake. All the important men in my life had made a mistake with me.

"Lyn, baby, I'm sorry I did that here – in broad daylight. I'm not sorry I kissed you – not at all." His hands moved reverently over my cheeks and down my neck, as if he just needed to put his hands on any part of me available. My eyes closed at the feeling of his rough and calloused hands moving over my sensitized skin. "I've wanted to kiss you since I first met you. I've been trying to read you, trying to figure out if you'd want that." He swallowed thickly and I watched his Adam's apple bob, biting my lower lip to keep myself from moving my mouth toward it. "Tell me you wanted it," he whispered, his eyes darting back and forth between mine, anxiety apparent in his expression.

I moved my own hands up to wrap around both sides of his thick, corded neck, making sure I said my next words with as much conviction as I could muster. "I've never wanted anything more than for you to kiss me."

He breathed out a sigh of relief and wrapped his arms around me, holding me for a few minutes, letting both our bodies come down from the kiss-induced high we'd climbed to just moments before.

"You're a fantastic kisser," I said, my voice soft and playful, hoping to lead us out of the thick and heavy moment and back into the light. He squeezed me a little tighter and I felt a slight laugh rumble through him, doing absolutely nothing to calm the arousal I was trying to keep at bay. He leaned back and then gently tucked another tendril of hair behind my ear.

"I must have been inspired."

"Well, here's hoping you get inspired again sometime." I winked at him and this time he let out a legitimate laugh. And just like that, we were back to the easy lightness we'd shared with him all day. One minute he was kissing me like he needed to devour me and the next we were laughing and making jokes. Something in the back of my mind told me *this is how it's supposed to be. It doesn't always have to be hard or sad or forced. Happiness is light.*

I shook my head, trying to free my mind of the profound thoughts making themselves known while I was sitting on an attractive man's lap.

I stood up and grabbed my camera, draping it around my neck again, and then Nate stood and took my hand, grabbed his backpack, and led me out of the cavern, back in to reality.

Chapter Fifteen

Present Day

"Well, here we are again," Nate said as he put his truck into park. The afternoon sun was shining through the windshield and his cheeks were just a little pinker for spending the day outdoors.

"Thank you for a great day. It was a lot of fun." I fiddled with my camera, trying to make it seem like I was putting things in order, when really I was stalling, not ready to leave him yet. When I felt his fingers under my chin I stilled, then lifted my eyes to meet his, which were a lot closer than they just had been.

"I'd like to see you again. Soon." His face was achingly close, his thumb and forefinger putting just enough pressure on my chin to make my insides melt.

"I'd like that too," I breathed.

He waited only a moment before he leaned forward and pressed the softest and most patient kiss against my lips. It was a far cry from the urgent kisses we'd shared behind the waterfall. There was still need, but it was simmering instead of boiling. When he finally pulled away, I was breathless. His body moved and I opened my eyes fully, and then realized he was pulling his wallet from his back pocket. He flipped it open and produced a business card.

"This has my cell number on it. I already have your number, now you have mine. I'd like you to use it. I'll do the same."

"Okay," I replied, taking the card from his fingers. I held his gaze for a moment, and then turned to reach for the door handle.

"Hey," he said softly, making me turn in my seat. "Soon." That one word sent shivers all through my body and made the air stall in my lungs. I nodded weakly then opened the door and climbed down from his truck. I walked to the door of my studio, noticing that my clothes were completely dry. I was glad for that because I didn't want to have to go home just yet. I wanted to get some work done.

My mind was still back in the truck with Nate and his kiss, his hands on me, and I didn't notice that only the bottom lock was turned. Didn't even pick up on the fact that the deadbolt was unlocked. I did, however, notice the lights were on. I stopped only a few feet in the studio when I saw Devon sitting in my fancy chair behind my desk.

"Devon," I said, shocked to see him. "What are you doing here? How'd you even get in?"

"You said you were working today." His voice was calm and almost sad. He sat with his hands folded together atop my desk, but he wouldn't look at me. "I left the kids with the neighbor girl across the street and came here to talk to you, to try and work some things out, but you weren't here." He paused for a moment and took a breath, then his face lifted and his eyes met mine. "I waited here because I thought, surely, you'd be back soon. You told me you were working."

"Devon," I said quietly. "How did you get in?"

"Liv had a key."

Of course she did.

"I was working," I lied. I held up my camera. "I did a nature shoot. Went for a hike."

"With him?" His words were colder, but not any harsher. If anything, he sounded sadder with every word.

"Devon, please-"

"I don't understand. I didn't think it was possible to be hurt by loss again."

His words opened up a deep and gaping hole, right in the middle of my chest. My lungs collapsed. My knees begged to give out, to bring me straight to the floor.

"I thought when Olivia died that would be the end of the loss. Do you know what I mean?" He looked at me again, pleading with me to understand what he was saying, but I knew his loss was something I'd never be able to comprehend. "I always imagined, at least in the last couple of months, that grief was like a basket or a bowl." He held his hands up, as if he were holding an imaginary bowl in his arms. "My bucket was full of grief. I couldn't fit anymore in there, Evie. It was filled to the brim. And it was heavy. I had to carry it everywhere."

I wanted to go to him, to wrap my arms around him and try *anything* to make him feel better, to make his hurt go away. But there was a notably distinct and solid wall of emotion around him and I didn't know how to break through or if it was even a good idea.

"But every day it got a little lighter, and the bucket got a little smaller. No less empty – the grief and sadness were still there – still just as real, it just became easier to carry. Every day when you would come to our house and make life easier, Evie, the grief became *less*." He shook his head and dropped it into his hands. His next words were mumbled, his voice quiet and aching. "It didn't occur to me that you were mine to lose, too."

"That's a lie," I rasped at him, my whisper angry and insistent. "You've known from day one, the day you realized I was your girlfriend's best friend, that I was yours. I've always been yours, even when I shouldn't have been." My body, which had previously been weak and empty from his presence, was now alive and filled with electricity coursing through my veins. "You chose Olivia."

"I wasn't given a choice!" His words were punctuated by his hand slamming down on the top of my cherry-colored desk. "I was with her and then you appeared, like I'd been wishing for, but I was already with her. I couldn't break up with her to be with you; that would have ruined your friendship." He slammed his other hand down, only this one was fisted, making a louder thump than the other. Then he fisted both of his hands in his hair, resting his elbows on the surface of the desk. "Besides, I cared about her," he whispered.

"I know. You loved her." My words came out with a sob I thought I would be able to keep under control.

"I did love her, Evie. God," he took in a stuttering breath, "I loved her." His voice broke as he started crying, and I just couldn't stay on the other side of the room any longer. Nothing in that moment was going to keep me from him. I rushed to him, knelt at his side, offering anything I had to make him feel better. The instant I was there, he turned and wrapped his arms around me. He buried his face in my neck and cried.

I ran my hand down the back of his head, smoothing over his hair, murmuring quiet words to him. Telling him it was okay, letting him cry. I tried to be the strong one, tried to keep my tears in, but I found myself with a few errant ones slipping down my cheek.

"She wasn't supposed to die, Evie," he cried. "She wasn't supposed to leave me here wondering what in the hell it was all for."

"I know, Devon," I whispered, not knowing what else I could say to him.

He pulled away slightly, his mouth just barely at my cheek, breath feathering over my skin damp from both our tears. "I was so content. I was so used to loving you both. Having her with me and you just out of reach." He sucked in a fast breath, but I couldn't get my lungs to work at all. I felt his hand come to the side of my face, his skin warm and familiar in a completely foreign way. My whole body seized up and I recognized what I was feeling as fear. Everything was about to change, to go down a completely unpredictable path. "I'm so confused," he whispered, his lips so close to mine I could feel the heat radiating off them, a hair's breadth from mine.

When his soft, wet lips made contact with mine, a few things happened all at once. First, I had an instant in which I understood I was living a moment I had thought was an impossibility. I paid homage to the fact that Devon's lips were pressed against mine, that he had consciously made the decision to kiss *me*. My heart swelled, the butterflies took off in droves, and my whole body sagged in the relief his kiss brought me. The next instant, all of that came to a jarring halt.

I pulled away from him, my hand coming to my lips. I didn't know if I was trying to keep a part of him on my lips, or if I was ashamed they'd been there to begin with. All I knew was that it was wrong. It was all wrong.

"Evie…" he pleaded.

"No," I said, shaking my head and getting to my feet. His hand reached out and grabbed my arm, spinning me around to face him again.

"Evie, please, you have to know I've wanted that for so long."

"No," I said again. We would not have that conversation. I couldn't. I pulled on my arm, trying to free myself from his grasp, but he held strong.

"Please, don't pull away from me. I couldn't bear to lose you too."

"You have to leave," I said, my words muffled through my hand still covering my mouth.

"Talk to me," he pleaded.

"You have to go." I pulled my arm free with a hard tug and then walked quickly to the bathroom. I pushed the door closed behind me, locked it, and then leaned my forehead against it as I finally let the cries out.

Chapter Sixteen

Olivia and Devon's Wedding Day

"You doing okay, Evie?" Olivia's voice floated through the hotel room and brought me out of my daze. My mind was elsewhere. Probably because a large part of me wanted to be anywhere but there. I knew watching Olivia marry Devon would be difficult, but she was my best friend and I wanted to be there for her.

My eyes moved down to my ring finger and focused on the square-cut diamond solitaire engagement ring I was still trying to get used to wearing.

"I'm fine," I said without any kind of feeling or conviction.

"Were you surprised?"

"By what?" I asked, still staring at the ring, trying to convince my mind that it was, in fact, my finger on which the ring was situated.

"By Elliot's proposal. Duh," Liv giggled. She was sitting in a chair across the room while a stylist worked on her hair.

"Oh. Right. Yeah."

The truth was, I'd never been more confused in my life.

The night before, at Devon and Olivia's rehearsal dinner, Elliot had stood to make his speech as best man. I hadn't thought much of it. He was doing a great job – talking about how Devon had been smart not to let the woman he loved get away, that when you know you're with the one you want to spend forever with, you should grab hold tight. The next thing I knew he was at my side, down on one knee, with a little black velvet box in hand, asking me to marry him.

I'd never felt more guilty than when my eyes fluttered over his shoulder and met with Devon's.

But Devon didn't stand up, and he didn't shout to me not to do it. Not that I expected him to. But I did see him swallow hard and it kind of looked like he wanted to throw up. *Me too.*

"Babe?" Elliot asked, still holding my hand, waiting for me to tell him whether I'd spend the rest of my life with him or not.

I looked into Elliot's eyes and said the only thing I could think of. "Yes."

He pushed the ring onto my finger and stood up, hugging me, lifting me into the air and kissing my cheek. He seemed so happy.

"Evelyn," Liv's voice cut through my mental fog again. "Earth to Evelyn," she giggled. "You guys must have had a lot of engagement sex last night."

I forced a laugh, trying to seem like she'd hit the nail on the head. I wanted her to believe I was tired because I'd spent all night having passionate sex with my new fiancé. I didn't want her to know I'd lost sleep because I was trying to come up with any feasible reason to get out of it without hurting anyone.

Elliot was a great guy. I loved him. He'd been good to me. But everything about the night before only solidified for me that it was over a long time ago. When someone asks you to marry him and the first thing you feel is overwhelming dread, that's when you know it's time to move on. I couldn't marry Elliot. I couldn't do that to him. He deserved someone much better than me, someone who would love him with as much enthusiasm as he loved them.

Two hours later, I watched my best friend exchange vows with the man I'd been in love with for years, a love I knew I'd never get the opportunity to express. Never get the opportunity to stand up in front of a group of people and hear him vow to love me until death parted us.

Because I was the maid of honor, I faced Liv's back with my eyes locked on Devon.

He said his vows and I could see the love radiating from him. I watched as his eyes lit up with his words, how his voice grew sharp with promises and emotion. And when the tears slipped down my cheeks, I plastered on a fake smile so that people would think I was crying happy tears, not sad, devastating ones.

I watched with a painful ache in my chest as Liv kissed her new husband.

Suddenly, the years of longing and the way I'd resigned myself to simply being around him without ever feeling his hands on me was all too much. I was realizing that I would be living this way *forever*. Just as he'd taken the vow to love Liv until the day he died, I realized it would never end for me.

This had always been my reality, but faced with an eternity of never being with Devon was too much to handle in that moment. I walked behind the happy couple, hand in hand with Elliot, trying to keep the devastation from my face as I followed them back down the aisle. When we made it right outside the doors of the church, Devon and Liv stopped to share a kiss, his hands framing her face, and her eyes filled with actual tears of happiness.

I took a sharp right turn and headed toward a restroom I'd seen before the ceremony, ripping my hand from Elliot's.

"Evie!" I heard him calling from behind me, but I couldn't turn and look him in the face. I made it to the restroom, locked the door, and then put down all the barriers I'd had up for so long. I let my guard down, let the wall down around my heart, and I cried. I sat on the toilet, face in my hands, and cried loud and gut wrenching sobs. My mind was torturing me with images of Devon looking at his bride with love, holding their baby, spending a wonderful life with her, my best friend, and my soul shattered like a sheet of ice, fragments shooting in all different directions, with sharp and jagged edges.

I don't know how long someone had been knocking on the door – I was unaware of my surroundings – but when the knocking turned into banging and shouting, my brain finally recognized the sounds of someone on the other side of the door.

"Evie, I'm worried about you. Please, open the door." Elliot's voice was loud and, indeed, worried. I stood, my legs shaky and weak, and walked to the sink, wetting some paper towels. I heard Elliot's muffled voice talking to someone else and then suddenly the door burst open. I saw a man in a blue jumpsuit with a nametag that read, "Bud," and Elliot barrel through the door past him. "Evie," he said, my name like a prayer on his lips, rushing toward me.

"Are you all right?" he asked as his hands came to my shoulders, his eyes running up and down my body, looking for any kind of injury or clue as to why I would have locked myself in the restroom.

My first instinct was to tell him that I was fine; old habits die hard. But the words wouldn't come. I couldn't bring myself to lie to him, or myself, any longer. So instead, I shook my head. Immediately more tears sprung to my eyes.

"What's wrong, babe?" His words were soft and concerned and the weight I was carrying around shifted, becoming altogether heavier with his sweetness.

"I can't marry you." I'd spoken the words without really thinking about them and instantly wished I could take them back, rephrase them, and soften the edges a little, instead of just blurting out the words that I knew would leave his soul entirely shattered as mine was, even if for different reasons.

He was shocked for a moment, but then he moved closer to me, bringing his body within inches of mine, bending at the knees to look into my eyes.

"Evelyn, let me take you home. You're obviously upset about something. I don't think you should be here. Let's go." His eyes were pleading with me to let him take care of me, to let him smooth over whatever I was upset about, and that would have been easy. Obviously, he was just as good as I was at pretending everything was all right, because if he weren't we would have ended long ago. We'd both been pretending, but I knew he was only biding his time, hopeful I'd eventually return his feelings with the same depth and investment he had shown me. But it had to end.

"I can't go with you, and I can't marry you. It wouldn't be right. We both know it."

He was quiet for another moment, and then he took a step backward, his hands dropping from me. I'd never felt as cold or empty as I did the moment the warmth of his hands faded from my bare skin. That warmth might have been the last time I felt a man's hands on me, and even though I wasn't in love with him, his touch had never been anything but wonderful.

"This is about Devon," he accused. I shook my head.

"No, this is about me. About us. It's got nothing to do with him."

"Bullshit." His voice was laced with an anger I'd never heard from him before. Gone was the Elliot who wanted to care for me and he was replaced with someone filled with fury. "You think I'm stupid enough to believe it's a coincidence you're having a breakdown at Devon's wedding? For Christ's sake, Evelyn, don't insult me by playing dumb." He took in a deep breath and seemed to calm down a bit. "I thought you were coming around, thought you'd realized what we had was a good thing." He moved closer to me again, but I took a step back, which only made him inhale a sharp breath. I'd never pulled away from him before.

"I don't think you're stupid, Elliot. And I do think that what we had was a good thing. But, I can't live like this anymore. I can't keep hoping that one day I'll move from loving you – and I *do love you* – to being in love with you."

"You mean you were hoping you'd fall out of love with Devon."

I opened my mouth, but I had no words to argue with him. He was right, but I couldn't bring myself to admit it. My hands dropped to my sides, and more tears sprung from my eyes.

"He's in love with Olivia. He just *married* her."

"I know," I whispered, still not looking him in the eye.

"She's your best friend," he said, the accusation implied – I was in love with my best friend's husband; it was the ultimate betrayal.

"This doesn't have to do with either of them," I cried. "Yes, I'm in love with Devon, but it doesn't matter. The only part that matters right now is that I'm not in love with you." The words came out harsher than I would have liked. I would have loved to make it through this exchange without hurting him at all, but in that moment I felt careless and horrible. "Devon isn't what's important here," I said as a way of trying to redirect the confrontation. "I care about you, Elliot, but it would be wrong of me to marry you when I'm not in love with you. I'm sorry. That's the truth. *I am sorry.* I wanted to be happy with you. You don't know how many times I've prayed that I would find my way to the place you seemed to get to so easily, a place where I could fall in love with you, but it never happened."

"So that's it?" he asked, pain and anger prevalent in his words, his fists clenched at his sides.

"Yeah," I said through more tears, "I guess it is."

"Two and a half years together and you're going to end it because you had a breakdown?"

"This isn't just a breakdown. This has been eating away at me for months. I can't do it anymore."

"I knew you had some weird thing going on with him, Evie. I could tell by the way you two would look at each other, or go to great lengths to never be alone together; it wasn't a particularly well-kept secret. But I never thought you'd be stupid enough to risk everything for him. On his wedding day, even." He shook his head and backed away from me.

"Elliot, please, if nothing else you have to understand that this has *nothing* to do with him. I've always been faithful to you. Nothing has ever happened between Devon and I. I promise. Please, just understand that I can't marry someone I'm not in love with." I took in a deep breath, trying to push past the sobs that were threatening again. "You're a fantastic man. You need to find someone who will love you better than I can, someone who gives you every part of them."

"I gave you everything," he whispered sadly.

"And I don't deserve it."

Chapter Seventeen

Present Day

The next day, Monday, I didn't go to Devon's house. I was up hours earlier than normal, pacing back and forth in my room, trying to decide what to do. I worked myself up so much I made myself sick. I didn't want to see Devon, didn't want to face his devastation again, but I felt terrible for essentially leaving him in a bind. Then, the other side of my brain would tell me that, surely, he wasn't expecting me, and he'd figure it out on his own. Then, the tiniest part of my brain, the evil part, would whisper that it was about time he was the one to get his kids ready for school and out the door without my assistance.

Finally, twenty minutes before I would have usually left and headed to his house, I forced myself to take three shots of tequila, purposefully taking away my ability to drive. I took the shots, turned off my phone just in case he tried to call – which I knew he wouldn't – and crawled back into bed. The tequila took me away in less than twenty minutes, and I spent the rest of the day in bed.

The next morning didn't go much differently. I worried myself into a fit about whether to go or stay, but finally convinced myself to go to work instead and catch up on what I'd put off Sunday and Monday. Once at my studio, I relaxed a little, but every time my phone rang I expected it to be Devon. But he never called. That fact both relieved and worried me.

Wednesday and Thursday, the same thing happened. I made myself go directly to the studio, never hearing from Devon. But on Thursday, I did hear from Nate. Honestly, I'd been too preoccupied with everything, and too unsure about men in general, to contact him. My mind would drift from the life-altering kiss with Nate under the waterfall back to the even more shattering kiss I shared with Devon, and all those thoughts would always be followed with shame. I shouldn't have been kissing anyone.

My phone buzzed in my desk drawer. I'd tossed it in there hoping it would keep me from checking it every three minutes to see if Devon had reached out to me. I opened the drawer and saw a text from Nate.

Hey.

That titillating text was quickly followed up by –

Did you like that first message? It took me three days to decide on it. Didn't want to seem too eager. How'd I do?

I couldn't help it; I giggled. Then I frowned. God, I was fucked up. I couldn't even let myself laugh. I stared at my phone for a few minutes, trying to figure out what the hell my next step should be. Eventually, I decided to approach the situation like you would a Band-Aid. I was gonna go the quick and direct route.

I can tell you put a lot of thought into it. Listen, I had a really great time with you the other day, but I think it's best if we not see each other again. I'm not really as available as I thought I was. I'm sorry.

I sent the message and held my breath. I didn't know what I was expecting. He could respond a million different ways. He could be angry, hurt, indifferent, offended. His response, however, wasn't anything I could have anticipated.

You can tell yourself whatever you want, Lyn, but you were fully available to me on Sunday. I think your brain is talking you out of it now. See me again and let me remind you how good we are together.

My jaw dropped after I finished reading his text and, even though it totally added an unwanted layer to my confusion, my heart sped up at his words, too. Before I could even fathom a response, another text came through.

Just meet me for dinner. In public. Nothing physical can happen in the middle of a restaurant. I'll behave. I just want to see you. Even if it's just for you to tell me we can't see each other again.

I knew, deep down, I didn't owe him anything. One date didn't obligate me to any further contact with Nate. But then I thought about the way his hands felt running up and down my back, how his lips pressed so softly and familiarly into mine, and I gave in. In truth, I wanted to see him one last time too – even if it was only to say goodbye. I typed my response.

When?

Tonight. 6pm. At Xavier's.

I'll be there.

I breathed out a large sigh, and then put my phone down, hoping to concentrate on some work – or at least pretend to. A few minutes later, my phone buzzed again with another text from Nate.

Thank you.

I let my phone fall from my hands and dropped my head into my palms, letting out a frustrated groan. I couldn't fathom why I was surprised. It seemed my super power was finding seemingly perfect, good, smart, sensitive men, and finding ways to make it impossible to be with them.

That evening I walked into Xavier's and, once I told the maître d' who I was meeting, was led to the far back corner of the restaurant where Nate was sitting at a small table for two. He stood when he saw me coming, his face holding tension and looking worried. He stepped behind the vacant chair and pulled it out for me. I gave him a smile, it was not lost on me that he was going above and beyond to be nice. The waiter walked away as Nate pushed my chair in, but before I could even say hello to him, Nate pressed his lips just below my ear and whispered to me, "I'm glad you came."

My skin prickled at his words and my breath caught. Then I tamped it all down because I was here to tell him goodbye. I was not here to imagine his lips moving up and down the skin of my neck, whispering words against me.

Before I could respond, he was sitting in his chair across from me, his long legs brushing mine under the table as he folded himself into the chair. Almost instantly, our waiter appeared and Nate was ordering a rum and coke. He looked at me expectantly and I found a way to make the words "Vodka Sour," slip past my lips. When Nate gave me a wistful smile, I nearly crumbled. I was just seconds from grabbing my purse and leaving, unable to look at him, knowing it was the last time, thinking about everything that we'd never have together, when I heard his voice.

"Stop overthinking this, Lyn. We're only having a drink. Ordering dinner. I'm not here to pressure you into anything or make you feel guilty or sad or angry. I just want to talk. And, this might be stepping past my boundaries, but I feel like you need someone to talk to. Let me be that person."

I let out a breath and nodded, a little relieved that he hadn't planned some big speech about going out with him again.

"Tell me about Devon." He'd just delivered the most surprising and unexpected request in the history of fucked up relationships.

My eyes darted to meet with his and I must have looked panicked because he held up a hand, almost like he was trying to defend himself.

"I know you probably don't want to talk about him with me, but I know everything you're dealing with right now is centered around him." He stopped talking as the waiter appeared, leaving both our drinks on the table. Before I could stop him, Nate ordered dinner for both of us, then sent the waiter on his way. He'd ordered us steaks, which normally I'd be excited for, but I didn't feel like eating. As the waiter walked away, Nate reached his hand over the table and gently wrapped it around mine. "It's okay to tell me about it all, Lyn. If you keep it all bottled up, it'll just eat you from the inside out."

Is that what's been happening to me for the last nine years? I'd been slowly hollowing out? That seemed like an apt description. How much of me could there possibly be left? How much longer could I live like this before I disintegrated entirely?

"Start from the beginning," he said softly, with so much kindness I wanted to cry. He was so *good*.

I took a deep breath and decided to give him exactly what he wanted. "I met Devon my freshman year of college. Some guy dumped a soda down my shirt and Devon gave me the shirt off his back. Literally. He was nice and funny and sweet, and when I walked away from him, I was smitten. I looked for him everywhere for the next few weeks. Walked through the same café where we'd first met, hung out in coffee shops, casually asked my friends if they knew who he was. I was consumed with him. I wondered who he was, what he was going to school for, if he had a girlfriend. He became almost mythical to me. Like some magical college-boy apparition." I stopped and lifted my glass to my lips, needing both the liquid courage and to wet my mouth for the speech I was about to deliver.

"I had nearly gotten to the point where I didn't believe he actually existed, until one day my best friend introduced me to her new boyfriend, and it was him."

"Ouch," Nate said just before sipping his drink. He didn't seem put off by the beginning of my story, didn't seem to mind too much that I was telling him about my infatuation with another man, so I continued, feeling like I was already a little lighter after letting some of the words out.

I went on to tell him everything. Every single detail I could recall. We ate. We drank. He listened attentively, almost raptly, asking questions when I left out something he couldn't piece together, nodding and sincerely paying attention to my crazy story.

"One night, at Liv and Devon's rehearsal dinner," I said, trying to gather the courage to tell him one of the most shameful parts of my past, "Elliot proposed to me." I inhaled, and then took another sip of my drink, despondent to see the glass was empty. Nate raised his hand and gestured to the waiter that we needed another round. I smiled at him, my head a little light and fuzzy from the alcohol, but not lit enough that I wasn't in control. I knew, even then, that Nate was giving me a gift.

"I said yes, but I shouldn't have. I shouldn't have given him that hope. I just didn't know how to tell him no in front of the entire dinner party. However, even though I might have had the best intentions, what I did the next day was even worse." I felt the tears welling in my eyes, the sharp pinching in the back of my throat, and I knew tears were imminent. I dropped my head into my hands and tried to keep the tears at bay. I didn't want to cry in a restaurant in front of Nate. I'd cried so much in the past few weeks and months, crying should have felt unremarkable and unsatisfying to me, shouldn't have been the release it was. I should have been immune to crying by that point. But I wasn't. I was still on the verge of tears and knew the release would feel like a weight lifting off me. Problems weren't solved by crying, but sometimes the only thing to make you feel better was to let the cathartic tears fall and the sobs break free.

"I watched Devon marry Olivia, lost my shit, and ended the engagement in a bathroom right after the ceremony," I sobbed the words out, not even trying to maintain any kind of façade of composure. Nate had given me free rein to open up to him, and for better or worse, my floodgate was officially wide open. He let me cry, let me weep quietly, and when I looked back up at him I didn't get the look of contempt I was expecting. I didn't wilt under his stare of disdain. Instead, he was looking at me with calm compassion. He looked as though he wanted to wrap his arms around me, but didn't want to frighten me away.

"I'm sorry," I whispered. "I've never told anyone about that before. It was, uh, a little overwhelming." I reached for my purse, grabbing a tissue, and blotted my face.

"So, you've spent the last nine years in love with your best friend's husband?"

"Give or take a year, yeah." I nodded and pushed back the tears. Hearing someone else say the words, having someone else acknowledge everything I had been dealing with was a heavy feeling. And the fact that he said the words without judgement, made it that much more difficult to hear. I wanted him to be disgusted with me, to be angry, to tell me that I deserved all the unhappiness I was feeling. I wanted him to help with the hollowing-out process. I nearly handed him a proverbial shovel and said, 'Here, dig out every good thing I have inside of me, every happy memory, every moment of contentment, and get it out. Then, bury me under it, so all that's left is a shell of a shitty person, buried underneath everything she ruined.'

"That sounds terrible," he said sincerely. And it was then I was convinced that Nate couldn't be a real person. He simply couldn't be that perfect.

"It was terrible," I said through a sniffle, and I caught the tiniest hint of a crooked smile pull up on one side of his mouth, but he pushed it back. "But then, the most terrible thing of all happened."

"She died," he said with a nod. I frowned, unable to stop them, more tears spilled. Nate got up, moved his chair so he was next to me, and then let me cry on his shoulder as I wept for my friend. I'd not had one person let me cry for her. I'd helped so many other people deal with her death, but no one had ever just wrapped their arms around me and let me mourn her, my best friend.

"Olivia died and we all just ended up in this really weird state of limbo. I stepped in to help because that was the one thing she'd asked me to do. I helped him because it's what I thought she wanted. But the longer I was there, even before you came into the picture, the more wrong it felt."

"I get that." Of course he did. "It must have felt strange, maybe even wrong, to be with him, almost in a domestic way, in her absence."

"Yes," I cried, my voice louder than I intended. "In the years before she was married, I would have given anything to take her place, but after she died, I didn't want to be her replacement." I wiped the puffy skin under my eyes, realizing I must have looked like some sort of soggy raccoon, and tried to continue. "I loved her," I whispered. "Even more than I loved him."

"I know," he whispered back to me.

"So now he's upset because he knows I went out with you, even though, he and I, we're *nothing*. We never were anything, except, maybe, a ruse. A sick, weird, twisted, relationship."

"Do you love him?" Nate asked the question with gentleness and genuine curiosity, and I felt like I owed him at least the truth. Or my own personal version of it. I wanted to give him the most truthful answer I had.

I took a moment to think about his question, because I wanted to give him the most honest answer I could. "I thought I did. Nate, I *really* thought I did. But, I want to believe love doesn't make someone feel this way."

"I want to believe that too."

We took a break from talking, letting everything I'd said sink in, and ate our meal. The quiet, which usually would have made me uneasy, was welcomed and not at all awkward. He continued to sit next to me, although he moved over a little to give me room to eat, but I liked that he was so close – that he hadn't taken the first opportunity to move away from me, to distance himself. When our knees brushed under the table, I tried to ignore the fact that I liked it.

"I'm sorry you had to listen to all that," I said, finally, after the waiter had taken our dinner plates away. "But, obviously, you can understand why I'm unavailable right now."

"I can understand why *you* think you're unavailable, yes." He picked up his linen napkin and wiped his mouth, his eyes giving away that he was getting ready to say something of importance. "I think," he said, putting his hands down and looking me straight in the eyes, "you're confused and sad and probably dealing with a little bit of depression following the death of your best friend."

I couldn't argue with him, but I also couldn't fathom where he was taking me with his words.

"The way I see it, in this moment, you've never been more available. At least, not since you met Devon."

I opened my mouth to argue that point, but he continued to talk, cutting me off.

"It sounds, to me, like you're holding all the cards, Lyn. Maybe you're not used to the feeling, seeing as how you've been playing by everyone else's rules all this time, but you're in a position to *choose* now."

I listened to his words, but didn't really take them in, couldn't comprehend them. It had been a long time since I felt like I was in the driver's seat of my own life, and if this was what it felt like, I wasn't ready to drive.

"Lyn," he whispered, placing his hand over mine again, gently rubbing his thumb on the top of my hand, sending shivers straight up my arm. "Do you want to spend the rest of your life being someone's second choice?"

I froze. "It's not like that," I whispered, my voice so low I wasn't sure he could even hear me.

"It is like that, babe," he said sweetly. But the sweetness with which he said the words did nothing to lessen the devastating effects they were having on me. "If your friend was still alive, he wouldn't be with you. The last decade of your life shows that." His thumb was still moving over my skin, but I was no longer feeling tingly. I was feeling emptier and emptier by the minute.

"I think I need to go," I rasped, reaching for my purse, starting to stand, until his grip tightened on my hand. My eyes flashed to him.

"Please, I'm sorry, don't go yet. I'd feel terrible if you left upset. Just…sit. We can talk about something else."

"Talk about something else?" I asked, my voice growing angrier. "You basically just told me that I've spent my entire adult life as insignificant."

I didn't know what I was more upset about: that he'd said those words to me, or that they were true.

The truest words I'd ever heard.

He was right.

I was insignificant.

And I did it to myself by allowing it. I let myself be his second choice ever since the beginning.

I collapsed into the chair, bringing my free hand to my mouth, wondering how I'd spent the last nine years being *nothing*. Nate still held my hand, still tried to comfort me, as I came to the most desolating revelation of my life.

After a few minutes, I felt Nate's other hand come to my shoulder as he gave it a gentle squeeze.

"You deserve to be someone's first choice, Evelyn." After his words, his hand dropped from my shoulder and I missed the warmth and the pressure immediately. I wanted him to hold me again and just comfort me, but I couldn't ask him to do that; it wasn't fair. Instead, he also pulled his hand away and moved his chair back to the opposite side of the table.

"So," he finally said, his voice light and airy, as if I hadn't just had an emotional breakdown. "I think, after listening to your story, I'd have to agree with you that you're not really available right now."

I quite nearly laughed at his words. In fact, a little sputtering chuckle made it past my lips through the tail end of my cries.

"However, I don't think you're as big of a lost cause as you seem to believe." He paused and I watched as his eyes fell to the table, his fingers fidgeting with his napkin. "Look, you're worth so much more than you're asking for. You ask people for the bare minimum, and then thank them when they give it to you. You deserve more."

His words were sending shockwaves of warmth through me, igniting the tiniest flame inside me. It was hard to believe the words, but they meant a lot coming from his mouth.

"Let me see your phone," he said gently.

I raised an eyebrow, questioning him.

"Trust me on this."

I relented and handed him my phone, watching as he lit up the screen and moved his thumbs quickly over the screen.

"Okay. In exactly one month, an alert is going to come up on your screen. All it's going to say is 'Nate.' That is just me, checking in. If you're in a better place and feel like giving me a call, I'll be waiting. If you see my name and cringe, then don't worry about me, just keep moving forward and I'll wish you all the best. The ball's in your court."

"Nate, I don't-"

"Nope," he said, cutting me off. "You don't get to turn me down now." He said all that with a smile. "When that alert comes up on your phone, decide then. And I promise, whatever you decide, I'll be okay with, as long as it's your first choice."

"Okay," I whispered, unsure of what he thought would come of waiting a month. I was broken on the inside. He shouldn't want anything to do with me.

"I'm glad you agreed to meet me tonight, Lyn. I'm grateful you told me your story. But, I think you need to rest."

He wasn't wrong. Realizing your life was in shambles, and you'd spent it practically begging everyone to see you as worthless was exhausting.

"That sounds good."

He walked me out of the restaurant and continued with me to my car. I opened the door and turned back to him, ready to thank him for dinner and tell him goodbye, but he surprised me by being only inches from me. Our eyes met and I stilled as his hand came up and pushed my hair behind my ear.

"Any man who wouldn't pick you, wouldn't wait for you, is an idiot, Evelyn." His hand dropped slightly, and his thumb feathered over my bottom lip. Then his fingers gently tucked under my chin, pushing it up just barely. "You get yourself sorted out, and if you feel like you want to give us a second chance, call me when you see my name on that phone."

He leaned closer and I breathed in right as his lips pressed against mine.

"Talk to you later," he said after he pulled away from the softest and sweetest kiss I'd ever been given.

"Bye," was all I could say as he walked away from me. A rather large part of me hoped in a month I'd see his name and want to call him. But in that moment, I knew I had other things to take care of. The first being me.

Chapter Eighteen

Three Days After Jaxy's Birth

I knocked gently on the door, opening it a crack and peeking in. I didn't want to wake baby Jax if he was sleeping, and I definitely didn't want to wake Liv. But the door slowly opened and I saw Liv with her back against the headboard, baby cradled in her arms, and a broad smile painted on her face.

"Hey, Evie. Come on in," she said in a whispered voice.

"Is he sleeping?" I asked, also whispering.

She scrunched up her face then looked down at the baby in her arms. "Sort of? He's kind of eating until he falls asleep, and then sleeping until he realizes he's not eating, and the cycle starts all over again. I feel like my boob is in his mouth too much."

"Men," I said with a smile, rolling my eyes.

"Too true, girlfriend."

I took a seat in the overstuffed chair angled toward her bed, where I'd sat during a lot of her pregnancy with Jax. He'd given her a run for her money and she'd been on bed rest for a while toward the end. I took a moment to examine my friend and, not surprisingly, she looked incredible for a woman who just three days prior had given birth. Her skin was all aglow and there were no signs of sleep deprivation. Yet. I knew, as I'd been around for Ruby's first year as well, the hard times were coming. Three-day-old babies seemed to be cake compared to the ones who were teething and growing and vocal about their unhappiness.

"How are you feeling?" I asked.

"I'm a little tired, and still a little sore, but doing well, I think. Much easier than with Ruby. She tried to kill me. I'm sure of it now."

We both laughed because it was true. Ruby hadn't wanted to come out and meet the world and put up a good fight until the very end.

"Do you want to hold him?" she asked me, her eyebrows raising.

"Duh," I said, smiling wide. I stood up and walked to her bedside, leaning down to take the precious baby in my arms, and then carefully sat back down in the chair and got comfortable.

"If he starts looking for your boob, just give him back."

I laughed. "Can do." I looked down at Jax and still couldn't believe how perfect he was. I'd seen him just minutes after he'd been born, and every day since, but I was still in awe of the perfect little person Liv had created. Well, Liv and Devon. Mostly Liv though. "I think he got cuter since yesterday," I said quietly, running just a fingertip down his surprisingly chubby cheek for a three-day old.

"If he's anything like his father, he'll just get cuter and cuter until we're beating teenage girls away with sticks and restraining orders," Liv said, laughing as she rolled to her side and snuggled in with the plethora of pillows she slept with.

I thought for a moment about how most appropriately to respond. I didn't dare comment on how he got his handsome looks from his father. "The two of you make good-looking children."

"So, Evie, does holding him make your ovaries throb in your belly?"

I laughed gently, trying to rein it in and let the baby sleep. "My ovaries haven't turned on me yet."

"You'd be such a good mom, Evie. Seriously, I know you're not dating anyone right now, and you seem to like leading a lonely life, but it would be a waste for you to go through life without becoming a mom."

I didn't look up at her. I couldn't. She knew I wanted kids. We'd talked about it hundreds of times since we'd been fourteen. We'd both had life planned out – husband, two kids, white picket fence, golden retrievers. We'd even planned to force two of our kids to fall in love and get married, making us legitimately related. It had been our silly, teenage-girl dream. And it hadn't died, we'd just never talked about the possibility of the two of us falling for the same amazing man.

As if he'd been waiting for his cue, Devon opened the bedroom door and my heart stalled at the sight of the man I'd only ever dream about being with coming into the room with Ruby wrapped around his hip.

"Hey, Evie," he said with a nod and a small smile. I gave him a four-fingered wave, hoping he'd think I was being quiet because of the sleeping baby in my arms. The reality was that I couldn't speak. His strong arm was holding a darling little girl and he looked so incredibly happy. And happy looked *good* on him. I couldn't say anything. I was feeling too much.

Devon walked with Ruby to the edge of the big bed, his knees stopping when they hit the mattress.

"I'm gonna take Ruby to the park and then for some ice cream," he said, and we all laughed when Ruby's eyes lit up with excitement.

"Yay, park!" she said, a little too loudly, but the baby remained sleeping.

"Need me to bring you anything, baby?" he asked Olivia, his voice sweet and loving. He was obviously in a babymoon, totally enthralled with the woman who'd given him a son. I completely understood, but it also totally sucked. He would never look at me that way; never see me holding our baby. That thought, above all the others floating around my brain in that moment, caused the most pain. I could always see Devon, be a part of his life, perhaps even be considered a part of his family, but I'd never have that connection to him. He looked at her as if she gave him the moon.

"No, I think we're good."

"Okay, we'll be back soon." He leaned over to kiss Liv and I had to look away. I usually did. I could tolerate a lot, but I tried to spare myself as much pain as possible. I heard him move across the room toward me and my eyes snapped up to find him, sure enough, walking my way.

His eyes locked on mine and something in them changed. They softened a little. And if I wasn't mistaken, they got a little sad, too. He stopped when he was right next to my chair and then he dipped low and placed a soft kiss on top of baby Jax's head. When he stood up, his eyes found mine again, and something passed between us. The only way I could describe it was a wave of regret. Almost as if he'd seen me holding his darling baby boy, but had the same realization as me: that this could never, really, be us. It had never occurred to me that seeing me with his children would affect him the same way as it did me. It never occurred to me he could feel that way about me.

Suddenly, my ovaries were aching. Throbbing, actually. Every part of me was in pain, screaming out for an ending I'd never have. And I found myself, for the millionth time in the last five years, telling myself it was okay. That I was okay. That I could deal with my life, if this was it. It was enough.

"Evie," Liv's gentle voice broke through my mental breakdown. My eyes snapped up to hers and she looked concerned. "Listen, I know that for a while I was pretty messed up. I went through a rough patch, and Ruby came along before I thought I was ready, but I'm telling you – don't give up hope. If I can be this happy, so can you. In fact, I owe you my happiness. Well, you and Devon. You guys never gave up on me, even when I was less than a good person."

"Liv, we all have our bad days."

"Or bad years," she said sadly, which made me even sadder.

"Liv, what's important is who you are now and who I always knew you were. You're happy, and kind, and a good wife, and a great mother," I said, looking down at her beautiful baby in my arms.

"You can be all that too, Evie." Her voice was so soft and so maternal. Soothing even.

"I'm happy," I said in my own defense, even if it wasn't with much feeling.

"You're content with the status quo, Evie. I just want you to find the happiness I have."

I finally raised my eyes to meet hers. I knew she'd never let it go if I didn't look her right in the eye and lie to her face.

"I'm happy, Liv. I promise." The words stung just saying them. It made me wonder if she could tell I was lying. "If, someday down the line, I find the man I'm supposed to marry and start a family with, then I will. But I've got too much going on to worry about it. I like to leave it up to fate. If he's out there, he'll find me."

"Not if you're hiding."

I scoffed. "I'm not hiding, Liv. I'm working. There's a difference. I don't have a regular nine-to-five job. I have to hustle to make ends meet. If that means weekends and late nights, then so be it."

"Okay, I know, but promise me you're not shutting yourself off to new people or new experiences?"

"I promise."

"You know I love you, right?" Liv asked. And even though it wasn't a crazy question, it caught me off guard anyway. She'd never seemed so intent.

"Yeah, Liv, I know you love me. I love you too." And I did. God, I did. She was my best friend, and the only way I was ever going to have a niece and nephew. She was my family. And it really sucked that I was in love with her husband.

Suddenly, the tiny baby in my arms started wiggling, moving his head from side to side, mouth open, and face looking angry.

"Uh oh," I said nervously, "I think he's looking for the boob."

Liv rolled her eyes, "Men."

I laughed and then slowly got out of the chair and handed her the baby who had started vocally announcing that he was, indeed, hungry.

I watched with wonder as Liv fed her son, marveling at the beauty of it, longing for that connection with a child of my own.

"I have this feeling, deep down in my soul, that everything is going to work out the way it's supposed to," Liv said, looking at me with a smile so genuine and heart-warming, I could do nothing else besides return it.

"I hope so."

Chapter Nineteen

Present Day

The next evening, after I knew the kids would be in bed, I drove to Devon's house. It took me all day to work up the nerve, and I wasn't even completely sure what I was going to say to him when I got there, but my conversation with Nate had struck a chord.

I stood on the front porch and sent him a text message, not wanting to wake the kids by knocking or ringing the doorbell.

I'm on your front porch. Can we talk?

It took a few minutes, but eventually I heard footsteps coming down the stairs and then the door opened.

Devon looked just as incredible as he always had. His blond hair was still pushed back, pink lips fuller than most women's but still irresistible, but his eyes were missing the spark he'd had for most of the years I'd known him. He'd lost it by the time Liv passed, but I hoped the dimness behind them was also attributed to my absence as well. I didn't want him to hurt, but I wasn't too proud to admit that I wanted him to miss me. It wouldn't change anything, but it would have been the first time I would have felt that from him and a part of me wanted that desperately, even if it was fleeting.

"Evie," he said, his voice sounding so different than I remembered. It'd only been a week, but he seemed like a new person to me. His face looked almost pained, as if I was doing injury to him by merely standing on his doorstep. "I was beginning to think I wasn't ever going to see you again."

I was starting to think you'd never seen me from the beginning.

"I'm sorry I disappeared. I just needed some time to think and sort things out in my mind. Can I come in?"

"Of course," he said, stepping backward into his house and giving me more than enough room to enter without brushing past him. I noticed he didn't smell the same. Or rather, he did, but it didn't catch me at all. The scent didn't grab ahold of me, as it usually had, and remind me of all the times I'd smelled him and wanted to bottle his personal scent. He just smelled like Devon.

I walked past him and sat on the couch, my eyes darting up the stairs, wanting badly to sneak into Ruby and Jaxy's room. To kiss their heads and run my fingers through their hair. I'd missed them terribly throughout the week, but knew it had been best to take a step back.

"How are they?" I asked, still looking up the stairs. I heard him take in a deep breath and the sound was like a vice grip around my heart. I'd never wanted to hurt the children.

"They were a little confused at first, Jax especially, but by Wednesday, they were mostly back to their old selves again."

"Did you have a hard time managing?" I didn't want to add 'without me' at the end of my question, but it was implied. The idea of asking if he'd managed without me was more pain and torture than I wished to endure.

"It took a bit of shuffling, but I found a solution. In fact, Evie, I'm glad you're here. I need to tell you something-"

"Devon, if it's all the same to you, I'd like to go first. Otherwise, I'll lose my nerve and I really need to get this out." He didn't say anything, but he did nod his head and then took a seat in the club chair just opposite me.

I took a deep breath and then started the speech I'd gone through a million times in my mind.

"I met Olivia on the first day of high school. I was fourteen and she was the first person to speak to me. She went out of her way to make me feel welcome and comfortable in a notoriously uncomfortable situation. From then on, she was my very best friend. I never could have dreamed up a better friend than her, Devon. She was sweet and loyal, beautiful but not vain, outgoing and inclusive. She was friends with everyone and everyone loved her. *I loved her*. Even when she started dating the guy I'd fallen for at first sight my freshman year of college, I still loved her." I took another deep breath, trying to keep calm even though speaking about Olivia always brought me tears. "I watched the two of you build a life together, Devon. I was here throughout everything. And even though I *always* had those feelings for you, always knew that if given the chance, I could make you so happy, I never once wanted that."

My eyes lifted and met his gaze and I was flooded with warmth. His eyes held only sympathy and compassion. Of course, he probably already knew everything I was telling him, but he could have easily stopped me before either of us became uncomfortable. But no, he knew it was important for me to say what I had come there to say and, perhaps, he was feeling the same thing I was; as if Olivia's death hadn't been the *end* we'd all built it up to be. I had thought her death might be the end of suffering, or the end of heartache. Liv had mercifully been relieved of all her pain and struggles, but the rest of us remained to trudge through what was left behind in her absence. And I'd taken that as the perfect opportunity to lock myself in the same cage I'd been circling for years.

I looked at my, arguably, inappropriate and, definitely, unhealthy relationship with Devon, and clung to it, hoping it would keep me afloat.

All I wanted now was to be able to float on my own.

"Liv asked me to look after your family, and I'll never regret the time I spent here with Ruby and Jax. I'll always love them, but I have to move on, Devon."

I'd tried so hard not to cry. I wanted to sound firm and certain during my speech, but the way my voice warbled and broke on his name, only made me sound weak and unstable. He quickly moved to sit next to me on the couch, wrapping both his arms around me, pressing my face into his neck, trying to comfort me.

"She told me to be happy," I cried, both my hands pressing against his big shoulder blades. "She told me to be happy, and I just don't think that's possible with you."

My fingers cinched the soft cotton of his t-shirt, and I burrowed my face farther into his neck, trying to inhale his scent and commit it to memory, my body trying to imprint the feeling of his against me on my skin forever. This was it. It was all we would ever have. A decade of longing and a few months of angst-ridden uncertainty.

I felt his hands move up my arms and then his neck was gone, only to be replaced by his face so painfully close to mine. We were breathing the same air, my hands still on his shoulder blades, but his gently gripping my face on both sides. Then, suddenly, he was kissing me.

I knew, as it was happening, it would be the one and only real kiss I would ever share with him, so when it didn't stop at a polite, "Thank you for taking care of my family" kiss, and moved more toward an, "I've been waiting to kiss you for a decade," kiss, I didn't try to stop it. I let his tongue move over the seam of my lips and I opened for him, letting myself take that first – and last – glorious taste of him. He tasted exactly like he smelled: of skin and sweat and soap. He tasted magnificent.

A small groan left me as his hands gripped me just a little tighter and tilted my head to get more of me. He wanted more, so I gave it to him. I tried to give him every part of me in that kiss I'd been trying to keep from him for years. Every pass of my tongue was one I'd been hoping for. Every tug at his shirt I was trying to get him as close to me as I'd always wanted. I inhaled his scent. I took note of the way he tasted, trying to ingrain it in my brain. I let my hand wander through his blond hair, realizing it, indeed, did feel as soft as it looked. The sounds he made as he kissed me were a lullaby I'd play that night as I tried to fall asleep, hushed groans and strangled moans, not wanting to wake the children.

It was the kiss to end all kisses.

When he pulled away I wasn't quite ready, but I might not have ever been. For him to kiss me was like coming out of a dark room to a world lit with prisms. Then again, there was a time when I was sure I'd never want a kiss from Devon to end. Kissing him wasn't the end though. No, this felt more like a beginning. He'd taken off my blindfold, let me out of my darkened room, and given me the colorful light I'd need to make the next step in my life. No, it wasn't an ending. However, his next words had the power to end me entirely.

He pulled his face away, only far enough to press his forehead flush against mine, and whispered, "I'm leaving, Evie."

My heart halted, stuck halfway between beats, unsure of its next move and all my blood froze in my veins.

"Leaving?" I whispered, my mouth so close to his I could nearly feel the magnetic pull between us bringing me closer.

Then, in that instant, the spell was broken.

He let go of me, took his hands off my skin, moved to the other side of the couch, and left a wide, gaping, crevasse between us.

"What do you mean you're leaving? You mean on a business trip?" I asked hopefully. I'd come over with every intention of telling him we'd never be together, but not in a million years did I expect that kiss and then those words. It was like a one-two punch. He faked left, and then jabbed right. Direct hit. Total knock out.

He ran his hands through his hair with frustration, and then heaved out a big breath. "No, not on a business trip. I put in my letter of resignation today. I'm quitting my job, selling the house, and moving to Florida to be near my parents so they can help with the kids. *That* was the rearranging I did while you were away."

"You're leaving?" I whispered, still unable to completely process his words. I'd heard him, understood him even, but refused to think about the fact that he was leaving with Ruby and Jax.

"I'm sorry," he said softly. He dropped his head into his hands and I could tell he was just as emotionally wrecked as I was, and that tore me up. I didn't want him to hurt. In fact, I wanted the hurting to end. I wanted him and me both to be happy again. He had a bumpy road in front of him, but I knew he could find happiness. I also knew, me being there every day, reminding him of Olivia, of her absence, was like pouring salt in his wounds. And I loved him enough to let him go.

"You don't have to be sorry. I'm glad you're going to be near your parents. That will be good for Jax and Ruby. I'm just really going to miss them." Even though my throat felt as if someone was making a slice right through it, I kept the cries in. I was not going to make him feel worse by crying in front of him about missing his children. No. I would cry in my bed for weeks, alone, about that.

"It was unfair of me to lean on you all this time. I apologize for that, Evie. I really do. But pretending like she isn't here isn't helping any of us. And, when you disappeared, it forced me to think about our lives realistically. I need help. Help you aren't obligated to give me. I never want to feel like an obligation to you."

"You don't. You couldn't. Ever. I love them."

"I hope you'll come see us. After some time though. After the kids have settled. I want you to be a part of their lives, a big part. I just want it to be healthy for everyone."

"I'd really like that," I said, damning the lone tear that slipped away down my cheek.

A silence fell between us as we looked at each other.

I didn't know myself without Devon. My entire adult person had been built around him, Olivia, and the weirdly beautiful, although ultimately destructive, relationship we'd all had. And, decidedly, that was the problem.

"I could never wish I'd never met her," he finally said, quietly, almost as if he wasn't talking to me, but more to himself. "I've thought about what would have happened if we'd done things differently. If I'd asked for your number, or broken up with her when I found you again. We all could have taken so many paths, even ones that didn't end with Olivia's death. But even with that alternative, I can't imagine ever going back and doing anything differently, Evie. The path we all went down brought us Ruby and Jax. So, as bad as I feel about what happened between us, and that we all had to watch Olivia suffer and die so tragically young, I can't, not even for one second, wish it were any different."

"I know." I swallowed over a large lump, not wanting to think about a world without those two beautiful children. "I agree. And I know Olivia would too."

Then, as if on cue, we both turned our heads as we heard Ruby's voice drift down the stairwell.

"Daddy, I can't sleep."

I couldn't help but smile at the sounds of her sweet, sleepy voice. It washed over me and made me feel a peace I hadn't known in years. Devon was going to do what was best for his children, and if I didn't love him before, I loved him now.

He looked at me with apology in his eyes, and I smiled, silently telling him I understood. Ruby couldn't know I was there, then she'd never go back to bed. I watched as he stood and walked up the stairs to help his little girl fall asleep. And when all was quiet, I snuck out the front door, feeling lighter than I ever had.

Devon stayed in town until the kids were done with school. So I had three glorious weeks of just being Aunt Evie. I took them to movies in the evenings and to the park on Saturdays, but never showed up to get them ready for school or to make them dinner. They never asked why, and I never offered an explanation. The time we spent together was bittersweet because we all knew, soon enough, they would be moving. But it didn't stop me from spending time with them and showering them with affection.

The day they left, I stood in their driveway blowing kisses at the back of their SUV, waving and shouting, "I love you." Then I sat on their porch and cried.

When I heard my cell phone ping, I picked it up from the passenger seat and saw an alert that, at first, didn't make any sense. I saw the word "Nate," flash across my screen. Then, all at once, I remembered. I found the nearest exit, pulled into a parking lot, and then stared at my phone.

His name kept flashing, over and over again, and it came with an alert that sounded a lot like a hurricane siren. That was fitting, actually.

When that alert comes up on your phone, decide then. And I promise, whatever you decide, I'll be okay with, as long as it's your first choice.

I closed my eyes and tried to listen. I tried to hear that inner voice that would guide me, tell me the right thing to do. I sighed, and then, dragged my finger across the screen, dismissing the alarm. I gently tossed my phone on to the passenger seat again, and then rested my head against the headrest. I took in a few deep breaths, and then gripped the steering wheel. I checked my mirrors, making sure I could see all the way to the end of the U-Haul trailer I was pulling behind me, and then I pulled back onto the freeway and left my old life behind.

I did not call Nate.

I'd done exactly as he'd told me.

He wasn't my first choice.

Chapter Twenty

Two Years Later

Present Day

"Sylvia," I called out, trying not to sound as completely flustered and nervous as I felt. "Can I get the lighting on this one taken down a bit and the print lowered just a smidge? It's being washed out entirely."

"Absolutely. No problem," she replied with confidence, even though I knew I was handing her a task she was going to pass off to someone else.

I flipped my wrist over looking for a watch I never wore then cursed myself for never wearing a watch. "What time is it?" I asked impatiently.

"We've got plenty of time," she said with a genuine smile, placing a friendly hand on my shoulder, trying to calm me.

I breathed out heavily, attempting to expel all the butterflies taking up residence in my belly. They didn't go anywhere. Bastards.

"Okay, let's get this one fixed then everything looks great."

"No problem," she replied, again with confidence.

"You know," I said, an easy smile coming over my face for the first time that evening, "I almost believe you're not just as nervous as I am."

"That's my job. To de-stress you. But trust me, I'm nervous as hell. But it's a good nervous, more excitement. I just know this is going to be your night." Her eyes lit up with contagious excitement, and I smiled back at her, this time my smile stretching my cheeks and raising my eyebrows.

"Thanks."

She winked and then walked away faster than anyone should have been able to walk in her death-trap heels. I walked back to my office, a room I'd neglected until about three weeks ago when the idea of my gallery filled with patrons and clients made me organize the mess I'd made there in the last year and a half.

Sitting atop my desk was a crystal vase filled with all different pastel colors of peonies. I smiled as soon as I saw them, remembering the happiness I'd been overwhelmed with when they'd arrived. I picked up the card leaning against the vase, and allowed the words written on it to calm me a little.

We're so excited for you, Auntie Evie. Good luck with your show!

The card was signed with an XOXO, and then names signed by little hands, Ruby and Jax.

I held the card close to my heart, trying to let their love wash over me. I missed them terribly. I hadn't actually seen them, face to face, since they moved to Florida, but we Skyped weekly. Devon had never denied me them and, in fact, had bent over backward to make sure I was still a part of their lives. I loved those two kids so much, it sometimes hurt to be away from them. But, I knew the space for Devon and me was important.

We'd had civil correspondence in the last two years, but nothing in depth and nothing meaningful. We were both moving on, trying to build new lives. He had spent a few months after moving focused on being with his children, and in those months I saw the kids respond well to having their father back. Then, he'd gotten a new job, and only a few months ago, he'd purchased another house, making Florida their permanent residence.

Still, it was very thoughtful of him to send the flowers. He knew how much it would mean to me. In moments like that I couldn't regret the way my life had played out. Devon was a good man. He just wasn't *it* for me.

I sighed and put the card back, then bent and smelled the flowers. It had worked. I was slightly less frantic than I had been five minutes ago. Mission accomplished. My eyes flitted to the hanger on the back of the door, which held my dress for the show. This show, my very own gallery show, was what I'd been working toward since I left my life behind two years ago. In my mind there'd been only two places I could go to make my dream a reality: New York City or Los Angeles. I'd done my research and decided LA was a safer choice. Plus, the weather was warmer.

So, I'd packed up my whole life, selling everything I couldn't take with me, and left for California. I'd spent the last two years focused on my craft, working tirelessly to make it as a photographer in one of the toughest cities in the country.

About eight months before, I had submitted a few photos to the Kontinent Awards. It was a fine arts series of four photos, all of which I'd taken on a hazy summer morning. Wildfires were running rampant through southern California. One morning, instead of evacuating as I'd been told, I grabbed a model, put her in a red gauzy dress, and placed her precariously close to smoke and flames.

When I was taking the photos, I knew they were special, but I had no idea they would launch my career. I'd won the award for my category and the images had become, in the world of photography, famous. Suddenly, I was selling photographs for more than I was used to making in a month. I invested in myself and started looking for a place to open my own gallery. Tonight was my inaugural show. I was beyond nervous. I wanted the show to go well, but more than that, I wanted to be taken seriously. I wanted to be recognized as an artist.

I slipped the red dress out of the garment bag, freshly steamed from the tailor, and it looked magnificent. I wanted to look professional, yet still young and fresh. I'd just turned thirty, and I was trying to embrace the 'Thirty and Flirty' mantra. My twenties were definitely something I wanted to leave behind, so I was looking forward to the next decade with exuberance. I locked my door and undressed, then slipped the silk dress over my head, loving the feeling of the material sliding down my skin, which I'd had buffed, primed, and polished in anticipation of this event.

I was, possibly, in the best shape of my life. I'd never taken such good care of my body than I had since I moved there. I was stronger in many ways, but my body was reaping the benefits of the gym I'd joined and all the hiking I did to get my shots. I also did small things to take care of myself. My nails were polished, my hair was highlighted, and I'd developed a habit of waxing. I was smooth everywhere and something about that always exhilarated me. And it was, indeed, just for me. I'd not been with a man since I had moved there.

I'd barely slipped on my black stiletto heeled shoes when I heard a small knock at my door.

"Come in," I called out, smoothing the fabric of my dress down my thighs, pulling on the hem where it lay only a few inches above my knees.

"Hey, famous photographer lady."

I turned at the excited declaration and saw Shelby standing in my doorway, an enormous smile on her face.

"Oh, my God! Shelby!" I cried, rushing toward her. "What in the world are you doing here?" I wrapped my arms around her, not believing she was actually standing in front of me.

"You said you were having your first show, so, of course I came! I'll get to tell everyone how I knew you when!"

"I can't believe you came all the way to LA for a gallery show." It had been a while since anyone had done something that nice for me.

"Well, I'll be honest, I can't afford to buy anything because you're so famous, your prints are selling for an arm and a leg, but I'm here to show my support."

I leaned in and hugged her again. "Thank you," I whispered.

I'd made a small group of friends in LA. Lainey was my neighbor and lived in the townhouse next to mine. She'd introduced me to her friends and, luckily for me, I had fit right in. They were all in their early thirties, single, and trying to do the responsible, working adult thing. I'd made some great connections with some models in the city, using them for my shoots, building relationships with them, but Shelby was more than just a model to me. She'd helped me through some tough times and I was thrilled she was here. I couldn't wait to introduce her to my LA friends.

"I'll let you finish getting ready and see you out there," she said with a smile before she gave me another quick hug and disappeared. I took in a deep breath and let it out. Something about having a familiar and friendly face there made me feel better, a little more relaxed, as if I could actually pull the show off.

An hour later, I could hear voices filling the gallery space. Lots of voices. I'd done a lot of legwork for this show, trying to make sure that anyone and everyone was invited. Editors from prominent magazines and newspapers had given me indications they'd be attending, other photographers whose endorsement could mean a lot to me, so many people who could be right in the other room. I almost couldn't bring myself to leave my office. But eventually, when I was sure there wasn't a hair out of place, I took a deep breath and walked out of my safe office and into the gallery.

I'd seen the set up for weeks now. Heck, I'd designed it. But seeing the show in full swing, lighting up, people milling around, drinks in hand, pointing to my photos, well, it seemed like a dream come true.

I grabbed a glass of champagne off the tray of a passing server, giving her a smile, and then slowly strode through the open gallery showroom, trying to take in bits and pieces of what people were saying to each other about my photos.

"Breathtaking," "beautiful," "soulful," and "exquisite" were some of the words floating through the air as I passed by, and the smile that spread across my face was genuine and pure. This was what I'd worked so hard for these past years.

I spotted Sylvia and made my way to her, grateful for a friendly face. Her eyes lit up when she saw me and greeted me with an excited smile.

"Oh, my gosh, Evelyn, so far everyone is in awe of your work." She placed her hand on my arm just below my shoulder and gave me a gentle, supportive squeeze. A few heads around us turned at Sylvia's words and once people's eyes found me, I was suddenly surrounded by people – fancy, glamorous people – who all wanted to talk to me about my "talent."

Over the next two hours, I was happily cornered by some of the most impressive people I'd ever hoped to meet, let alone talk with about my photographs. Someone from Time

Magazine spoke to me for ten whole minutes about using my photos for a regional edition and I nearly stopped breathing. Whose life was I living?

Shelby found me, champagne in hand, and gave me another enthusiastic hug.

"Evie, these photos are incredible. You've done such phenomenal work in LA," her eyes continued to wander around the room, taking in all the photos that hung from the wall.

"You saw that one, right?" I asked, pointing to the wall on the east side of the building. Hanging there was a large print of the photo I'd taken of her at the falls just weeks before I left town.

"I did see it," she said with a smile. "I also saw the little sticker next to it that indicated it had been sold." Her voice was nearly at a squeal.

A new wave of emotions rushed over me. While talking with all the exciting people about what my next step as a photographer would be, and where my art would take me, I'd totally forgotten that my work was for sale. If I sold even a few pieces at the prices posted, I would be set for months.

"Are you serious?" I balked.

"Totally. I saw quite a few stickers already. You're doing fantastic!"

Another server walked by and we grabbed more champagne, quietly toasting, my smile growing wider by the minute. I kept Shelby near me, glad to have a friend there, and we slowly made our way through the gallery. I accepted compliments with as much grace as I could muster, feeling my cheeks heat every time someone said something I wasn't sure I'd ever hear.

"You're a magnificent artist."

"The way your photographs capture light, it's amazing."

"Where have you been hiding? Your work is incredible."

I was floating on a cloud of realized dreams and bubbly champagne when I suddenly felt the hairs on the nape of my neck raise, standing straight up, and goose bumps spreading across my skin.

"You're a difficult woman to get ahold of."

I heard his wonderfully deep and gravelly voice from behind me and my breath caught in my lungs. My mouth parted, waiting for words that weren't anywhere near ready to come. I registered Shelby's wide eyes, but I was too focused on all the exciting responses my body was having to his voice to care.

My heart rate thundered through my veins, my breath started moving in shallow pants, and every nerve in my body was tingling with just the sound of his voice. I felt him step up closer, his front barely brushing my back, and I had to fight every instinct to lean into him.

"This one is my favorite," he said, his voice a low whisper, his hand coming up, finger pointing toward a photo on the wall a few feet in front of us. My eyes were trained on his hand. His skin was tanned, palms looking rough and worn, but he was obviously strong. Then, my gaze moved to the photo he was pointing at and I felt a small smile pull on the corner of my mouth.

It was one of my favorites too.

A black and white image of a man, standing atop an unusual, yet amazing, formation of naturally fallen logs. Even though it was a black and white image, the sunlight was flooding the frame, making his face impossible to see, but illuminating every other part of him.

"That was one of my most favorite days," I managed to whisper. I remembered that hike, remembered him fondly, and thought of him often.

"Mine too," he whispered so close to my ear I could feel his breath passing over my cheek. I turned my head slightly, and took in his incredibly handsome face with bright eyes smiling down at me. He was just as I remembered him. Dark hair, a little unruly, deep brown eyes, arresting smile.

"What are you doing here?"

"My favorite photographer announced on her website a few months ago that she was going to open her own gallery. I made it a point to come and support her. She's an incredible artist."

"Nate," I whispered, unable to make it past his name, overcome by his sweetness and the absolute shock of seeing him again. Something in my belly flipped at the thought of him looking at my website, of him thinking about me after not seeing each other for years.

He stepped around me so we were face to face, and his thumb and forefinger gently gripped my chin, his touch light and comforting. "How've you been, Lyn?" His eyes sparkled with his question, his smile widening. He was the only person who ever called me Lyn, and I liked it. So much. Too much.

"Good," I breathed. "I've been good."

"Hmmm. I can tell." His words flowed through me, my eyes drinking in the beauty of his face right in front of me. His hand moved to my shoulder, then slid softly down my arm until my fingers were in his hand. He lifted my left hand up and examined it, running his thumb over my ring finger. "You're not wearing a wedding ring, and I haven't seen any men lingering near you. Is it possible you're single?"

"She's totally single," Shelby offered from behind me, her voice way too enthusiastic for the message she was delivering. I rolled my eyes.

"Thanks, Shelby," I laughed, but then turned back to Nate. "I still can't believe you're even here. I never really thought I would see you again."

"I don't want to monopolize you on your big night, but I was hoping we could catch up later."

"Um, sure," I said softly, realizing I was a little disappointed he wouldn't be monopolizing me. "But you'll hang around?"

"I wouldn't miss it," he said, squeezing my hand one more time before stepping away toward the bar. I couldn't take my eyes from the man who I had only seen in clothes fit for hiking or construction, now standing before me in an incredibly sexy suit, complete with slick, skinny black tie. My mind was whirling, wondering what in the world he was doing there.

"Did you tell him about this?" I asked Shelby as soon as Nate was out of earshot.

"Absolutely not. I haven't seen him since that one time in your studio back home. I can't believe he showed up here, all hot for you, checking out your ring finger. He's on a mission, Evie."

My eyes flitted back to him, standing at the bar, back to me. A considerably large part of me wanted to stare at him for the rest of the evening. My body was remembering, slowly, the one real date we'd had, the one kiss we'd shared under that waterfall, and the way it had made me feel. Before my thoughts could carry me too far away, I was being beckoned by Sylvia to chat with an editor of LA Times, wanting to do a story on my photographs and me, so I had to put my work face back on.

My body, however, was always aware of Nate. So much so, it seemed to vibrate with the awareness. I knew where he was at all times: which photos he was looking at, which people he was talking to, which corner of the gallery he was standing in, watching me from afar. It was the most brutal and beautiful form of torture. As much as I was aware of him, he definitely seemed to be tracking me as well. Electricity flowed between us like a hot current, and I was surprised people inside the gallery weren't fanning themselves. I found my cheeks warm and my core even warmer. My belly clenched every time we made eye contact, my breath caught when I saw him taking in one of my photos. I'd never experienced foreplay from a room apart, but what was happening between us definitely qualified.

I sipped cool champagne, trying to calm myself. Obviously, my body was on high alert, suffering from withdrawals. I'd only gone on a few dates since moving to LA, and definitely hadn't slept with anyone. And it had been a long while since I'd slept with anyone even before the move. I was in a serious dry spell and my mind was telling my body to prepare.

I was almost embarrassed. He'd said twenty words to me. He could have been in a relationship for all I knew. But deep down I knew he wouldn't have come to my show, especially alone, if he'd been in a relationship. Regardless, my body was onboard and primed to devour his.

Despite the distraction of Nate, I managed to put on a good show. I spoke with many important people who could all have a significant impact on my career path, and I felt as though I'd made a good impression on everyone. Overall, it seemed to be quite a successful night. It was easy to keep a smile on my face as people began to leave, showering me with compliments and congratulations.

My eyes wandered to Nate and I saw him talking with Shelby, both of them stealing glances my way. I didn't know what she would have to say to him, but I wasn't too worried about it; Shelby had always been a good friend. I watched as she leaned forward and pressed a friendly kiss to his cheek, and then made her way back to me.

"I'm beat. I'm going back to my hotel." She opened her arms to me, wrapping me up in a hug and whispered in my ear, "I'm so proud of you, Evie. You've accomplished so much since you've been here. Now, let that man love on you a little."

I laughed, not at all surprised by her forward demand.

"Thank you for coming," I said as I pulled back from her embrace. "It means a lot that you were here. Make sure you call me before you head home so we can get coffee or lunch."

"I'll call you tomorrow, but not too early," she said with a sassy wink.

I gave her a natural, warm smile as she left, feeling particularly lucky to have made such a good friend in her. As a few more people left, I felt the tension in the room grow between Nate and me. Soon enough, there were just ten or so people with us. My breath stalled when I saw him making his way to me, a small glass of amber liquid in his hands.

"Hi," he said, his smile easy and sexy.

"Hey," I breathed, a peculiar combination of relaxation and anxiousness coming over me. Something about him calmed me and amped me up simultaneously.

"I'm sorry I ambushed you." He looked down at his glass, swirling the liquor in it slightly. "I should have reached out to you and told you I was coming, or even asked if it was all right for me to be here." I smiled, not really knowing how to respond. If he had told me he was coming, I would have been even more nervous than I was before. And even though his presence was distracting, it wasn't unwelcome. Not at all. "I was pretty sure if I called, well, I was sure something would have kept me from coming to you."

I felt my eyebrows draw together and a confused expression pass over my face. "What do you mean?"

"I thought if I called, you'd either tell me you were married or dating someone, or worse, tell me you didn't remember me." He shrugged. "I just thought something would keep me away. After I never heard from you…" His voice trailed off and I could tell he was waiting for me to start explaining myself, to give him some sort of information about my life and how it had changed since we saw each other last.

"Nate, I have to close up the gallery," I said with regret. "But, can we talk about everything? How long are you in town?"

He ran his free hand through his hair and I remembered, instantly and with arousing detail, what his hair felt like between my fingers. "I didn't buy a return ticket," he said, not looking me in the eye.

Excitement shot through me, followed quickly by apprehension.

"Don't worry, I didn't abandon my life to come to LA. I wasn't sure what I would find when I got here, so I wanted to be able to either go right back to the airport and fly home, or stay a few days if things worked out."

"Abandoning life and coming to LA worked out pretty well for me," I said, smiling again. "But we can talk about that too. Tomorrow, maybe? Where are you staying?"

He laughed at my question. "I'm not sure yet. Know any good hotels in the area?"

"Are you serious? You don't have a hotel room somewhere? It's Friday night in LA. The only places you'll be able to find an available room are places you don't want to be."

"Again, I wasn't sure what my plan would be. I've got a rental car and a suitcase."

"I have a spare bedroom. You can stay with me if you'd like." The offer was out of my mouth before the words had even formed in my mind. The majority of my brain was eagerly hoping he would accept, that I would have unlimited access to him until he went home, whenever that would be. The idea of him in my home was causing warmth to spread through me, laced with excitement. But a tiny part of me was screaming, albeit quietly, to not invite practical strangers to my house for an undetermined amount of time.

"Are you sure? I don't want to impose. Honestly, I thought I'd come here and find a good reason to turn around and go home."

"Do you want to go home?" *Please don't say you want to go home.*

His eyes remained on mine, not blinking, and he softly said, "I don't want to go home yet."

"Okay then, you can come stay with me."

Chapter Twenty-One

Present Day

I'd spent the entire drive back to my townhouse wondering who in their right mind invited perfect strangers to stay in their house. Granted, Nate wasn't actually a stranger. I'd been on a date with him once upon a time. And he had travelled all the way to see me and my gallery show. And, if I were being completely honest with myself, after our date two years ago, had I stayed in town, I probably would have slept with him. After that one date, I wasn't sure how much longer I would have waited.

But things happened and my life changed course and in that moment, I was standing on my porch trying to use trembling fingers to unlock my door while I could feel the heat from Nate's body standing deliciously close to me.

"Let me," I heard his deep timbre voice say just before his hand clasped over mine, taking the key from me, and effortlessly unlocking my door. He pushed it open and I turned back to him with a smile.

"Thank you. I'm still a little keyed up from the show." I led him inside, closing the door behind him.

"This is a great place," he said, turning in a slow circle, taking in my home.

"It's not as decorated as I would like it to be, but I've been really busy pretty much since I moved here."

"I see you found time to hang some photos though," he said, still smiling. He'd been smiling practically the entire night and the sight of his smile, easy and sexy all at once, and his body encased in his gorgeous suit, with his eyes and his hair, in my house…well…it was nearly overwhelming.

I laughed a little, trying not to be completely obvious that his mere presence had me nervous and excited. "Hanging photos was the first thing I did. I had pictures up before I had my bed put together." I flipped on the light switch at the entrance of the kitchen and walked to the refrigerator. "Would you like something to drink? I've got a bottle of wine, but that's about it."

"Water would be great." He followed me into the kitchen, his eyes still roaming around my space as if he was looking for clues or information about me based on my living space. He'd be sorely disappointed; my house didn't say much about me besides the fact that I wasn't there a lot.

I opened the fridge, pulled out a bottle of water, and handed it to him. He took it, and then proceeded to unscrew the lid and bring the bottle to his mouth, taking long, thick swallows. It was too much for me to watch, so I let my eyes wander down his front, taking in the way his chest just barely fit into his suit. His arms snuggly filled the sleeves of his jacket as well.

I had to say something to distract myself from everything about him that was enticingly sexy.

"I need to go in to the gallery tomorrow. There will be a lot of people trying to get in contact with me, so it's best I'm there for the day. I'm sorry. I don't want to abandon you."

"Hey, don't worry about me. I'm the one who totally ambushed you."

I turned around quickly, reached into my junk drawer, and pulled out my spare key.

"Why don't you take this," I said, holding out the key for him. "You can leave the house and go do whatever you want and still be able to get back in."

"Are you sure?" he asked, tentatively taking it from me.

"Definitely," I said with an assertive nod. "Here, let me show you to the spare bedroom." I practically jumped away from the counter, making sure I passed by him without letting our bodies brush against each other. Looking at him was torture enough. To accidentally press myself against him and then have to pull myself away again was more than I could handle.

I started up the stairs and could feel the heat of his gaze on my backside. I knew, without a doubt, my red silken dress made my ass look outstanding. I'd purchased it mainly for that exact reason. My body was alight with the idea of him taking in the sight of it. I simply couldn't handle the tension, couldn't deal with him and me, alone, in my house, with me in my 'come and fuck me' dress and him in a 'you know you want to come and fuck me' suit. It was just *too much*.

"Here you are," I said, my voice too breathy, chest rising and falling too quickly. My arm, out slightly, was motioning toward the open door, but he didn't go in. No, he stopped when his body was right in front of mine. My eyes, naturally meeting his chest, followed his tie up to his face, and when our eyes met, he didn't look away.

"Looks fantastic."

He was so close I could smell him. When his fingertips wrapped around my hip, my mouth fell open and a tiny whimper escaped me. His grip tightened and he pulled me even closer to him. I had to tilt my head even farther to keep my eyes trained on his.

"You look fantastic. You *feel* fantastic. Lyn, Christ, I've been thinking about you for two years."

His words sent a slight panic through me. He'd been thinking about me for two years? Flattering as it was, it was also a little overwhelming. I'd compartmentalized my old life when I drove out of town. I'd made a conscious decision to leave it all behind. Sure, I still spoke to the kids, and Shelby was still my friend, but it was almost necessary for me to start over to move forward. He must have sensed my unease because his intent stare turned into a questioning look.

"I'm sorry, I'm not trying to make you uncomfortable," he said, taking a small step backward, his hand leaving my hip, my body shouting at me not to let him back away. I could feel the pull to keep his hand on me, to reach up and pull on his jacket so our bodies were pressed together, but I ignored the impulse and took my own step backward.

"It's been a really long day and I think I just need to go to bed."

He was quiet for a moment, but then he smiled.

"Will you have dinner with me tomorrow night?"

I let out a relieved sigh at his request. I could do dinner. I wasn't sure I could do his hands on me in the dark hallway. I wasn't ready for that yet.

"I'd love to do dinner." I smiled at him, still a little unbelieving that he was even there, but then I went into hostess mode. "There's a bathroom at the end of the hall, and there should be towels in the cupboard next to the sink. Feel free to help yourself to anything in the kitchen, although, there's not much there." I laughed, realizing I was ill prepared for company. Then I laughed because I hadn't been expecting company, but there he was. And even though he made me nervous, I was touched he'd come. "Thank you for coming to my show, Nate. It was truly a surprise."

He only nodded, then said a soft, "Goodnight, Evelyn."

I gave him a small wave, then turned and headed down the hall to my bedroom. I closed the door softly, and then leaned back against it. Nate, for however long he decided to stay, was going to give my nerves and my heart a run for their money.

Chapter Twenty-Two

Present Day

The next morning, I tried to be as quiet as possible when getting ready to leave for the gallery. I was used to traipsing through the house in my pajamas, not paying attention to noises or floorboard creaks. But with Nate asleep upstairs, I was trying to be as mouse-like as I could, quietly scurrying through the kitchen to make my coffee and bagel, then get to work.

I was telling myself I didn't want to disturb him, but in reality, I was pretty sure I just wanted to avoid an awkward situation. And all that really meant was that I didn't want to see him comfortable, sleepy, in his pajamas with bed head in my house. How could I ever love my house again after seeing him like that? It would never be the same. It would always be lacking. So I had to make it out of the house before he woke up.

I had packed my travel mug, I had my bagel, and I was just leaving him a note when I heard his door open and his footsteps start down the stairs.

"Shit," I whispered to myself, looking toward the door to gauge whether I could make a clean getaway before he appeared. I quickly realized, unless I wanted him to see me dashing for the front door as if the kitchen were on fire, I would have to face him. I grabbed my bagel and took a bite, trying to appear comfortable in my own kitchen, and probably failing spectacularly.

He came around the corner and I knew I was doomed. He looked exactly as I was afraid he would. Sexy. Rumpled. Sleepy. Lickable. Damn.

"Morning," he said in a rough, sleepy voice.

Damn.

"Morning," I said, forgetting I had bagel in my mouth, crumbs shooting forward and landing on the floor. I covered my mouth quickly, rolling my eyes at my own ineptitude. "Morning," I tried again once my mouth was empty.

He laughed and pointed toward the coffee pot. "Do you mind if I grab a cup?"

"No, no. Please, help yourself." I watched as he opened a cupboard, guessing their location correctly on the first try, and pulled out a mug. He poured the coffee while I stared at his broad shoulders. The t-shirt he was wearing was just tight enough to show his muscles flexing in a delicious way.

He turned back around and I suddenly found my shoes extremely interesting, moving my eyes away from his body as fast as I could.

"You're up early," I managed. "Especially considering the time change."

"I'm used to getting up early in my line of work. Generally, you want to get a lot of the work done before the day gets too hot. Also," he said, a playful smirk spreading over his mouth, "I heard you trying to be quiet." He laughed a little as he brought the mug to his lips, and then sipped. "You whisper to yourself. Did you know that?"

"I do not," I cried, but tried to think back over my morning to see if I could recall whispering anything.

"You do, actually. You narrate your morning. Or, at least you did today. I heard you tell yourself it was time for a shower and also when it was time for coffee." His smile grew wider and he crossed his legs at the ankle as he leaned back against the counter. "I thought it was adorable."

This was exactly what I was afraid of – him, being cute, comfortable, and cozy in my house. No, this wouldn't do. "Well, I'm going to go whisper to myself at work then," I said, my voice strained. I was caught somewhere between completely aroused and extremely uncomfortable *because* I was aroused. "Do you need anything before I take off?"

"I just need to know what time you'll be home to make plans for dinner."

"I'll be back around five. Again, help yourself to anything in the house. I'm sorry I have to be gone, but today will be a busy day because of the show yesterday. I'm expecting lots of phone calls and emails and things of that nature." I said all this while backing up toward the door. I kept my eyes on him, talking to fill the space between us, half-afraid that if I didn't slowly escape, he was going to eat me alive.

"See you at five," he said, his smirky, sexy grin still plastered across his face.

I turned abruptly and quickly opened and closed the door, breathing out a sigh of relief when I'd made it outside.

"Make it through the workday and then dinner and everything will be okay," I whispered to myself as I walked toward my car.

The day passed at a fast pace. As I expected, I was inundated with phone calls and emails, all contacts who'd been at the show the night before wanting to make plans for future projects. Sylvia had been nice enough to come in on her day off to assist me, and around ten a.m. came in to my office with a wonderfully large cup of coffee.

"You're the best assistant I've ever had." She handed me the cup and I noticed there was extra ice – just the way I liked it.

"I'm the only assistant you've ever had."

"That's irrelevant." I took a sip of the too sweet coffee concoction I loved and then let out a happy sigh. "Okay, now that I'm caffeinated, what's the word?"

"The word is you made thirty thousand dollars last night."

"Shut the fucupcakes." My mouth gaped open.

"I will *not*. I'm not even sure I know what that means."

"Thirty thousand dollars? As in, one thousand dollars thirty times over? As in one dollar thirty thousand times?"

Sylvia laughed as I gaped.

"That's exactly what I said. Thirty thousand dollars. That's a lot of money for one show, Evie." She raised her eyebrows at me. She was pretty much telling me 'I told you so,' without saying the words. I gave her the satisfaction anyhow.

"You were right," I breathed, leaning all the way back in my chair.

"With that kind of money, you can pay someone to manage the gallery and spend more time taking photographs," she said, her voice soft and easy, as if she was afraid I wouldn't like her suggestion.

My eyes grew wide.

"I can buy a better camera."

Again, Sylvia laughed. "Yes, you sure can."

"I can't believe it." Even to me, my voice sounded far away. Sure, I'd priced all the photos. I knew what they all would go for, but I'd never allowed myself to imagine a scenario where I made my old yearly salary in one night. That didn't happen to people like me.

"This is the next step in your career, Evelyn. And it's a big step. You've got enough money to take your business to the next level, and you've got jobs now lined up for months that are going to pay you *really* well." She paused and looked at me for a moment, a thoughtful expression across her face. "All the hard work you've done since you got here is paying off. You did it."

"I did it." My voice was wistful and unbelieving. For one moment, I forgot about the man waiting for me back at my house.

"So, what happened with you and that ridiculously handsome man you left with last night?"

"He's an old friend," I said, trying to avoid talking about him because I had no idea what I was supposed to say. I couldn't very well tell her that, aside from Devon, he'd been the only man in almost a decade to turn me inside out.

Then, a smile spread over my face when I realized that thinking about Devon no longer turned me inside out. In fact, the only thing I felt when I thought of him was fondness. I let out a breath, glad to have confirmation that moving to LA, changing my life, and going in a totally random yet wonderful direction had been the best decision I'd ever made.

"We went out on one date a few years ago." I decided to elaborate, and took great pleasure in the fact that just the one sentence about Nate brought on the butterflies. "But I wasn't in the right mindset to start dating someone. When I left to come to LA, I lost touch with him."

"So," Sylvia started, a confused look on her face, "how did he know about your show last night?"

I shrugged. "He said he saw it on my website."

Her eyes went wide.

"He's been cyberstalking you?"

"He's not stalking me," I said, defending him. "He's not a creeper."

"No, that's not what I meant. I just meant he's been investigating. Gathering information. It's cute when guys do that. Unless they're creepers."

I nodded, looking at the clock, and then realized I'd been looking at the clock often. It was quite a while still until five o'clock.

"So, you didn't know he was coming to the show?"

"No. I hadn't spoken with him since before I left. I came to LA and changed my phone number. It was a complete surprise."

"A good surprise?" Her voice sparkled exactly like the smile on her face. Her eyebrows were high, as were the corners of her mouth.

"I'm not sure yet, but I'm hoping so." That was, possibly, the most honest sentence I'd uttered all day. I shook my head, trying to break apart all the thoughts of Nate flooding my brain. I had work to do. "Let's get back to work. I'll keep returning phone calls, if you can work through my email."

"Done. I'll step out in about an hour to get you lunch."

"You know what, Sylvia? I think I'll go out myself. I need to make a stop somewhere."

"Okay," she said, her voice knowing and singsong.

Three hours later, I found myself inside Agent Provocateur, thinking perhaps I was in over my head. I didn't know for sure what was going to happen that evening between Nate and me, but I knew what I *wanted* to happen. I knew it involved removing clothing. I also knew I hadn't purchased new lingerie in years. This occasion definitely called for something black, lacy, and new.

I'd found the perfect set, something I would feel comfortable wearing under my clothes. It was simple and classic. Almost innocent. If lingerie could be innocent and sexy at the same time, that's what I bought. I also found myself, thinking about the enormous paycheck coming my way, purchasing a week's worth of new panties. Some innocent, some not. But simply knowing I had them made me feel more feminine than I had in a long time.

On the drive home that evening, my heartbeat thrummed through my veins and my belly flipped with the thought of going out to dinner with Nate.

His car was still parked at the curb in front of my house, but all the curtains were closed. I opened the door and walked in, my breath caught, eyes wide.

Votive candles were placed randomly throughout the bottom floor, casting a romantic light throughout the house. Soft music was playing, but it was wordless, beautiful piano pieces. I walked slowly through the house, wondering where I would find Nate, my heart pounding. I found him standing at the stove, cooking. His back was to me, and I wasn't sure he knew I was there, so I took a moment to drink him in.

He had on jeans that clung to every curve of his thighs and ass, leading down to what appeared to be cowboy boots. His black shirt had long sleeves, but they were rolled up, allowing me to see his forearm working as he stirred whatever was making my house smell delicious. His dark hair was barely dusting over the collar of his shirt and I was a little upset I couldn't see a bit of skin there.

"I can feel your eyes on me, Lyn."

His voice startled me, and heat spread over my cheeks with the realization I'd been caught. He obviously liked it though; he let me stand there and ogle him for a good half minute before interrupting me.

"It's not every day I come home to a handsome man cooking in my kitchen."

He turned his head to look at me, his brown eyes captivating against the black of his shirt. Then I noticed his shirt was a button-up, and it was tucked in. He was dressed up. He looked fresh, all but for the stubble on his chin, which I never wanted to see him without. In fact, I wanted to feel it up against my skin: on my fingers, my mouth, my thighs.

A new heat ran through me with the thoughts of his stubble against my skin.

"I'm not going to pretend like that statement doesn't make me happy," he said with an easy smile. "Dinner will be ready in about thirty minutes if you want to relax for a little while."

I looked down at my jeans, flip-flops, and t-shirt and decided to change. "I'm just going to go freshen up," I announced. But before I made it out of the kitchen, I stopped and asked him a question. "I had no food in my house. What in the world are you cooking?"

"I went to the store. Don't worry about anything. Tonight we're celebrating."

"Okay," I replied, my voice a whisper. He winked at me and I nearly died, every muscle in my body contracting.

The next thirty minutes was spent in a dizzying dash around my master suite. I'd never been so glad to have an attached bathroom, as I was running in and out, trying on different dresses, trying to decide exactly how I wanted the evening to play out.

In the end, with my hair smoothed out, fresh makeup applied, and new underwear on, I decided to take a cue from Nate and wore a black dress just a notch or two up from casual. It wasn't fancy, but it wasn't something you'd put on to go to the grocery store, either. It was, perhaps, a third date dress. The one you'd wear to let a man know you wanted him to take you *out* of it.

I also put on high heels, even though I was only walking down the stairs to my own kitchen. The dress looked silly with anything but four-inch stilettos.

When I finally thought I'd made myself presentable, exactly twenty-eight minutes after I'd come upstairs, I took a deep breath and returned to Nate.

When I entered the kitchen, I marveled again at how gorgeous he looked, but was taken by surprise at his response to me. He looked stunned. He stopped, mid-stride, kitchen towel draped over his shoulder, pan in hand, and he took me in.

I tried not to shrivel under his stare and instead, tried to blossom. I pushed my shoulders back, lifted my chin, and pretended that I was totally comfortable with his eyes roving over me. I wanted his eyes there, but I'd never been so bold as to stand tall and let a man drink me in.

"It smells great, whatever you're making," I said, trying to break the tension building in our silence.

"Seafood Alfredo. I hope you like shrimp and scallops."

"I do," I said, pleased with his choice of meals. "Where'd you learn how to cook something like that?"

"Here," he said quickly, "sit down and I'll get you some wine. I bought white to go with the meal, I hope that's all right?"

"I love white wine," I said as I sat at my own table, but feeling like I was at a restaurant.

"Before I went to college, my mom taught me how to make seven meals." He opened the fridge and produced a bottle of wine, then moved to open it while he continued his story. "She figured if I could cook one meal for each day of the week, I might not starve."

"Did your mom know you'd be using your acquired skills to woo women?" I said the words quickly, before I could stop my mouth from spewing them out, and then panicked when I realized I'd insinuated there was more to this dinner than just two people sharing a meal.

A wicked smile grew on his face and I was fixated on it. He walked to the table with the wine bottle and two glasses in his hands. Placing one glass in front of me, and one in front of his spot, he turned back to me and poured the wine for me.

"If my mother knew you, I'm sure she'd approve of my attempt to woo you, cooking included."

"Oh," was all I could say as I brought the now full glass of wine to my lips. I took a sip of the cool, crisp white wine, loving the taste. "This is quite good," I said, setting the glass down.

"I'm glad you like it." He moved back into the kitchen and the next few minutes passed with silence as I watched him move around in my house as if he'd lived there with me for the last two years. He never once asked me where something was, or if I had a certain ingredient or utensil he was looking for. He'd seemed to have everything memorized.

Finally, he turned toward the table with a plate in each hand and placed one in front of me, then made his way to the other side of the table, sitting down with his plate in front of him. The meal looked as good as it smelled and suddenly, I was starving.

"I hope you like it," he said, his voice sounding a little shy and hopeful.

I took a bite and had to hold back a moan. It was delicious. I was a fan of Italian food, always had been, and that was the best seafood Alfredo I'd ever had.

"Wow. This is amazing," I said before piling more into my mouth, trying to walk the line between gross-food-shoveling and being the girl who wasn't afraid to eat on a date. "What else did your mom teach you to make?"

"If you'd like to know, you're going to have to go out on six more dates with me, at the very least."

"Oh, really? I see how it is," I said through laughter.

"My mother didn't raise a fool." He smiled right before he wrapped his lips around the tines of his fork and I nearly choked on my shrimp. I'd never considered eating an arousing activity, but I'd be damned if Nate's lips wrapping around something wasn't the sexiest thing I'd seen in a while.

"What did you tell your mom about coming to California? Did she think you were crazy?"

"No. I didn't tell her. I didn't tell anyone, actually."

"Oh," I replied. His answer had deflated me a little.

"I guess I was afraid that if I told my mom about how I was going after a woman, she'd get her hopes up. I didn't know how you were going to react to me showing up. I didn't want to have to go home and tell her I'd gotten my very first restraining order."

I couldn't help but laugh and thought he had a point.

"Nate," I started, but was stopped when he held up his hand.

"Whatever you're going to say, let's just wait until after dinner. I want to sit here, with you, in that amazing dress, and pretend like this is the dinner date we never got." The butterflies in my stomach took flight at his words, and the pounding of my pulse thrummed through my veins. I was in full swoon mode. "I promise whatever you want to talk about after dinner is fair game." It was a statement, but it was pleading. I nodded, then took another bite, conceding. "So," he said with a sigh, "how was work today."

"Great," I said, trying to sound nonchalant. "I made thirty thousand dollars." I said the words like they meant nothing, and then took another bite. I was aware he'd stopped moving, his fork stalled halfway to his mouth, eyes wide.

"I'm sorry," he said, coughing a little, putting his fork down, and taking a sip of his wine. "Did you just say you made thirty thousand dollars?"

I nodded quickly, too excited to hide it any longer. "I'm sorry, it's probably bad form to talk about money on a date, but I really wanted to tell someone." I took a breath and continued. "I made thirty thousand dollars at my show last night." I was nearly bouncing up and down in my chair, thankful to have someone to share the news with.

"Holy shit." His face was blank and his eyes were like saucers. "Holy shit, Lyn. That's amazing."

"It's really exciting," I agreed. "I'm not sure I've really grasped it yet, but I know I'm really lucky. A lot of people can't make it as a professional photographer and, well, I just secured my job for at least another six months. I feel really blessed."

"You're being humble, which is cute, but you're really talented." His words were insistent and genuine. I didn't get the feeling he was trying to be flattering, it felt like he was telling me the truth.

"Thank you." I blushed again.

"Wow, okay, now we've really got something to celebrate. I didn't get any champagne though. I thought we'd maybe gotten enough champagne last night."

"I don't need champagne," I said a little more dreamily than I had planned. My eyes were glued to his and I was already warm from the wine, and more than a little tipsy from his praise. I didn't need champagne. I needed exactly what he was giving me.

"So," I said, kicking off my heels and folding my feet under me on the couch where I'd just sat down, "let's talk about you being in California."

"Okay," he agreed. He was sitting on the opposite side of the couch, but it was a small couch, so he was only a few inches from me. The hand closest to me held his wine glass, and his other arm was stretched out along the back of the couch, draping down the arm. I looked at him over the rim of my own wine glass, taking in the way his shirt was stretched over his bicep. I couldn't be sure, but I was almost positive his muscles had grown in the two years since I'd seen him.

I wanted to reach over and undo a few of his buttons, maybe even all of them. He'd been eyeing me all through dinner and I knew he wanted to touch me too, but we were still going to talk. I got the feeling nothing would progress between us until that happened. And, honestly, I was okay with that. Things between us weren't exactly simple and the way I'd left him hanging, without even a goodbye, deserved an explanation. Especially since he'd come all the way to California to see me.

"The last time I saw you, before you left, you were in a rough spot emotionally."

I nodded, remembering our last encounter vividly. He'd been heartbreakingly sweet and very understanding.

"That day, it took everything I had in me not to wrap my arms around you and tell you how amazing I thought you were, and how dumb I thought Devon was for playing whatever role he'd played in your unhappiness."

I opened my mouth to argue with him, but then closed it because, well, he had a point. Devon had played a role in my unhappiness. I'd long since forgiven him, and myself, for the years of torture we'd put ourselves through. It was over now.

"It didn't feel right though." He brought his free hand up and threaded it through his hair, showing he was frustrated, or frustrated by a memory, perhaps. "I knew if I tried to swoop in and fix you, you wouldn't ever be mine." His eyes darted over to me, and I tried to keep my expression even. I didn't want him to know his words had opened me up. "Not really, anyway," he continued. "We might have hooked up, and we might have tried to date, but if we got together when you were still healing from something else, we would have been doomed." He took in a deep breath and then exhaled it out. "So, I did the only thing I thought was right. I gave you time." He shifted on the couch, turning in to face me a little more. I was glad to have more of his handsome face to look at.

"You know that saying, if you love something, let it go and then if it comes back to you, you'll know it belongs to you?"

I nodded.

"Well, I was trusting the wisdom of that stupid saying. I was hoping if I gave you space, you'd come back to me."

"Nate…"

"So, I guess what I'm saying is," he continued, talking over me, "I came to California to find out why you never came back to me." His eyes came up to meet mine and he looked so gentle and curious, with just the tiniest twinge of hurting there in the brown depths of his eyes. "I thought for a while that it was because you were with Devon. But then I found you on your website, and your name was still the same, and a small part of me held out hope." He stopped and shook his head. "I sound like a crazy stalker."

"No, Nate, it's fine. I can explain." I leaned forward and placed my wine glass on the coffee table, then moved so I was facing him fully, sitting with my legs under me. I met his eyes and smiled because I could see he was anxious about what I was going to tell him. The butterflies in my belly thought it was adorable.

"I never came back to you because of something you said to me that day."

His eyes grew wide and then confused. I could tell his brain was sifting through everything he'd said to me so long ago, trying to pinpoint what he'd said to make me run away.

"You put that alert on my phone and you told me, when it came up, to make a decision. You said you'd be okay with whatever I chose as long as it was my first choice."

I reached out and took his hand because I could see him as he took in my words, watching as he realized what they implied.

"And I wasn't your first choice."

"No, Nate, you weren't." I rubbed both of my thumbs over the top of his hand, loving the moment but also wanting to get past it because I could tell it was upsetting him. "My first choice was me."

I powered on because I had so much to say to him that I couldn't risk him butting in.

"For so long, I'd been everyone's second choice, just like you said. Then, you came along and you showed me what it was like to have someone see me first, to see me and make no qualms about wanting me. You were sweet and nice and *such* a great kisser." I blushed a little, but then linked my fingers with his, smiling when he didn't pull away, but gave me a gentle squeeze.

"I wanted all of that – wanted you – but knew it wasn't the right time or the right situation. That next night, after we talked, I went to Devon and we finally both ended everything between us. Not that there ever was anything, really. But we just couldn't do it anymore. He needed to move on with his life, and I needed to start mine, because I never really had. So, I left. I wanted to reach out to you, but I knew it wasn't right. I couldn't make you sit around and wait for me, especially when I had planned, from that moment on, to focus on me, on what I needed. And the last thing I needed back then was a man." I smiled at him, hoping he understood.

"But never in a million years did I expect to see you again, Nate. And I'll never be able to explain the way it felt when I saw you last night. It means so much to me that you came – no matter the reason behind it – it's the best thing anyone has ever done for me."

Our eyes were locked and his looked slightly worried and troubled.

I watched as his free hand slowly came across his body, gently finding my cheek, his fingers sliding back into my hair just slightly.

"And what about now, Lyn?" My eyes automatically closed at the feeling of his fingers floating over my skin. "Are you still your own first choice?" His words were whispered, and his hand put gentle pressure on the back of my neck, pulling me closer to him. His hand, which was clasped in mine, pulled loose and traveled slowly up the side of my thigh.

I nodded. "I have to be. No one else is going to put me first if I don't."

"What if," he said, his voice wavering just a little as his hand slid even higher up my thigh, then rounding up over my ass. "What if I told you I was interested in ranking a close second?"

"I'd say," I breathed, our faces only inches apart, "the position is all yours."

Our lips met in the slowest collision. When his mouth was finally pressed up against mine, I could do nothing to keep the relief from coming out of me in a moan. Granted, I never thought I'd see the man again, but that didn't mean I hadn't spent nights thinking about kissing him under that waterfall.

I'd missed kissing, sure. But I hadn't realized until that moment how much I missed kissing *him*.

Then, suddenly, we lost ourselves. I was climbing over him, straddling his legs, pulling his mouth to mine as if I could fuse him to me. His hands were roaming all over me, groping me over my dress, groaning as he squeezed the fleshiest parts of me.

After minutes of making out like teenagers, I felt him pull away and my lips felt like the rug had been pulled out from under them.

"I'm sorry, Lyn, I didn't mean to attack you like that. God, I'm sorry. You must think I'm an ass. I've been thinking about you for two years now, and all day today, and then you came downstairs in this dress," he said the last words as he ran his hands over my ass again. "I'm sorry," he said again, removing his hands.

"Nate, I climbed on your lap," I laughed. "You're not the only one who wants this." I bent low again, trying to coax his lips to come back to mine, but he pulled back again.

"I don't want you to think this is why I came here."

With those words, I pulled back even farther, trying to read him, trying to understand his hesitation.

"I've been thinking about you for so long. I dated a few women, but none of them compared to the woman I took on that hike, who lit up when a camera was in her hands. Who loved two children so dearly who weren't even hers. Who missed her best friend but did everything she could to carry out her last wishes. This isn't about sex, Lyn. Although, I can't deny that I want you. But, for me at least, this is way more than just sex."

My eyes darted back and forth between his, looking for some indication as to how to take his words.

"So, you *don't* want to do this?" I asked, my eyes drifting down to where our bodies were connected, yet still clothed. I could tell part of him wanted to continue.

His hands came to rest near my knees, a much safer place than my ass had been. I felt my heart deflate a little at the movement. I wanted him. I found myself unwilling to deny that fact, and also proud of myself for not shying away from sex. I'd spent a good portion of my life denying myself the pleasure of sharing my body with a man because the man was Devon.

"God, I want you, Lyn," he said, squeezing my legs with his hands. "But I want more than just sex."

"What more do you want?" I asked breathily, my heart rate spiking.

"I want you. I want us. We never got a real shot the first time – nothing was right then. But I want a second chance."

"You live very far away," I whispered, moving my hands up his arms, loving the way the cotton of his shirt slid along my skin. I wasn't denying him, not in the slightest, I just wanted to make sure he knew what he was getting into.

"There are planes, and Skype, and FaceTime. It'll be difficult, but it's got to be better than the last two years of only imagining what it would be like."

"It's got to be only me, Nate." My voice was suddenly serious. I hadn't meant for it to sound cold, but when the words escaped from me, they needed attention. "I won't be with someone who is also seeing someone else. I want to make someone, you, my priority, and I want that in return."

"You want me all to yourself?" he asked, a smile now spreading over his previously troubled face.

"Yes," I whispered. "And for the last two years I've been working so hard on myself, I want to give you all of that as well."

"I get the new and improved Lyn?" His smile grew even wider.

"If you'll have me."

Then, for just one moment, I was struck with panic. I panicked because for most of my life the person I loved wouldn't have me, and the one person who would, never knew the real me. This was the first time I'd come, essentially bare, stripped down and *real*, and offered myself to someone. And he could easily say no.

My breath was stalled, my skin vibrating with the agony of waiting for his response.

"I won't just have you," he said, bringing his hands to the back of my neck and pulling me down to his mouth, "I'll keep you this time."

I smiled as our mouths met, and the butterflies in my belly took flight again.

My smile quickly disappeared when Nate's arms wrapped tightly around my waist, lifted me, and lay me on the couch, his body fitting over mine. One foot was on the floor, his other knee wedged between my body and the back of the couch, keeping the brunt of his weight off me. But I could feel the pressure and the heat pressing me down into the couch, and it was wonderful. I wanted to feel everything: every breath he took, every move he made. I wanted to be fully present.

We kissed and my hands started to wander, wanting to familiarize themselves with him, wanting to touch and feel him. I managed to squeeze them between us and started working on the buttons of his black shirt. I pulled his shirt free from his pants at the same time, slowly peeling back the only layer of fabric between my hands and his chest.

He shrugged the shirt free after I'd released the last button and tossed it across the room, then his mouth found mine again. I wasted no time letting my hands roam freely over the chest I'd only imagined, in great detail, both two years ago and then all day today. And admittedly, more than a few days in between.

My fingers made their way down the defined valley that ran between his pectorals, then felt the rigid bumps of his abdominals, and somewhere inside my brain a very girly voice was screaming and hyperventilating about the V I felt running up the sides of his hips as my hands smoothed their way to his back.

The entire time I was caressing the muscular landscape of his top half, his bottom half was inching closer to mine. His foot had come off the floor and my legs instantly wound themselves around his hips.

"Lyn, God, I've wanted this for so long," he said before dipping back down and sucking my lower lip into his mouth.

I didn't have a response. Or, not one I would give him. He couldn't fathom how long I'd been waiting for someone to want *me*, to chase *me*. Nate was here, in my home, where he'd traveled a long way to be, and he wanted nothing more than *me* in that moment. His hands moved over my body and I knew, without one single doubt, no one else was on his mind.

And that, to me, was almost the best part. Almost.

My favorite part of our encounter kept being replaced by the moment that followed directly after it.

I loved the way his hands threaded themselves through my hair.

I loved the way he groaned a little in the back of his throat when I ran my fingernails down his biceps.

I loved the way my hips tilted to meet his, to bring him closer to me than any other man had been in so long.

I loved how, I knew, even if everything between us was brand new, I'd never given anyone what I was about to give Nate, which was all of me.

"I need you in a bed," he said suddenly, lifting off of me and taking my hand. I was pulled to my feet and led up the stairs, all the while watching the way each muscle in his back worked with those around it, a synchronized orchestra of sorts. It was hypnotizing and glorious. He pulled me into my room, didn't bother to close the door, and then started with the kissing again.

The man could kiss.

He didn't just kiss with his mouth. No. He kissed with his hands all over my body, with his breath panting heavily on my face, and with the most demanding and gifted tongue I'd ever encountered.

As he kissed me, his hands bunched up my dress, pulling it up higher and higher, until he was fisting the length of it in his hands at my thighs. He pulled his mouth from mine, stepped away slowly, and then inched the dress up and over my head. I closed my eyes, not able to handle the magnitude of the situation. I wasn't sure I could handle it if the first thing I saw on his face when he took in my naked body was anything less than the bulgy cartoon eyes I remembered from Saturday mornings. No. I didn't want to risk witnessing his disappointment.

I felt the fabric brush over my face. I lowered my arms to my sides, and then I stood in my bedroom in complete silence.

"Open your eyes, Lyn." Nate's voice was low and deep and rumbled through me. My eyes opened at his command and I was relieved to see what I imagined the opposite of disappointment would look like. He looked excited. His eyes were taking in each and every part of my body before rapidly moving on to the next. His fingers were moving back and forth just slightly as if they were itching to touch me. I watched as his chest expanded and fell in time with his breaths, which were coming fast.

When his eyes finally landed on me, he spoke.

"You're so much more than I could have ever imagined."

Without any thought, I looked down at my body, wondering what he saw that impressed him so. I, admittedly, had a critical eye. It was an occupational hazard. I saw shadows where there shouldn't be shadows, and dimples where I hated seeing dimples. I saw pointy angles were others might only see elbows. The point was, whatever I was afraid Nate was seeing, he obviously wasn't.

Thank you, Agent Provocateur.

He took the two steps back to me and gently placed his hands on my hips, his rough, calloused hands sending shivers all over me. One arm moved to wrap around my waist, lifting me off my feet, and my legs instinctively wrapped around his middle. He walked us to the bed, crawled across it, with my body still clinging to his, and then he gently lay me down. My hands immediately went to the closure of his jeans, pulling them open, button by button.

We were rapidly losing the few remaining pieces of clothing between us, but when we were both bare, skin to skin, my body seemed magnetized to his. I'd never experienced such a complete feeling as I did pressed up against Nate, feeling his hands wander over me, claim me, need me. It was intoxicating and beautiful all at the same time. Intoxicating because I wanted to die in that feeling, wanted to end on such a high that I'd never have to float back down, but beautiful because I knew he was just as high as I was. This wasn't one-sided. This wasn't forbidden or soul crushing. This was his body *finally* connecting with mine. And it was beautiful.

Epilogue

Six Months Later

"Are you nervous?" Nate's voice pulled my gaze from the door at the end of the path.

"I shouldn't be, but I am." My answer was honest and raw, exactly the way I was with Nate all the time. The last six months had been an awakening to reality. Suddenly, I was in a functional, adult relationship where I got out whatever I put in. It was astounding.

If I was open, honest, and real with Nate, he gave it back to me. If I told him I loved him, he always loved me back. If I went out of my way to show him I was thinking of him, he made damn sure I knew he was thinking of me too. Six months in and I couldn't imagine not being with him for the rest of my life, and because I was open and honest with him about it, I knew he felt the same way.

I didn't miss the angst at all.

"This is going to be one of the best days of your life," he whispered against the shell of my ear and on cue, I melted. I melted because he knew what the day meant to me, knew that it would be one of the best days of my life.

We made it to the door, hand in hand, and with a deep breath, I reached up and pushed the doorbell.

Within moments, I heard the sounds from inside the house that made tears form in my eyes and a lump lodge in my throat. Nate squeezed my hand, rubbing his thumb along my wrist.

The door opened and the world stopped spinning.

"Auntie Evie!" I knelt to the ground and small arms were wrapping around me.

Ruby and Jax smelled exactly the same. They felt exactly the same in my arms, but they did not look exactly the same.

Even though I would have stayed on the porch and let them hug me forever, I pulled back, leaving one of my hands on a shoulder of each of them. I took them in, smiling as tears streamed down my face.

"Oh, my gosh, look at you two," I said, trying to sound excited and not like I was sad, even though I was sobbing.

Ruby's brown hair was a little lighter, but still curly, and very long. She was ten now, and looked very much like a ten year old, perhaps even twelve. She had more freckles and tanner skin, which made sense living in Florida.

Of the two of them, Jaxy had changed more, but that was more because he'd gone from being practically a baby, to becoming a small child. It was amazing, but it was also sad. He was almost eight, his hair was buzzed short, and he was missing a front tooth. His baby voice was gone and his boyhood voice had taken its place.

They both looked at me as if I was the most amazing person they'd ever met and my heart could just barely take it.

"Okay, kids, let's take a step back, and let Aunt Evie into the house."

I heard his voice for the first time in almost three years. In all the time I'd been away, we'd never spoken on the phone. We'd only corresponded through email or text message, and any time my phone rang with his name on the caller ID, I knew it would be Ruby or Jax calling to chat. Never Devon.

His voice caused a few things to happen. First, I smiled. He sounded exactly the same, even if his children didn't, and that was comforting. Second, my eyes found him. I looked up at him and thought he looked great.

Just.

Great.

He did not look like the man I'd spend the rest of my life loving, and he did not look like the man I'd spent half my life pining over. He just looked like Devon. Third, I felt Nate's hand slide into mine and give it another squeeze. This caused the color in my world to brighten a little.

Nate wasn't trying to claim me, or give Devon some sort of signal that I was his. No. In true Nate style, he was showing me he was there supporting me.

"Nate, good to see you again." Devon said as he reached out a hand, wearing a genuine smile.

"Likewise," Nate replied with a matching smile.

"Evie, we've been waiting all day. The kids were nearly losing their minds with excitement." He stepped forward and opened his arms to me. Without hesitation, I met him with a few steps of my own and gave him a hug, my hands open and splayed on his back. He smelled the same, felt the same, even looked unaffected by time, not aging much since I'd seen him last. But everything else was different.

My heart didn't sputter when his arms wrapped around me, my breath didn't steal away, and there was no electric jolt that used to shoot through me at his touch. I was unaffected, other than the warmth that spread through me as I realized all of this.

I loved Nate. More than I ever thought I could love anyone. In six months we'd been able to build a stable and wonderful relationship, even with us living in different states. He was the most patient, loving, giving partner I could have ever dreamed up. But I would have been lying to myself if I said I hadn't been worried about how I would react to seeing Devon.

The last time we saw each other we were discussing how we'd spent ten years wanting to be with each other. Ten years is a long time. Much longer than six months. My worst fear had been that I would see Devon and something I'd worked so hard to fix over the last two years would instantly break and, in turn, I'd end up breaking Nate.

Hurting Nate was the one thing I never wanted to do. Intentionally or otherwise. So when no buried feelings started clawing their way up and through me, I realized, finally, that Devon was in my past.

Only the socially accepted rules of decorum stopped me from throwing my hands in the air and shouting, "I have no romantic feelings for you!" It was the biggest sigh of relief I'd ever let out.

Devon pulled away and held out a hand, motioning into his house. "Please, come in."

Without thinking much about it, one hand reached back and took Nate's, and then Ruby's hand was in the other.

"I can't wait to show you my room, Auntie Evie. Dad let me choose my own paint color when we bought this house and I chose this awesome, neon blue color."

"Wow, sounds exciting."

"Mine's green," Jaxy said from beside his sister.

I let the children lead me to the back of the house, leaving Nate and Devon in the living room. I worried for just a moment about the two of them alone together, but when I heard Devon's relaxed and friendly voice offer Nate a beer, I let all my anxiety go.

The next half hour was spent getting to know my Ruby and Jax again. Ruby's room was definitely a neon blue. I was honored to see a magazine story about my photography cut out and taped to her wall. I remembered being her age, and only really important things were taped to the wall, so I took it as a huge compliment. Her room was definitely that of a girl just barely creeping up on her teen years. She had a poster of a somewhat young-looking boy band, a beanbag chair, and pushed into the back of her closet I could see a large Barbie house that looked like it hadn't been played with in a while.

She had a white four-poster bed with gauzy fabric draping down the sides, which looked amazingly romantic. I knew that in a few years she'd appreciate the bed a little more than she probably did now.

Jaxy's room was a disaster, but that didn't stop him from showing it to me with pride. His walls were indeed green, but I couldn't have told you which color the carpet was, as it was covered from one end to the other in what could only be described as the litter of childhood. I stood in the doorway as he ran around and showed me all his "awesome toys."

Gone were the trains and stuffed animals I'd left him with; they were replaced with nerf guns, a handheld gaming system, and spy toys. Jaxy had gone and grown up while we were apart.

It was thirty minutes of me just watching them, memorizing their new faces and their new facial expressions. I hardly said a word, but enjoyed listening to them tell me all about who they'd become in the last two years.

Suddenly, like a tidal wave, I became aware that their mother was still missing the wonderful children they'd become. I tried to keep it together, not wanting to cry in front of them, and instead, I asked where their bathroom was.

I disappeared down the hallway, found the bathroom, and locked myself in.

Even though I'd spent two years trying to get over Devon, I had never gotten over Olivia. She was, and would always be, the very best friend I ever had. It was easier to push back all the sadness losing her caused when the life she was missing wasn't staring me straight in the face. I'd been so preoccupied with being able to deal emotionally with Devon, that I hadn't spent any time preparing myself for the inevitable onslaught of emotion that seeing her family thriving without her would cause.

The bathroom was barren, only filled with the necessities. No rug was beneath the toilet to keep toes warm, no decorative towels hanging on the towel bar, just mismatched towels that looked like they'd been used to dry children that same day. No candles, no matching cup and toothbrush holder. It looked like a man's bathroom.

That thought brought a smile to my face. He'd bought a new house and he was doing his best. It didn't look like a woman lived here because one didn't. He was a single dad and had given his family what they needed. A themed bathroom with matching accoutrements was not a necessity. Although, I laughed knowing Liv would die if she knew Devon had been letting company dry their hands on used towels.

I unrolled some toilet paper, because there was no Kleenex, and dabbed my face with it. Luckily, I'd worn waterproof mascara that day, so the damage was minimal. I cupped my hand under the faucet and brought some cool water to my lips, then took a few calming breaths.

I didn't want the kids or Devon to see me upset. That wasn't why I came to visit them today. And I knew later, while we were alone in our hotel room, Nate would hold me and let me cry all I needed. I needed to keep it together for a few more hours.

Once I felt like I was in control of my emotions, I flushed the damp toilet paper because Devon didn't have a garbage can in his bathroom. I nearly laughed. Then I thought I would have to tell him in an email soon that with a nearly pre-teen daughter, he'd better get a garbage can ASAP.

When I left the bathroom, I could hear the kids and their father's voice floating down the hallway from the kitchen. I started toward them, but I was caught by the photos hanging on the wall.

Most of them were the same photos that had been hanging in the house Olivia had lived in, but there were a few new ones. Jaxy's first day of first grade, Ruby and Devon at a father-daughter dance, both of the kids with an older couple I vaguely remembered as Devon's parents. It was a beautiful mixture of before Olivia and after.

At the end of the hallway was the living room, which I'd already walked through but hadn't gotten a good look at. Stopping, I looked around the room and took it in, gasping, bringing my hand to my mouth.

Above their fireplace, at the focal point of their living room, was a large, beautiful print of a photo of Olivia. A photo I'd taken the day of her wedding before the ceremony while she was getting ready. She was smiling and mid-laughter. Her hair was curling around her face in soft ringlets, and pearls at her neck made the photo timeless. The silken robe she wore looked entirely as soft and luxurious as her smile. She was happy. And beautiful. And alive. Alive with so much more than just breath and a heartbeat. She was alive with love and happiness.

Anyone would see that picture and think the woman in it was happy.

I looked at that picture and knew Olivia was filled to the absolute brim with happiness the day that photo was taken. I remembered her happy. She was radiating with it. As the photo so powerfully demonstrated.

I'd tried not to look at photos of Olivia in the past few years. It was a sure trigger for tears. I thought about her often, but since LA was so removed from my life with her, I never got the chance to talk about her much. Even Nate was post Olivia on the timeline of my life. He asked about her every once in a while, but I think he knew it upset me, so she wasn't a regular topic of conversation.

My eyes drifted from the happy photo and I noticed a few smaller photos throughout the living room. One was on the side table – a picture of Olivia hugging her children, both their faces smashed up against the sides of hers, all three smiling widely, Jaxy's eyes closed because he was smiling so big. Another photo of Liv and Devon, both dressed up and looking fancy, probably at some work function for Devon. But they were connected at the sides, his arm around her back, her arm wrapped around his waist. Her other hand was resting against his chest and they were looking into each other's eyes with obvious and abundant love.

That photo made me smile. Liv had loved him so.

On the back of their couch rested a blanket Liv had crocheted while on bedrest with Jaxy. I recognized it because I'd gone to the craft store and purchased all the supplies for it, then sat in her room, next to her bed, in a recliner Devon had moved in there just for me, as she crocheted nearly the whole thing.

It was worn and well used, and I spied some holes where the yarn had torn. Olivia had worked so hard on that blanket and then complained when no one had used it. It had been folded up in their linen closet for years, the kids complaining that it had been scratchy and always opted for other forms of warmth in the winter months.

Now, they lived in Florida where cold weather was practically unheard of, and the blanket looked worn and well loved.

Olivia was missing from this house, but she wasn't absent.

She was on the walls, and draped over the couch. She was in their hearts, on their faces, woven into their lives. She was not, however, anywhere to be found in the bathroom. And that was okay.

"Auntie Evie," I heard Jax shout from the entrance to the kitchen. "Dad says we have to have chicken for dinner, but Ruby and I want pizza." He came running out to me, instantly grabbing my hand without hesitation. "We asked Nate what he wanted, but he said something about not angering the beast, and that he votes whatever you vote."

I laughed and squeezed his hand, walking back to the kitchen. "I think chicken sounds pretty good."

"Aw, come on, Auntie Evie," Ruby said from the barstool she was sitting on, right next to the one Nate was atop. "Chicken isn't any fun. And we hardly ever get to eat pizza."

"You can't barbeque pizza, Ruby," Devon said with a smile. "We invited Evie and Nate over for a winter barbeque."

"She can probably barbeque in LA in the winter. She's not impressed with our weather, Dad." Ruby hadn't lost her trademark snark.

"She's got a point," I said, laughing. "I can barbeque in the winter in LA. But I never have, so this is going to be a first."

"See? We barbeque." The adults laughed while the kids sulked.

I lowered my voice and whispered, pretending Devon couldn't hear me. "Maybe if you're really good, your dad will let me take you both out for pizza tomorrow night."

Devon's smiling eyes met mine over the heads of his children and he laughed.

"Yes!" Jaxy shouted as he pulled a fisted hand down to his waist. Ruby clapped and bounced excitedly in her seat.

"Nate, would you like to help me get the grill going?"

"Sure thing," he answered immediately and with an exceedingly friendly voice.

"Great, I'll grab the meat tray if you want to grab the sauce tray."

Devon didn't have a toothbrush holder in his bathroom, but he had a separate grilling tray for meat and sauces.

The kids and I stayed indoors for a few minutes, but then I was taken outside because I had to see their pool and trampoline.

We ate some delicious chicken. The kids showed Nate and me all their cool trampoline tricks, and the three adults sat on the porch, slowly drinking beer and watching two well-adjusted children enjoy their backyard.

"Nate," Jaxy yelled from his trampoline.

"Yeah, buddy?" Nate called out, a smile on his face.

"Do you know how to play Minecraft?"

"Is that a board game?"

Jaxy's mouth gaped open in surprise and a tiny bit of dismay. "A board game? No, it's not a board game. Come on," he said, making a surprisingly graceful, bouncing dismount from the trampoline. He walked right over to Nate and put his hand on his shoulder. "I'll show you what Minecraft is. Dad doesn't like to play it with me. Says it's boring."

"I'm sure you'll enjoy it though," Devon said to Nate with a devilish grin. I tried to stifle a laugh.

Nate stood at the urgent pulling of his hand from Jax and was dragged into the house. Within five seconds, Ruby was trailing after them.

"Do not play on my game, Jax. I don't want Nate ruining my progress." More classic Ruby snark. That made it impossible to stifle my laughter any longer.

I heard the sliding glass door slam shut and let out a deep breath, my laughter ending. Then I realized Devon and I were alone, and I suddenly became tense.

I picked up my beer, which was nearly empty, but I pretended as if it still had a swig left in it and took a drink hoping to stall the awkwardness I was feeling.

"I'm glad you made it out for a trip. The kids have been bouncing off the walls all week waiting for you to get here."

"It's a little overdue," I said quietly, thinking about the long years between squeezing those kids. "I don't think I want another two and a half years to go by without seeing them, Devon." I knew it was completely up to him. I knew he could tell me that it was over, that the kids didn't need me in their life, that it was better just to say goodbye for good. "I love them, Devon. And they're the last piece of Liv I've got left."

"I know," he said, then surprised me by reaching out and giving my hand a squeeze. He didn't linger. He removed his hand and placed it back around his beer. "They need you too, ya know. You have stories about their mother I can't tell them.

They deserve that connection. And there are few people on this planet who love them like you do."

˙ I let out a stuttered breath, feeling a weight lift off me I hadn't realized I was carrying. Devon was going to let me keep seeing Jax and Ruby. I would get to be a part of their lives. There was something akin to sunshine bursting through me, warming me, calming me.

"Thank you," I whispered.

"No thanks necessary, Evie." He took a long pull from his beer, and then put the bottle down on the glass table next to him. "Will we be getting a wedding invitation any time soon?"

His question caught me entirely off-guard and it took me a moment to formulate an answer.

"You know, the first time I saw him in my house, I wanted to kill him," Devon said with a slight smile to his voice, like he was looking back on some fond memory. "For ten years you were a foregone conclusion. I assumed you would be there forever. Then Nate showed up with more plans than just to fix my house."

"Nate didn't take me from you, Devon," I said with as much gentleness as I could muster.

"No, I know that now." He was silent for a moment and I didn't know what to say or do to move the conversation back to a safe place. Besides that, Devon and I'd had decidedly few *real* conversations, and I wasn't trying to shy away from that one. "But, it felt that way at first, ya know? I don't know Nate, besides how much we've gotten to know of each other here today, but I know he's a good guy. You wouldn't be with him otherwise. But, him showing up at my house was the beginning of the end for us." He shook his head back and forth before I could even say one word in response. "And I know there wasn't an *us* in the traditional sense, but we had something, Evelyn."

I couldn't argue with him, so I nodded, looking him straight in the eye. "I know."

"I'm not saying I'm glad we haven't seen you in so long, but I can say I'm glad we've all moved forward in a healthy way. The kids miss you and I agree they need you in their life, so I'm looking forward to having a regular, healthy, friendly relationship with you." He took in a breath having plowed through his mini speech without taking one, and I could tell that was something he'd practiced saying, as if he knew he needed to get it off his chest. And I could totally appreciate that.

"I would love to be regular, healthy, friends with you, Devon," I said with a straight face, but when he started laughing, I joined in.

I thought for a moment about Devon and Liv, and about the big, stunning photo of her above his fireplace.

"Are you dating yet?" I asked the question, hoping it didn't make him uncomfortable. If we were truly going to be friends, then this seemed like a completely valid question to ask.

"Not ready," was his low and nearly whispered response. I didn't get the feeling he was uncomfortable with my question, but more so, that he was uncomfortable with the idea of dating someone.

"Liv would want you to be happy, Devon," I said gently, not wanting to overstep my bounds. Moments ago, we'd just solidified our friendship. I didn't want to make him regret reaching out the olive branch to me.

He sighed. "I know she would. That woman told me on her deathbed that I needed to remarry. She even imagined the woman I would meet. Described this imaginary woman, and had a good time doing it too." A few silent and pregnant moments passed, but when he spoke again, his voice was a little more strained than before. "She was lying there, no hair, a good thirty pounds underweight, skin so thin you could see all the veins running through her, describing some beauty queen who I was supposed to meet right after her funeral and move on with."

His voice was becoming ragged and I turned my head to look away from him, trying to give him a moment to compose himself, but he just kept going.

"All I wanted was the woman dying in that bed, Evie. She was all I wanted." He let out one racked sob and I immediately reached for his hand, grasping it tightly, trying to show him that he wasn't alone.

"She was only trying to make it easier for you. You know how she was: a little inappropriate. She would have given anything to be here with you and the kids. But she knew that wasn't in the cards. That was her way of telling you it was okay with her for you to be with someone else."

"I know," he said, composing himself. "She might have been inappropriate, but she was the best woman I'll ever know."

"I won't argue with you there."

He smiled at me, squeezed my hand, and then let it go. "You run a close second."

"I won't argue with that either."

"You happy, Evie?"

I could not, in a million years, have stopped the smile that spread across my face. "Yeah," I whispered.

"Good," he said, his voice just as whispered as mine. "That's all Olivia would have wanted for you."

"You don't mind us taking the kids out for pizza tomorrow, do you?" I called out from the bathroom at our hotel room later that night.

"Babe, we're here to see those kids. Of course I don't mind taking them out for pizza."

I leaned out of the doorway just enough to see Nate lying on the bed in his signature flannel lounge pants. I met his eyes and said, "You're the best."

"You say that like hanging out with those kids is a hardship. They're pretty awesome."

"Told you," I yelled again from inside the bathroom. Suddenly, he was in the room with me, coming up behind me, meeting my eyes in the mirror. I was startled at first, not expecting him, but then continued to floss.

He was right behind me, his front pressing into my back, and I soaked up the warmth he was giving me. He leaned down and rested his chin on my shoulder, his hands behind his back, and just looked at me as I slid the floss between my teeth.

After a moment, it became weird, the way he was staring at me and not speaking. I stopped mid-floss, and asked with a garbled voice due to the fingers in my mouth, "What?"

"Nothing."

"What?" I asked again, more insistent the second time.

"Have you ever played Minecraft?"

I rolled my eyes at him. "No, can't say that I have, what with being an adult and all."

"It's a pretty sweet game. Jax showed it to me. Ruby too."

"Glad you enjoyed your time with them," I said with a laugh.

"I did. But I felt bad, them showing me something special to them, so I had to show them something special too."

"Did you show them how you can fit your whole fist in your mouth?" I asked, letting out an exceptionally unladylike snort with my laughter.

"No," he said, all laughter gone from his voice. "I showed them this." As he said the words, one of his hands came out from behind his back, and it was holding a black, velvet box. Nestled inside the box was a solitaire diamond ring. Princess cut. Perfect.

"What is that?" I asked in a whisper, a piece of floss still wedged between two teeth. I quickly pulled it out and turned to face him.

"I'm hoping it's the ring you'll wear for the rest of your life." He slowly knelt to the floor on one knee, took my left hand in his, and looked up at me with the most intense but beautiful brown eyes. "Evelyn Marie Reynolds, I've been waiting my whole life to fall in love with you. I'd like to spend the rest of my life showing you how hard I've fallen. I can't promise it will always be easy, but I can promise it will always be better with you by my side. Will you marry me?"

He asked the question, but didn't wait for my response before he slid the ring onto my finger. My mouth was still gaping open, and I couldn't make any words come out. Tears welled in my eyes, making everything blurry, but I couldn't pull my gaze from the ring that sat on a previously empty and unadorned finger.

"I asked Jax and Ruby if they thought it was okay for you to marry me, and they were totally cool with it."

I blinked down at him. "You did what?" I said, my voice squeaky and sharp.

"Ruby and Jax give their blessing," he said, smiling at me and rising to his feet.

I couldn't hold myself back any longer. I flung myself at him, arms wrapping tightly around his neck and, of course, he caught me, holding me around my waist.

"I love you, Lyn." His words were a whisper against my ear. "I want to have everything with you. And I want to start now." He took in a breath, and then said, "Marry me."

I shook my head against his shoulder, trying, with terrible results, not to cry. He pulled away from me, his hands coming up to my cheeks, wiping away my tears with his thumbs.

"Don't cry, baby," he said. Then, after he'd finished drying my tears, he said, "I'd like to hear an answer." He was smiling, and even though we were in a bathroom of a hotel room, it was the most perfect thing I could have ever imagined.

"Yes, Nate. Of course, I'll marry you." I had no sooner said the words than he had me in his arms, lifting me up and spinning me around. When he set me down, I was on the countertop, his hips were between my knees, and he was kissing me.

"I love you," he said against my mouth between kisses.

"I love you too," I said, pulling back and looking him in the eyes. "I mean that, Nate. You're everything to me."

"I know, babe," he said with a brilliant smile on his face. "You're going to marry me."

"I am," I laughed. "And you're going to marry me right back."

He hauled me into his arms and carried me into the bedroom, flipping the lights off as he went, and tossing me onto the bed. I lost myself in a fit of laughter, but all the joking ceased as he appeared over me, his eyes dark and full of love.

Later that night as I lay in a foreign bed, in a foreign city, with Nate's arms wrapped tightly around me, holding me close, I found myself unable to sleep.

I lifted my hand up into the moonlight that shot through our room in rays, examining the beautiful ring that fit me perfectly. I couldn't remember a time when I was that happy.

Somewhere in the back of my mind, I heard my best friend's voice. *You're my very best friend, Evie. Promise me, you'll be happy.*

"I'm happy, Olivia," I whispered into the dark room. "I'm finally happy."

The End

*I hope you will all look forward to reading
about Devon's happily ever after in*

The Presence of Grace

Slated to release in 2016

Acknowledgements

I would first like to thank my readers. I know this book is a little different than my others, but those of you who dove in, enthusiastically, I love you so much. You make my job and life so amazing. Thank you.

To Lindy – thank you for your constant motivation and friendship. The last half of this book was written and inspired by all the texts we'd send back and forth, challenging each other, pushing each other, and teasing each other. I met you IRL while I was writing this book and it was awesome.

To my early readers, those who volunteered to read it when it was only half way written just simply to assuage my fears that it was crap – Leslie, Rachel, Kathy, and Joanne. Your love for the book made it possible for me to continue. Thank you.

To my eagle eyes – Jen, Andrea, and Kelly. THANK YOU for beta reading the book and helping me find the parts that needed work. I am so grateful to have people like you on my side.

Becca – Thank you for taking my words and making them beautiful with images and pretty fonts. You are so creative in a way I could never be. Thank you so very much for your support and help.

To every blogger and Give Me Books Promotions – Thank you for spreading the word about The Absence of Olivia. I am so appreciative every time sometime spends their precious time telling someone about my books; it means the world to me.

Other books by Anie Michaels

The Never Series

Never Close Enough

Never Far Away

Never Giving Up

The Never Duet

Never Standing Still

Never Tied Down – *coming soon*

The Private Serials

Private Affairs

Private Encounters

Private Getaway

Private Property

Stand Alone Novels

The Space Between Us

The Absence of Olivia

The Presence of Grace – *coming in 2016*

Please feel free to follow me on any and all media platforms!

http://www.facebook.com/AuthorAnieMichaels

https://twitter.com/Anie_Michaels

http://www.instagram.com/aniemichaels

Shoot me an email!

anie.michaels@gmail.com

Made in the USA
Charleston, SC
11 November 2015